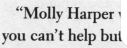
Praise for the Half-Moon Hollow novels

Where the Wild Things Bite

"This series has gotten more appealing over time and will satisfy readers looking to bite into a paranormal romance flavored generously with dashes of humor."

—*Kirkus Reviews*

The Single Undead Moms Club

"*The Single Undead Moms Club* is frequently hilarious yet surprisingly touching."

—*Single Titles*

"Molly Harper once again takes us on a hilarious tour to Half-Moon Hollow to meet the newest vampire on the block."

—*Heroes and Heartbreakers*

The Dangers of Dating a Rebound Vampire

"Harper can always be depended upon for a page-turning story with a lot of frisky, lighthearted humor, and *The Dangers of Dating a Rebound Vampire* is no exception."

—*RT Book Reviews*

A Witch's Handbook of Kisses and Curses

"Harper serves up plenty of hilarity . . . [in] this return to the hysterical world of Jane and crew."

—*Publishers Weekly*

"Clever wit and heart. . . . Fans of the series and readers new to Half-Moon Hollow will enjoy the fun and frivolity."

—*RT Book Reviews* (4½ stars, Top Pick)

The Care and Feeding of Stray Vampires

"A perfect combination of smarts and entertainment with a dash of romance."

—*RT Book Reviews* (4½ stars, Top Pick)

"Filled with clever humor, snark, silliness, and endearing protagonists."

—*Booklist*

Nice Girls Don't Bite Their Neighbors

"Terrific. . . . The stellar supporting characters, laugh-out-loud moments, and outrageous plot twists will leave readers absolutely satisfied."

—*Publishers Weekly* (starred review)

Nice Girls Don't Live Forever

RT Reviewers' Choice Award winner!

"Hilariously fun."

—*RT Book Reviews* (4½ stars, Top Pick)

Nice Girls Don't Date Dead Men

"Fast-paced, mysterious, passionate, and hilarious."

—*RT Book Reviews* (4½ stars)

Nice Girls Don't Have Fangs

"A chuckle-inducing, southern-fried version of Stephanie Plum."

—*Booklist*

Praise for the Naked Werewolf novels

How to Run with a Naked Werewolf

"Harper is back with her trademark snark, capable heroines, and loping lupines."

—*Heroes and Heartbreakers*

The Art of Seducing a Naked Werewolf

"Harper's gift for character building and crafting a smart, exciting story is showcased well."

—*RT Book Reviews* (4 stars)

How to Flirt with a Naked Werewolf

"Mo's wise-cracking, hilarious voice makes this novel such a pleasure to read."

—*New York Times* bestselling author Eloisa James

"A light, fun, easy read, perfect for lazy days."

—*New York Journal of Books*

Sweet Tea and Sympathy

MOLLY HARPER

G

GALLERY BOOKS

NEW YORK   LONDON   TORONTO   SYDNEY   NEW DELHI

G

Gallery Books
An Imprint of Simon & Schuster, Inc.
1230 Avenue of the Americas
New York, NY 10020

First Gallery Books trade paperback edition November 2017

GALLERY BOOKS and colophon are registered
trademarks of Simon & Schuster, Inc.

For information about special discounts for bulk purchases,
please contact Simon & Schuster Special Sales at 1-866-506-1949
or business@simonandschuster.com.

The Simon & Schuster Speakers Bureau can bring authors to
your live event. For more information or to book an event, contact
the Simon & Schuster Speakers Bureau at 1-866-248-3049
or visit our website at www.simonspeakers.com.

Interior design by Michelle Marchese

Manufactured in the United States of America

10 9 8 7 6 5 4 3 2 1

Library of Congress Cataloging-in-Publication Data is available.

ISBN 978-1-5011-5122-4
ISBN 978-1-5011-5132-3 (ebook)

To the Southern women
who taught me about bacon fat
and backchat

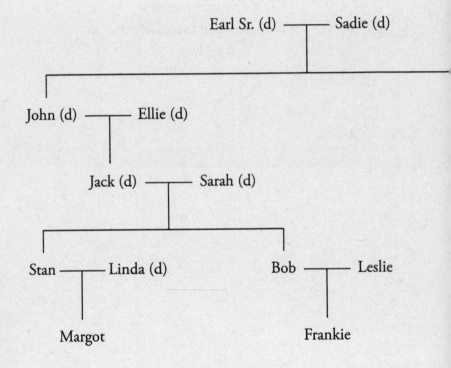

The McCready Family Tree

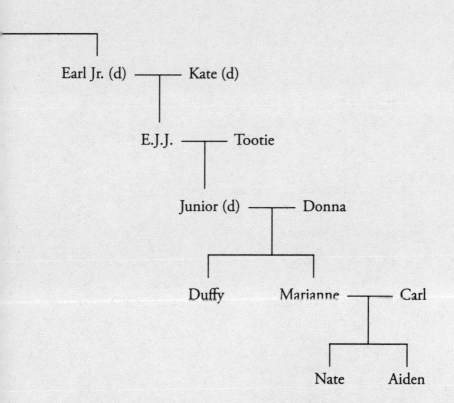

Earl Jr. (d) —— Kate (d)

E.J.J. —— Tootie

Junior (d) —— Donna

Duffy   Marianne —— Carl

Nate   Aiden

1

*M*ARGOT CARY LEANED her forehead against the warm truck window as it bounced along the pitted Georgia highway. She closed her eyes against the picturesque landscape as it rolled by. Green, green, green. Everything was so effing green here.

GREEN WAS NOT her lucky color. It certainly hadn't blessed the opening of the botanical garden's newly completed Wesmoreland Tropical Greenhouse. Maybe it had been a mistake to carry the green theme so far. Green table linens, green lanterns strung through the trees, down to emerald-green bow ties for the catering staff. Weeks later, she still remembered the terrified expression on one waiter's face when she caught him by the arm before he carried his tray of crudités into the party space.

Despite her glacial blond beauty, the younger man practically flinched away from her touch as she adjusted his tie. Margot would admit that she'd been a bit . . . demanding in organizing this event. She had taken every precaution to make sure that this evening's black-tie opening was as smooth as Rosaline Hewitt's recently Botoxed brow. She'd commissioned a silk-leaf embroidered canopy stretching from the valet station to the entrance to prevent the guests' hairstyles and gowns from being ruined by the summer rain. She'd researched each invitee meticulously to find out who was gluten-free or vegan and adjusted the menu accordingly. She'd arranged for two dozen species of exotic South American parrots to be humanely displayed among orchids and pitcher plants and a flock of flamingos to wade through the manufactured waterfall's rocky lagoon.

She was not about to have all of that preparation undone by a cater waiter who didn't know how to keep a bow tie on straight.

"Go," Margot said, nodding toward the warm, humid air of the false tropical jungle. He moved silently away from her, into the opulently lit space.

Margot turned and tried to survey the greenhouse as it would appear to the guests, the earliest of which were already filtering into the garden, *ooh*ing and *aah*ing. Calling it a greenhouse seemed like an understatement. The glass-paneled dome reached four stories into the sky, allowing the tropical plant specimens inside plenty of space to stretch. Carefully plotted stone paths wound through the flower beds, giving the visitor the impression of wandering through paradise. But knowing how much Chicago's *riche*-est of the *riche* enjoyed a nice soiree, the conservators had been smart enough to add a nice open space in the middle of the greenhouse to allow for a dance floor. She'd arranged elbow-high tables around the perimeter, covered in jewel-tone silk cloths. Gold LED lights cast a hazy sunset glow over the room, occasionally projecting animated fireflies against the foliage. And since society's ladies would never do something so inelegant as visit a buffet, the waiters had been informed to constantly circulate with their trays of canapés in a nonobvious, serpentine pattern around the enormous shrimp tower in the middle of—

Wait.

"No," Margot murmured, shaking her head. "No, no, no."

She snagged the next waiter to walk through the entrance and took his tray. The sweet-faced college kid seemed startled and alarmed to have the chief planner for this event grabbing him by the arm. "You, get two of your coworkers and very quickly, very quietly, very *discreetly* get that shrimp tower out of here. If anyone asks, just tell them that you're taking it back to the kitchen to be refilled."

The poor boy blanched at the brisk clip to her tone and said, "But—but Chef Jean was very specific about—"

"I don't care what Chef Jean was specific about," she said. "Get it out of here *now*."

The waiter nodded and pulled away from her into the gathering crowd.

Margot stepped forward into the fragrant warmth of the greenhouse, careful to keep her expression and body language relaxed. She was aware that, while professionally dressed in her black power suit, she was not nearly as festive as the guests in their tuxedos and haute couture gowns, but she was perfectly comfortable. She'd attended hundreds of events like this growing up. She would not be intimidated by some plants and a pretentious wannabe Frenchman. She pressed the button of her earbud-size Bluetooth and whispered, "This is Margot. I need to speak to Jean."

She could tell by the way her words were echoing in her own ear that the head chef of Fete Portable had taken his earpiece out—despite Margot's repeated requests to keep a line of communication open with her—and set it on the stainless steel counter in the makeshift kitchen. She blew out a frustrated breath. Jean LeDille was not her preferred caterer for high-profile events, but the de facto hostess of tonight's opening—Melissa Sutter, first lady of Chicago and head of the botanical garden conservators' board—had insisted on using him. So far he'd been temperamental, resistant to the most basic instruction, and a pain in Margot's Calvin Klein–clad ass. And when she was done with this event and had secured her partnership at Elite Elegance, she would have Jean blacklisted from every Chicago party planner's contact list. Theirs was a close-knit and gossip-driven circle.

Someone in the kitchen picked up the earbud and said, "Ms. Cary, he says to tell you he's unavailable."

Margot gritted her perfect white teeth but managed a polite smile to the head of the opera board and his wife as they passed. Jean wouldn't be able to get a job making a clown-shaped birthday cake by the time she was done with him.

"So I guess I'll just have to make myself available to him, then."

Margot's assistant, Mandy, a sleek brunette who reminded Margot of a Russian wolfhound in four-inch heels, fell in step behind her. "Make sure that tower is gone. You have two minutes."

"On it," Mandy snapped, and peeled off after the hapless waiters.

Margot pushed through the heavy plastic curtain that separated the greenhouse from the kitchen tent. Far from the muted music and golden-green light of the greenhouse, the tent was ruthlessly lit with fluorescents and heating lamps. Jean's shouts filled the air, demanding that the canapé trays be restocked tout de suite.

Jean was a stocky, balding man with thick, dark eyebrows and an unfortunate mustache. His chef whites were splattered with various sauces and he sneered—actually sneered—at Margot as she walked into his kitchen.

"What are you doing in ma' kitchen?" he demanded in an exaggerated French accent. "I tell you before. No outside staff when I am *creating*."

"Jean, would you explain to me why there is a shrimp tower in the middle of my venue?"

"I was overcome by the muse this morning. I decide to build you a shrimp tower. Only four hundred dollars extra. I do you favor, eh?"

"Wait. Is that shrimp salad on the crostini?" Margot asked, stopping a waiter before he left with his tray of appetizers. "Because we agreed on poached quail eggs. Mrs. Sutter, the hostess of tonight's event, whom you've cooked for on several occasions, is allergic to shrimp. As in, she can't even be around people who are eating shrimp because she might come into contact with the proteins. I wrote it on everything. *Everything*."

Margot motioned to the field refrigeration unit where she had taped a neon-green sign that read PLEASE REMEMBER THAT MRS. SUTTER IS HIGHLY ALLERGIC TO SHRIMP.

Jean waved her off. "I do not read the cards. My sous chef reads the cards."

"Jean. Drop the French accent that we both know is about as real as that ridiculous hairpiece and tell me what you are feeding the mayor's wife."

The chef, whose real name was John Dill, shrugged and in his natural, Midwestern voice said, "The market didn't have enough quail eggs, so I took the shrimp. It's not a big deal. If she's allergic, she'll know not to touch it. People make too much of their food allergies anyway."

"It's just lovely to know that someone with that attitude is making food for innocent bystanders," Margot snapped. She called out loud enough for the entire kitchen staff to hear, "Eighty-six the shrimp crostini. Throw them out and take the bags out of the tent. All of you wash your hands—twice—and any utensils that have touched the shrimp—also twice. I need one uncontaminated staff member to make a special shrimp-free plate of food for Mrs. Sutter so we can feed her tonight without poisoning her. Get it done, now."

Jean was seething, but Margot didn't give a single damn. Mandy popped through the plastic curtain, a stricken expression on her angular face.

"There's a problem with the tower," she said. "It's too heavy to move. But they're working on disassembling the shrimp trays to bring them back in before people notice."

"I don't care if it's made of concrete. I need it—" Margot's response was cut short by a strange honking ruckus from the greenhouse, followed by screams and crashing . . . and running?

One of Margot's golden eyebrows rose. "What is that?"

Mandy grimaced. "Don't flamingos eat shrimp?"

Margot dropped her clipboard and her headset to the ground and scrambled through the plastic curtain. "Oh, no."

The flamingos were making a run at the shrimp tower, pink wings flapping, pecking at the waiters who were attempting to remove the shellfish. The guests were falling all over one another trying to get away from the shrimp-frenzied birds and in the process had knocked over several cocktail tables and the votive candles on top. Those candles had set fire to the tablecloths, which set off the greenhouse's sprinklers and alarms. The parrots did not appreciate the clanging alarms or the sudden scramble of people. They broke free from their perches and were flying around the greenhouse, leaving "deposits" on the guests in protest. Oh, and Mrs. Sutter was purple and covered in hives.

Margot gave herself ten seconds to surrender to the panic. She let her stomach churn. She let her ice-cold hands shake. She allowed herself to hear everything and nothing all at once. In her head, she saw her career going up in flames with the tablecloths. The promotion and partnership she'd worked for were disappearing before her eyes in puffs of smoke. Everything she'd planned, everything she wanted in life, was slipping out of her fingers because of some misplaced shellfish.

And then Margot put a lid on her anxiety and did what she did best. She put out fires metaphorical and literal. She called an ambulance and the fire department, grabbed the EpiPen from Mrs. Sutter's purse, and jabbed her in the thigh. Hell, she even took off her pumps and wrangled the shrimp-seeking flamingos back into the lagoon.

But the damage was done. The news photographers who'd prepared themselves for a boring evening shooting glamour poses gleefully snapped photos of society matrons in soaked designer gowns and runny makeup dashing for shelter from the sprinklers. A guest who happened to be a member of PETA started screaming at Margot for mistreating the flamingos while trying to herd them away from (attacking) the guests. And a conservators' board member handed her an invoice for the thousands of dollars in rare orchid species that had been trampled in the melee.

The next morning, an exhausted Margot sat slumped in the

offices of Elite Elegance as her boss, Carrington Carter-Shaw, slapped newspapers with headlines like FLORAL FIASCO and REAL-LIFE ANGRY BIRDS! on her desk. One particularly cheeky tabloid had printed a picture of Margot beating the smoldering remains of a matron's hairpiece with a wet napkin under the headline FLOWER POWER F***-UP!

"How could you let this happen?" Carrington cried, her carefully blown-out dark hair dancing around her heart-shaped face. "We're the laughingstock of the Chicago social scene. Guests from last night are trying to stick us with dry-cleaning bills, medical bills—Michelle Biederman claims a parrot flew off with her two-karat diamond earring! The mayor's office has contacted us—twice—to call our business license into question. I had to move three guys from the mail room just to handle the incoming phone calls. Margot, you're my star! My rock! You can make a backyard potluck birthday party look like a black-tie gala. You're the planner I call when it's clear in the first meeting that the client is absolutely batshit insane. What happened?"

Margot wanted to blame the untested Chef Jean and his "inspired" impromptu shrimp, but ultimately the fault rested with her. She'd lost control of the party. She'd lost control of the food. She'd lost control of two dozen species of birds.

"I don't know," Margot mumbled, shaking her head. She took a prepackaged stain wipe out of her Prada clutch and dabbed at a questionable blotch on her lapel. "It all happened so quickly. I—I know, at this point, the partnership is off the table—"

"Partnership?" Carrington scoffed. "Honey, I can't even keep you on staff. You're professional poison. I'm going to have to fire you and do it in a very public manner—I mean, picture the polite urban equivalent of putting you in stocks in the town square and pelting you with rotten fruit—so people know that our company is safe to use again."

Margot let loose a breath she didn't know she'd been holding. She nodded. In some way, she'd been expecting this. She knew it would be rough for a while and she would have to put off some bullet points in her five-year plan, but she could handle this. She had contingency funds and a secret contact list of important people who owed her favors.

Margot cleared her throat and tried to straighten her rumpled suit jacket. "And what, you'll shuffle me out to one of the branch offices in the suburbs and I'll organize bar mitzvahs until this all blows over?"

Carrington frowned. "No, Margot. *Fired.* As in employment permanently terminated. The partners are willing to give you a three-week severance in recognition of the work you've done for us. And I'll write you a positive recommendation letter. But that's it."

"But I've worked here for almost ten years. I've put in eighty-hour weeks. Ninety during the holiday party season. I don't have a social life because I'm always here. I haven't been on a date in more than eight months."

"Yes, I know. That's why you get the third week of severance pay. Really, Margot, I think we're being more than generous here, considering the fallout from this fiasco."

As Margot walked out of Elite Elegance's plush offices with a banker's box full of her belongings and a severance check in hand, she told herself that it would be okay, that this was what backup plans were for, that this situation couldn't possibly get worse.

It got worse.

Stage one of Margot's plan had been to retreat to her apartment to regroup, polish up her résumé, and compose a list of companies she could apply to, but her unit's new tenants kept stopping by to measure for new flooring and curtains. Just a week before the "Floral Fiasco," she'd given up her lease in preparation to move to a newly purchased condo in Wicker Park. Between the down payment she'd saved and the raise she was supposed to get with her promotion, she would have been able to afford it. But the day after she was fired, she'd gotten a call from the mortgage officer handling her condo loan. Mrs. Meade had seen the news about the greenhouse incident and her firing, and informed Margot that without a job, the mortgage company could not guarantee her loan. The only good news was that the mortgage company was willing to return 70 percent of her down payment. So now, with her lease running out and her condo being sold to someone else, Margot was effectively homeless.

And still, it got worse.

Without a job, she couldn't get an apartment in a decent building. And the buildings where she could get an apartment were not places where she wanted to live. And she could not find a job. Anywhere. Receptionists laughed and hung up when she called the best event-planning companies in Chicago. Receptionists from second- and third-tier event-planning companies in Chicago also laughed at her. She couldn't get the companies in New York or Los Angeles to call back. Hell, she couldn't get companies in St. Louis to return her calls. She still had her savings, but thanks to Mastercard and her monthly expenses, they were dwindling quickly.

Her friends weren't returning her calls or messages, either. And she couldn't turn to her adoptive father for help. Gerald hadn't spoken to her since her mother's funeral three years before. And she'd promised herself that she wouldn't take a dime after her parents made their last tuition payment. She still had the shreds of her pride.

The shreds were costing her. She was three days away from living in the storage unit where she'd moved her stuff, sitting at her breakfast bar—because it was the only table space she had left—actually filling in a JobLink profile, when a Skype notification popped up on her laptop. The message said it was from "hotsy-totsy45."

Margot frowned. She used this account for after-hours and long-distance consultations with clients. She definitely would have remembered a client nicknamed hotsy-totsy45. Leaning back from the screen, she clicked *decline*.

Blowing a long breath out through her nose, Margot continued to fill out the JobLink form. Another notification from hotsy-totsy popped up.

"Still a 'no,' creep," she muttered, clicking *decline* again.

But hotsy-totsy would not be denied. And given the amount of chardonnay Margot had consumed just for the sake of not having to move it out of her apartment, it wasn't surprising that her hand slipped a bit and she clicked *accept*.

"Damn it!" she grunted, trying to close the chat window before it opened. She did not want to witness the latest in creative junk shots currently being embraced by the Internet's weirdos. But instead of the expected random nudity, Margot's screen was filled with the face of an adorable little granny lady with a cloud of snow-white hair and Dalmatian-print reading glasses balanced on the tip of her nose.

"Hello?"

A brilliant smile lit up the granny lady's face, showing teeth too white and too even to be original parts. "Well, hello there! It took me a little while to track you down, but here you are!" the lady crowed in a Southern drawl so pronounced that Margot had trouble processing what she was saying at first. "You look just like I thought you would. A lot like your mama, mind, but you got a bit of your daddy in there, too. Of course, I thought you'd be a little more polished up, but I'm guessing you haven't left your house in a while."

Margot caught sight of her appearance in the little preview window in the corner of the screen and winced. She looked like someone who was unemployed. She was wearing a grubby Northwestern sweatshirt. Her carefully highlighted blond hair was piled into a haphazard topknot. She was wearing her thick-rimmed black glasses, making her hazel eyes look owlish and too big for her face. She hadn't worn makeup in days, so her skin had taken on a cheesy appearance in the blue light of the computer screen.

"I'm sorry, do you know my parents?" she asked. As friendly as this lady might be, she didn't exactly look to be Linda and Gerald's speed. Linda McCready, a nobody from nowhere with traces of a Low Country accent and a toddler daughter in tow, had managed to snag Gerald Cary, MD, while she was working as the records clerk in the hospital where the handsome British expat practiced surgery. She had spent considerable time and energy clawing her way into the upper middle circles of Chicago society. Linda Cary would have gone blind before she wore Dalmatian reading glasses.

"Well, your mama and I were never close, but your daddy is my nephew, so I guess you could say I know that sad-sack face of his pretty well," the woman said with a chuckle.

Margot's jaw dropped. Her stepfather had adopted her when

she was four years old. But considering that he was from just outside London, it was unlikely he had relatives in Georgia. "You know Gerald?"

"No, honey, your *daddy*. What do you young people call it—your 'biological father.' Stan McCready. I'm your great-aunt Tootie."

"Beg pardon?" Even Margot couldn't be sure which part she was questioning—the "biological" bit or the ridiculous nickname. Even in the South, people knew better than to name their children Tootie, right?

"I'm Stanley McCready's aunt, honey."

Stanley McCready. Margot slumped on her bar stool. She'd never met her father's family. Linda had made no secret of her "unfortunate" first marriage to a man named McCready, but she'd referred to it as a youthful mistake she'd corrected when Margot was barely three years old. Stanley was a heavy drinker, Linda had insisted, a train wreck of a man who couldn't provide for them. After Linda left, he'd almost immediately given up his rights to his daughter without so much as a court motion.

Margot didn't know where he lived. She couldn't remember what he looked like. Her mother had never even shown her a picture, insisting that it would be disloyal to Gerald. Neither Mr. McCready nor his family tried to contact her in thirty years, which was fine with Margot. She didn't have room in her life for an irresponsible drunk who couldn't be bothered to send so much as a birthday card. And frankly, she resented the idea that her father's family only reached out now, when she was at her lowest.

And it wasn't even her father, just some wacky great-aunt with a ridiculous name.

"You know, I thought you'd have that nasal-sounding Chicago accent, but you sound like you should be having tea with the queen. So proper and prim. I suppose that's your mama in ya. Did she make you take those diction lessons?"

"No, I just like using all the letter sounds."

The woman snorted a bit and said, "My point is, honey, I've been looking for you for weeks now, after I saw the video of your party on YouTube. I spotted you and knew you had to be Linda's daughter."

"YouTube?" Margot winced. "How many hits did it get?"

"Hundreds of thousands! Honey, you're your own meme!" Tootie exclaimed. Suddenly, a window popped up in the corner of Margot's screen, showing one of the press photos of Margot herding the flamingos away from the shrimp tower with giant print reading NO CAN HAZ SHRIMP, FLAMINGOZ! NO CAN HAZ!

Margot buried her face in her hands. She'd spent most of her twenties carefully policing her own social media posts so as not to damage her professional reputation. And now this. Also, her great-aunt seemed to be awfully tech savvy for a woman who looked to be in her eighties.

"Well, thanks for contacting me and mocking me with age-appropriate Internet humor . . . and dredging up a bunch of unresolved emotional issues," Margot muttered. "But I'm going to have to sign off now."

"Oh, sure, honey, I'm sure you're busy with your job search. How's that going?"

"I've submitted quite a lot of résumés," Margot said, trying to sound casual.

"Any interviews yet?" Tootie pressed.

Margot floundered a bit while searching for an answer. "It's still early. You don't want people to think you're too eager."

"Not one callback, huh?"

Margot pursed her lips. "Not one."

"Well, that's just fine, because I have a proposition for you."

Margot's instinct to say no right that second was quelled when the bank paperwork that showed her checking account balance caught her eye. "What sort of proposition?"

"We need an event planner here at the family business. We'd be willing to provide room, board, and a generous salary."

"How generous?"

"Well, now, you've got to remember that the cost of living is much lower here as opposed to the big city," Tootie cautioned.

"How generous?" Margot asked again, and Tootie's blue eyes sparkled behind those reading glasses.

"Here, I'll send you the compensation package the family put together."

Another box popped up on Margot's screen. She clicked on the file and grimaced at the salary, which was about one-quarter of what she'd made at Elite Elegance. "How *much* lower is the cost of living there? Also, where is 'there'?"

"Did you notice that the package includes health insurance?" Tootie asked. "When does your coverage run out?"

"Soon," Margot grumbled. "Also, I noticed you didn't answer the question about location."

"And I'm guessin' from the packing boxes in the background that your lease runs out pretty soon, too. So really, I could see why you would want to stay where you would be homeless and at risk of huge medical bills, in a city where you could be mugged or run down by a taxi or have a windowpane fall on you from twenty stories up. That's far preferable to coming down to Georgia, to a town where the crime rate is next to zero."

Margot had never passed the Mason-Dixon Line, not even to Florida. Her mother had always insisted on family vacations to Lake Geneva, to New York, to France. Anyone could go to Disney World, she'd told Margot; Linda was trying to give Margot the *world*. Margot didn't know how well she would function in a rural environment, much less a place where she would constantly hear the banjo music from *Deliverance* in the back of her head.

"But my life is here. My friends are here. I need to stay where the jobs are. And right now, that's in Chicago."

"So you lay low for a few months in God's country, get to know your kinfolk, get that city air out of your lungs, and then relaunch yourself at people who will have forgotten your foul-up once someone else messes up worse. It will be good for you," Tootie told her.

Margot stared at the offer. Tootie had thought of everything: financial compensation, meals covered, a clothing allowance, and health insurance. She'd even attached a picture of a small cabin on the edge of a lake, labeled *housing*. And another photo of a huge family posed in front of a lakeside dock. Tootie stood with an older man, holding his hand. Two couples in their fifties stood behind them next to a man with deep frown furrows barely touched by his lopsided smirk. His arm was thrown around a twentyish girl with purple-streaked hair in pigtails wearing a black T-shirt with a pink radiation symbol on it. Another couple stood on the far left, a man in his thirties with curly reddish-blond hair hugging a laughing blonde. The sun was setting behind the family and they looked so happy together, so at ease with one another. And it felt like a punch to the chest. These people didn't miss her at all. They didn't feel a Margot-shaped hole in their family, they'd just moved on without her. It shouldn't have hurt as much as it did. She'd spent a lot of time on visualization exercises so it wouldn't hurt. And yet . . .

She cleared her throat. "The whole family put this together? Even my . . . even Stan?"

"Everybody," Tootie said emphatically.

Margot skimmed the top of the document and caught sight of the letterhead, which read *McCready Family Funeral Home and Bait Shop.*

"Funeral home? Wait, you run a funeral home? And a bait shop?"

"Well, it's more of a full-service marina, but yes! For four generations now! You're part of a Lake Sackett institution, hon."

"Why would a funeral home–slash–bait shop need an event planner?"

"Well, the baby boomer generation is dropping like flies around here, so we've got more business than we can handle. We've needed to add another planning consultant for a while now, and when I saw your video and looked up your background, I knew you'd be perfect."

"I'm an event planner. For major society parties, galas, charity balls, that sort of thing."

"Well, a funeral is a kind of event. And some of the considerations are the same—timing, speeches, music, food, and such."

"Oh, I just don't think I could—"

Suddenly, the lights flickered out and her refrigerator died with a whine. Because she'd shut off utilities in preparation for the move to the condo that was supposed to have taken place the week before. But she had nowhere to go. And no health insurance.

She pursed her lips. "When can I start?"

AUNT TOOTIE—MARGOT was still refusing to call her that out loud, on principle—had been very helpful in organizing her immediate move to Lake Sackett. Using her above-generational-average tech skills, Tootie arranged for a local company to ship the few belongings Margot was bringing to Georgia. Tootie booked a flight from Chicago to Atlanta and then assured her that she'd have a car pick her up at the airport and drive her the two and a half hours to the lake country.

Tootie was just *so* efficient.

Three days later, Margot's flight was taxiing down the runway at Hartsfield-Jackson Atlanta International Airport and she was clutching her cell phone to her chest. Margot had no idea what she'd face when she deplaned. She'd intentionally avoided reading up on the funeral home or her new base of operations because she was afraid that additional information would convince her to cancel the whole agreement.

Margot managed to find her bags without problems, but she couldn't find the car service at the arrivals terminal. She scanned the little signs held by the handful of drivers near the exit. Not one of them said *Cary*. Maybe Tootie hadn't sent anyone, she thought. Maybe she could take the airport transit system to the departures terminal and book a flight back to Chicago. She didn't believe in signs, but maybe this was an omen. Maybe she wasn't meant to meet her father's family. Maybe she wasn't supposed to live in Georgia. Maybe she should step back on the sidewalk before that enormous green truck barreling through the pickup area squashed her flat.

The battered early-model truck skidded to a stop in front of her. The side door was marked MCCREADY FAMILY FUNERAL HOME AND BAIT SHOP—LAKE SACKETT, GA in bold gold print.

Margot murmured, "Oh . . . no."

Tootie hadn't arranged for a car service. She'd sent a family member to pick Margot up. A stranger in a pickup truck. Everything inside of Margot seemed to tense at once. She'd thought she'd have at least a few more hours to pep-talk herself into the right frame of mind to meet any of her extended family—not to mention the little bottle of vodka she'd purchased on the plane to help prepare her to meet her father. But here it was, spewing exhaust at her, while the driver's-side door opened. The windows were tinted too darkly to allow her to see the driver. Would it be Stan McCready? Was she ready for that? Was it too late to run back into the airport and hide behind the baggage carousel?

A man in his thirties—the man with curly reddish-blond hair from the family photo she'd studied relentlessly for the last three days—popped his head over the truck frame and grinned at her. His eyes, the same ocean blue as Tootie's, glowed with amusement as he held up a poster-board sign that read WELCOME HOME, COUSIN MARGOT! in bright red glitter letters. The sign had been decorated with balloons and glittery star stickers. He waved it madly and yelled, "Hey!"

Definitely *not* her father, then. Margot stepped back, eyes wide, and in a move natural to someone who spent most of her life in a major city, pulled her purse closer to her body.

The bearded man scampered around the front of the truck and threw his arms around her. "Hey, cuz!"

"Who . . . are you?" Margot whispered as he squeezed her tight. His T-shirt smelled of citronella and sunscreen, a pleasant combination, but she generally liked her personal space bubble to be a little more . . . bubbly.

"Oh, I'm sorry! I'm Duffy McCready, your cousin. Well, my grandpa is your grandpa's cousin, which always muddies the waters with third cousin and once-removed and all that. So we'll just keep it simple and say 'cousin.'"

"And Tootie McCready sent you?" she asked, just in case there was some other half-wild McCready picking up his long-lost cousin at the domestic arrivals terminal.

"We're so excited that you're here," he drawled in his heavy Georgian accent. "I'm sorry I'm late. I had this nightmare customer, refused to give up the search for Billy the Mythic Large-mouth Bass. And then Atlanta traffic is always awful."

"You're still hugging me," she noted.

"Sorry," he said, detaching himself from her. He was a pleasant-enough-looking guy, thin but nicely muscled, with a cheerful face. He was dressed in well-worn jeans, work boots, and a plaid shirt over a forest-green T-shirt that read MCCREADY FAMILY FUNERAL HOME AND BAIT SHOP.

He attempted to take her Vuitton suitcase from her and she held firm to the handle, shaking her head. "I've got it."

After he realized that she was not, in fact, going to let go of her luggage, he raised his hands in surrender. "Suit yourself. I just can't believe I'm finally getting to meet you," Duffy said, opening the passenger door for her. "Everybody's excited that you're comin' back home."

"Everybody?" Margot whimpered.

2

THE MCCREADY FAMILY had a compound.

An honest-to-God backwoods compound.

Duffy had called it that with absolutely no irony.

The ride to Lake Sackett started optimistically enough. Atlanta was a bustling metropolis, almost comparable to Chicago.
Margot recognized various department stores and clothing
shops, so at least she wasn't stuck in a fashion desert. But then the
buildings got a little less polished and fewer and farther between.
Pretty soon, all she could see whizzing by were scrubby pines
and sunbaked red clay, broken up by the occasional run-down
gas station or pecan stand.

She had never been this far away from any city. She'd never
felt so alone or out of place. And she wasn't entirely sure this whole
Aunt Tootie job offer wasn't some sort of ruse to lure her into the
middle of nowhere so her paternal family could sacrifice her to
Lake Sackett's forest god like something out of *The Wicker Man*.

While she was suffering this crisis of identity, Duffy continued to chatter to fill the silence. Where was her father? Duffy
seemed nice enough, but there was this unspoken distance

between them, the strange knowledge that they *should* know each other better but didn't, for reasons beyond either of their control.

"We didn't want to crowd you. Tootie said you weren't used to a big family fuss. We figured it would already be pretty overwhelming for ya, new state, new place, and all. Everybody's at Mr. Allanson's visitation—working as usual—so you have some time to settle in, get some sleep before you go through the full McCready roll call."

Some small part of Margot would admit that she was relieved. She didn't think she'd be able to handle meeting the entire family en masse at the moment. She'd barely handled meeting Duffy, and he'd been insistently sweet. She also noted that he hadn't mentioned where Stan was, that he hadn't even made an excuse for her father not being present. What did that mean? Had her father not even tried to make it to see her for the first time in almost thirty years?

Margot realized Duffy was staring at her with an expression both troubled and expectant. She tried to muster some semblance of a polite smile and said, "Thank you, that's very considerate."

"You'll meet 'em all soon enough. Grandpa E.J.J. couldn't be more pleased. He wanted to add you to the company letterhead right away, but we convinced him that might be jumping the gun a little."

"Grandpa E.J.J.?"

"Technically, he's Earl Edward McCready the Third, but everybody called him Earl Junior Junior. E.J.J. My dad was called Junior. And my mom said the whole damn thing was becoming too confusin' so they named me after her side of the family, the McDuffs."

"So my grandfather's name is Earl?"

"No, E.J.J. is *my* grandpa. *Your* grandpa was his cousin, Jack. He and Grandpa E.J.J. were the ones who really got the business thrivin'."

"I think I'm going to need a chart," she muttered.

"It's actually not that hard to remember. McCreadys have lived in Sackett County since before there was a lake. Our branch comes from a pair of brothers, John and Earl Jr. Now, back in 1916, Earl came home from World War I minus several toes and half an ass cheek and built a little bait shop on the shore of the lake selling night crawlers, plus homemade lemonade and sandwiches that his wife, Kate, made. Now, John never had much interest in fishing, but he could make the sturdiest cabinets you ever saw. The Spanish flu epidemic hit Lake Sackett real hard. John had to stop makin' cabinets and start makin' coffins. And it turned out he was an even better coffin maker than he was a cabinetmaker. With all the coffins the town needed—"

"Due to a plague decimating the town's population?"

Duffy smiled brightly—perhaps too brightly, in light of the pandemic discussion. "Yep. With all the extra orders, John had to have more space to work and Earl let him use the back of his store as a workshop. They'd always gotten along real well and liked having each other nearby as they worked. The bait shop grew, because people loved Kate's sandwiches and Earl's fishing stories. And the coffin business took off, because, well, everybody dies eventually. Earl and Kate had E.J.J. John and Ellie had Jack. They all added to the business over time, offering full funeral services and guided fishing tours and such. And they added their own kids with Sarah and Tootie—my dad, Junior, came from E.J.J., obviously. Your dad, Stan, and Uncle Bob came from

Jack, who passed on years ago. Bob and his wife have our cousin, Frankie. My parents have my sister, Marianne, and me—clearly the better child. My dad passed away about five years ago. Mom's still a bit touchy on the subject. Marianne's the only one of our generation to get married and have kids, so far. She and her husband, Carl, have two boys, Nate and Aiden."

"I will definitely need a chart," she said.

"Marianne already made you one. She hung it up in your cabin." Duffy gave her a goofy half smile. "It's a lot to take in, but you'll get it. The most important thing to remember: Nate's a biter."

"I will try to remember that," she promised. "So I noticed that you didn't mention Stan with a second wife or more kids. Um, I guess my father never remarried?"

"No." For the first time in their acquaintance, Duffy's expression was not the picture of boyish excitement. He looked almost offended on Stan's behalf that Margot was questioning her father's loyalty. "He never even looked at another woman after your mama left."

Margot frowned. She'd been counting on some sort of story about a cruel stepmother who wouldn't let her father contact his only daughter. As a child, she'd spent a lot of nights coming up with elaborate reasons why her father never called or wrote. He was a spy. He was an amnesiac prince. He was in the Witness Protection Program. Gerald was a decent man who had always treated her civilly, if a bit coldly. But she'd needed some reason to excuse Stan's silence. And then her mother had given her the full awful explanation about Stan's drinking. Margot had spent years in therapy—sessions starting in college that she'd never told her mother about—working through those excuses. And to find that there was no story, no spies, no amnesia, no evil step-mother? It was more than a little deflating, especially when he'd failed to come pick her up. He'd finally had the chance to start making up for years of absence and he hadn't shown up.

"He's been sober for a long time, you know," Duffy added. "We had a big party for his twenty-year chip and everything. Mama said he was a real mess when we were little. Hell, nobody really blamed your mama all that much for takin' off. I mean, it sucked she never let us see you, but Stan was in no shape to be a daddy to you. We understood that. We just wish she woulda told us where she was goin' with you so we knew you were all right. And it still took years after that for him to clean up. But once he got on the path, he stayed on it. Hasn't had a drink since."

"Good for him," Margot said blandly. "So, is there a reason my father isn't here to pick me up?"

Duffy glanced into the rearview mirror and switched lanes, as if he was stalling. "Uh, well, I think he's seein' to Barbara Lynn Grady. He got called to pick her up a couple of hours ago. It's a bit of an occupational hazard. Death doesn't stop for holidays or airport pickups. He probably won't be home until late tonight."

Margot nodded. While she was hurt that she wouldn't see her father that day, she was also oddly relieved. And then she felt guilty for being impossible to please. To distract herself from these rapidly realigning feelings, she pulled out her iPhone and checked her messages.

"Oh, you're gonna have a hard time gettin' much of a signal up here," Duffy said, waving his large, calloused hands at her smartphone. "It's better closer to town, but the hills between us and Atlanta make it pretty hard for the towers to get through."

She dropped her phone in her carry-on bag. "Of course."

"So, Grandma Tootie says that you're going to start tomorrow. She said you didn't seem the type to want to take time off to rest after your move. E.J.J. is going to do his best to teach you all he knows about the 'people' side of the business. Uncle Bob is a dab hand at handlin' the logistics: paperwork for the coffins, the cremations, arranging the burials, workin' with the police on traffic arrangements, and all that. But he's all thumbs with non-McCready people, even if he's known 'em all his life. If you're not family, he just blurts out the most accidentally offensive things you can think of, because he doesn't know what to say. And that is not the guy you want talkin' you through one of the roughest times in your life."

Margot swallowed heavily. She hadn't thought that part of the job through, dealing with those who were handling the deaths of their loved ones. She'd thought her job would mostly involve ordering flowers and discussing casket linings. She was used to guiding clients through happy occasions. She'd been to only a handful of funerals herself.

No, no doubts. Margot could do this. It wasn't as if she knew these people. She didn't have to worry about what they thought of her handling of their grief. Hell, she'd gotten Miriam Schram through two "thank God the divorce is final" parties, including a custom piñata made to look like her soon to be ex-husband. Margot could handle funerals.

"How does that work, exactly?" she asked, watching as the trees became thicker and the roads seemed to get steeper. "The two businesses together. Don't the bereaved bring down the festive vacation mood for the boaters? Aren't the mourners offended by coolers and pool noodles being carted through the parking lot?"

"The way your grandpa Jack set up the parking lot, they come in through totally different entrances, plus the boaters tend to stick to the lake side of the building anyway. And people seem to like the novelty of it, the tradition. Knowing that yeah, today might suck and you're going through something hard, but better days are coming, and eventually, you're going to be back to living. And Frankie likes to think the funerals help remind the boaters not to be jackasses about wearin' their life vests."

"Does it?"

Duffy pulled a frown. "Not particularly. No."

Duffy easily guided the truck around a bend in the road and a huge glittering blue-green lakefront came into view. For the first time in about a week, Margot's smile was genuine. Lake Sackett seemed to be shaped like a fern, all irregular inlets with the occasional tiny island breaking up the glassy expanse of water. The water was teeming with sailboats and speedboats towing water-skiers and inner tubes full of screaming kids.

"Crowded," Margot observed, searching the shoreline for resorts and hotels. But she could find only small clusters of cabins here and there along those oddly shaped bays.

"Nah, this is nothin'," he said. "You should have seen it a few years ago, when the tourists were really flockin' in. This is the dregs. It's drivin' Uncle Bob just about nuts. Him and the town council, they're pullin' out what little hair they've got left trying to figure out how to get them back."

"Why? Where did they go?"

"Here we are." Duffy ignored the question and nodded his head toward two stone columns that seemed to pop up from out of nowhere. The neatly masoned columns, each with McCREADY carved into the rock in bold letters, flanked a gravel drive nearly hidden by the thick trees.

"The old family compound," Duffy said, steering the truck over bumps and craters in the drive as if they were nothing. Meanwhile, Margot bounced her head off the passenger-side window hard enough to make her teeth rattle. "McCreadys first cleared it as a homestead back in the 1840s. Barely held on to it over the years, to be honest. Turns out we're good at fishing and burying people—we are not great at farming. It wasn't lakefront back then, mind you. We were lucky that the water stopped short of the houses when they dammed up the river in the fifties to make the lake. A lot of people were 'encouraged' by the Corps of Engineers to move along. It's made for what you might call a historically ingrained distrust of outsiders."

"Oh, good." The corners of Margot's mouth tilted up, but by the time she'd finished forming the expression, it was enough to make Duffy recoil.

"Hey, now, you're not an outsider. You're a McCready. Even if people in town don't know you, they're gonna know you. Know what I mean?"

Margot drew back against her seat. This was a mistake. She needed to tell Duffy to turn the truck around and take her right back to the airport because there was no way she could plan funerals and be some sort of minor redneck celebrity.

And she was about to tell him just that when they drove over another rut and she whacked her head against the window again. She opened her eyes just as they topped a rise in the gravel. The trees seemed to melt away to reveal a chain of log cabins grouped along the lakeshore, centering around one large two-story cabin. Each one seemed to have its own personality while sticking to the rustic aesthetic. There was just enough space between so the occupants would have some privacy but still be able to shout for help when the bands of roving rednecks inevitably raided the countryside. Each cabin had flower boxes blooming with yellow and purple Johnny-jump-ups and trailing fuchsias. The cabins had obviously spread out, with new ones added over time, from a huge log structure with a wraparound porch and three eaved windows springing from the roof. Each was recently painted and neatly kept, except for a slightly dingy-looking yellow cottage with a peeling green shingle roof at the end of the road.

Duffy eased the truck past the main house and parked in front of an adorable specimen with a bright blue door. He reached behind the seat to pick up her suitcase, but she opened the back door and grabbed it. "I've got it, thank you."

"You have trust issues in relation to your luggage, huh?" Duffy observed.

"I don't mean any offense," she told him. "I just . . . This is so sad, but I don't have much left in the world. I sold a lot of my things before the move."

Duffy grinned. "Well, this place is all yours. It's one of the newer additions, used to be my sister's until she and Carl got married."

He opened the cabin door and ushered her through. The cabin was basically an overgrown dollhouse, like one of those trendy tiny homes without the pretentious storage solutions. There was one room divided into kitchen and living space, with one bedroom off to the left. A folding privacy screen, painted like the green mountains surrounding the lake, separated the bathroom from the bedroom. Margot got a look at the fairly new soaking tub, with its handheld showerhead but no shower curtain. She suspected it had been chosen because it was the only thing that would fit into the tiny plumbing footprint. "That is going to be an adjustment."

At this point, she was just glad there was a functioning toilet.

A few of the things she'd shipped here were already arranged around the cabin. Some of her clothes hung in the wardrobe. Her Northwestern mugs were washed and ready on the counter of the kitchenette.

"Tootie put the linens and towels out for ya. You should be all set." Duffy backed toward the door. "Well, I'll leave you to your unpacking. Get plenty of sleep tonight. You'll start your training first thing tomorrow. No worries. Bob's real patient. Hardly ever gets ruffled, not even when both of Curtis Taggerty's wives showed up to make his arrangements."

"Ex-wife versus current wife drama?" Margot asked with a yawn.

"No, they were both his current wives," Duffy said, shaking his head. "They just didn't know it."

"I would give that the reaction it deserves if I wasn't so tired," Margot said as she hung her suit bag in the tiny closet. Somehow, leaving a few things in her suitcase helped her feel like this wasn't a long-term situation, like she could throw her stuff in her bag at any time and use her open-ended ticket back to Chicago.

"Also, I've meant to ask: what grown adult woman allows people to call her 'Tootie'?"

Duffy snorted, his big blue eyes twinkling. "Her real name is Eloise. When she was little, she took these tap-dancing lessons and that was one of the songs they learned the basics to. 'A tootie-tah, a tootie-tah, a tootie-tah-tah.' And she would just drive her whole family nuts, tapping up and down the hallway, up and down the stairs, up and down the sidewalk. 'A tootie-tah, a tootie-tah, a tootie-tah-tah.' They started calling her 'Tootie' to try to tease her out of it. But she's so stubborn, the name-calling just made her do it more. And eventually the name just stuck. Heck, we don't even call her 'grandma.' She's always been Tootie."

"Well, when your name is Tootie, what other qualifiers do you need?"

"That about covers it," Duffy said. "The spare key's on your nightstand there. And if you hear something that sounds like two rocks being banged together, don't panic. It's mostly harmless, just . . . don't go outside on your own. Really, it would be better if you just waited for one of us to come get you in the morning."

"Okay," Margot said, flopping down onto the mattress, making the springs squeal. The sheets smelled freshly laundered, that airy clean scent that came only from drying on a line in the sun. She'd smelled it once that she could remember, when her mother's Whirlpool dryer broke down and the appliance store took two whole days to deliver an upgraded replacement. The blue-and-green quilt was handmade, she could tell from the irregularity of the fabrics and the stitching. And she tried not to be touched that these strangers had taken the time to make her bed with sun-bleached sheets and an heirloom coverlet, but she was.

Her great-aunt had put a much-loved quilt on her bed, but her father hadn't even bothered to pick her up at the airport. That helped squelch the warm fuzzy feeling spreading across her chest. He didn't want to see her. After all this time, when he finally had the chance, he still didn't want to see her. Why did that hurt so much? She was a grown woman. She didn't need her "real" daddy to hug her and kiss her boo-boos. So why did the rejection leave an acidic burn that made her rub the heel of her hand against her sternum in the search for a deep breath?

Eyes watering with exhaustion and unshed tears, Margot buried her face into her pillow and inhaled the spring-fresh smell of linens dried in the sun.

Until her head popped up from the pillow. "Duffy! What do you mean 'mostly harmless'? . . . Duffy!"

MARGOT RECOGNIZED THE telltale sign of cramps before she even woke up.

Face still buried in the pillow, she knew she was starting her period, way off cycle, on the first day she was supposed to work in a funeral home. Because this was her life.

She was completely without supplies, beyond the emergency tampons in her purse. Duffy had left his spare truck key with her and told her to use his vehicle anytime. But could she even find a store if she wanted to? Her phone had GPS, but her signal was at about half a bar. She remembered the small group of lakeshore buildings she'd spotted on the drive in. Surely she could reach that if she just kept turning left. That was a sound navigation plan, right?

She sighed, hauling her ass out of bed and wincing at the soreness in her legs and back. Too much time on an airplane, not enough Pilates over the last few weeks.

She glanced at the mirror on the wall, surrounded by beaten tin, and blanched at the scarecrow hair sticking up around her head. She spent a few minutes rifling through her suitcase for some yoga pants and a hair elastic. She didn't bother with makeup. It was six in the morning in the backwoods; there was no one to impress.

Margot paused at the door, suddenly remembering Duffy's warning not to leave her cabin on her own. Was that an all-encompassing warning, like "Don't leave your cabin until one of us comes to get you to protect you from the mountain mole people," or more of a predawn warning, like "Don't leave your cabin until after sunrise, because *they* can't survive in sunlight"? Were there bears here in Lake Sackett? Would they attack her because of her lady issues?

"Oh, for God's sake," she huffed, throwing the cabin door open. She was greeted by the glorious sight of fog rolling across the surface of the lake, the misty blue skies opening up to make way for the sun. Margot paused for a second. She'd thought she would be immune to the views of Lake Sackett. How could it compare to the oceanic majesty of Lake Michigan, after all? But there was a certain appeal to being able to see across the lake to the trees. A cozy, protected feeling she didn't get staring out at the vastness of a great lake.

Duffy had thoughtfully parked his truck halfway between her little dollhouse and his more rugged man-cabin, which seemed to have a giant fishing lure–shaped birdfeeder and a set of wind chimes made of beer cans. Margot was glad she'd met Duffy the day before, because she probably would have judged him pretty hard based on the wind chime thing.

The truck did not roar to life so much as purr, something she was sure her family/neighbors—scary combination—probably appreciated. She slowly crept over the lumpy driveway and eased the truck onto the highway.

"Please, God, don't let me mess up my cousin's truck," she

muttered, letting the pickup trundle down the road. "I don't know what the punishment is for truck injury in Georgia, but I'm sure I wouldn't like it."

Her plan to "just keep turning left" was unnecessary because there was nowhere to turn—the road was one long loop around the lake, leading right into the center of town. There wasn't even much town to navigate, really. Tiny houses sprawled away from the empty main street with its two gas stations, a bakery, a golf cart dealership, a diner, and a shop called the Jerky Jamboree devoted entirely to exotic animal jerky. The darkened buildings seemed to stick with a log cabinish, rustic theme, stacked up next to one another like cracker boxes. But the buildings had clearly seen better days. The roofs were peeling and the signs needed some refreshing. Also, none of these businesses were open, save the Rise and Shine Diner, and she was pretty sure they didn't sell feminine supplies.

And then she spotted the squat plank building flanking a two-story wooden bear holding a LAKE SACKETT GENERAL STORE sign. Miracle of miracles, the lights were on and Margot thought she spotted a red OPEN sign in the bear's mouth. The bear theme was really not making her feel better about her current state.

Margot aimed the truck at the ursine mascot and walked across the gravel lot. (Was everything gravel here?) The general store lived up to her every expectation. It was a sort of aisle-less mishmash of essentials and pretty, useless trinkets. It looked like the old "cracker barrel" type stores you'd see on shows like *Little House on the Prairie*, but with dishwasher pods and K-cups mixed in with the kitschy lake decor. This was probably the sort of place most of the tourists used to stock up before heading to their cabins, for the charm factor alone. The locals used the more modern Food Carnival grocery, but Margot wasn't in the mood to drive an extra ten miles just for tampons.

Chuck, who accentuated his name tag with both suspenders and a belt, oversaw the mostly empty store. He barely glanced over his copy of the *Lake Sackett Ledger* as she walked into the crowded space. The feminine supplies were crammed in next to a display of swimmer's ear remedies and beer koozies.

Not wanting to repeat this experience anytime soon, Margot stocked up. Her little basket was overflowing when she rounded the corner toward the tiny pharmacy section and walked face-first into a man's green utility jacket. Peeling her face off the material that smelled of April-fresh fabric softener, she dropped the basket to the floor.

"Ooof," she grunted, taking a step back and rubbing her nose. "I'm so sorry."

He was tall, and broader than she normally appreciated in a man, with a narrow waist and long, rangy arms. His sandy hair was windswept in that far-too-flattering-to-be-an-accident way, and he had a thick dark-blond beard covering his cheeks. And despite the fact that she'd hated full facial hair ever since beard mania took root in the city's hipster population, she found that she liked it now. It suited his whole "lost soul" aesthetic.

He looked . . . haunted, like he was carrying an awful weight around on his shoulders. It was so different from the glib, polished princes she was used to dealing with in the city, so concentrated on projecting an image of unaffected success that they wouldn't dare frown. Who was he? What had hurt him so much? How was it possible to be that attractive while basically looking like a homeless loner?

"Hi," she breathed, sounding much huskier than she'd intended. His brow furrowed and he bent to pick up the basket. As he leaned closer, she caught the crisp, clean scent of shampoo from his hair. She grabbed a nearby rack of shelves to keep her knees unjellied.

He rose, and his eyes went wide at the array of tampons from her basket as he wordlessly handed them back to her. She grabbed items from another shelf—a few scented jar candles and a blue glass bird attached to a suction cup—to try to cover up the smorgasbord of feminine protection.

"It's not all for one . . . week," she said before pressing her lips together.

Maybe she could toss the basket down the aisle as a distraction and run away.

Green Jacket grimaced and said, "Good luck with that."

And before she could come up with a clever answer—or any answer, really—he eased past her and headed for the coffee section. She hid behind a stack of beer cases, watching as he picked out grounds and filters and then checked out without a word to Chuck.

Margot tiptoed toward the checkout. The man crossed the street, coffee supplies in hand, to walk into the Rise and Shine. Could she follow him? Maybe she could get some fruit and granola. That was reasonable, right, making excuses so she could follow a handsome stranger in order to reassure him she wasn't some menstruating monster?

"You gonna pay for them lady things?" Chuck asked. Margot realized she'd drifted toward the door and now appeared to be shoplifting sanitary supplies. Her head dropped and she slumped back to the register to pay. She really hoped this was not the sort of story that circulated on the local gossip circuit.

As she climbed into the truck, she spotted Green Jacket through the front window of the diner, hunched over a cup of coffee. Who went out for coffee after buying their own coffee supplies? He looked so miserable, so alone, even in that dining room full of customers. Margot felt all her city-born "mind your own business" instincts evaporate and she had the urge to walk into the diner and hug him.

She forced her eyes away from the window and started the truck.

"There's probably a dozen available men in this town and you zero in on the depressive lumberjack," she muttered.

3

$\mathcal{M}$ARGOT STRAIGHTENED HER black Armani and smoothed her chignon in the tin mirror. The tailored pants combined with the low-heeled pumps made her legs look impossibly long and her waist slim. She was overdressed—she knew that—but the suit was her favorite and felt like slipping on armor. Nothing could hurt her when she knew that she looked this good.

She leaned over her sink to get the right angle in the tiny vanity mirror to apply her eyeliner. Just as she touched the tip under her lashes, a braying bark from what sounded like the hounds of hell made her hand jerk up. The liner left a wide black smear above her eye. The howls and barks were growing closer, but Margot was focused on the thick black smudge caked across the smoky eye she'd just spent five minutes perfecting.

"Augh," she groaned, keeping her raccooned eye shut while she fumbled for a tissue. "What in the bluest of hells?"

In the mirror, she saw a single small black-and-tan dachshund trotting through her bedroom. She whirled around and watched as the dog sniffed the borders of her room. How had it gotten in? Had she left the door unlocked when she'd stumbled back into her cabin that morning? Also, how did one dog make all of that—

Margot shrieked as a dozen dogs of all breeds and sizes gamboled through her door, crashing into her little cabin like a tidal wave of slobber and yapping. A Dalmatian with a spade-shaped ear made himself comfortable in her only chair. A bulldog wearing a lampshade collar ran at her armoire. Two dogs of a fluffy indiscriminate breed, with identical brown and white markings, beelined for her wastebasket. A sable pit bull wearing a pink tutu hopped up on her bed and circled until she plopped down in just the right spot. The rest were a furry blur, swarming around Margot's legs, sniffing from all angles. Margot froze and kept her hands at crotch level. It was her only defense.

The dachshund ringleader sat in the middle of the room, observing this melee with no small amount of canine smugness.

"So many dogs," she marveled.

Tootie shuffled into view, wearing a PETA T-shirt and bright purple Bermuda shorts.

"Oh, y'all calm down and act like you've been in company before!" she cackled.

Margot squeaked, still unable to process the doggy chaos. But when the bulldog nosed her armoire open and started sniffing, she yelped, "No! Not the wardrobe! That's where my shoes live!"

Margot dashed past Tootie, shooed the dog out of the way, and snapped the door shut.

"Oh, don't mind Dodger. He's not a chewer. Now, Lulu," Tootie said, nodding toward the tutued pit bull lounging on Margot's bed. "She has real expensive taste in shoes. Watch her like a hawk."

"Or, you know, they could just, I don't know, stay outside, away from my shoes," Margot said.

"Fair enough." Tootie didn't seem at all offended as she opened the door. "Come on, now, all of you. Git. Go have your breakfast."

At her command, the pack leaped to their feet and scrambled out the door. Margot breathed a little easier and stretched a more friendly "professional" smile across her face. She crossed the tiny room and extended her hand. "Hello, I'm Margot."

"Oh, honey, don't try puttin' on any of those airs; come here." And just like that, Tootie dodged Margot's hand and wrapped two surprisingly strong arms around her. "I'm so glad to see you again."

"Thank you so much for your generous offer. I'm not sure what I would have done without it."

"Stop with the interview talk, honey, you have the job," Tootie retorted, pulling a small brass name tag out of her pocket. "Speakin' of which, Bob had this made up special for ya."

The tag read MARGOT—ADMINISTRATIVE OFFICE. Margot noticed that her last name had been omitted, but she wasn't sure if that was because her father's family didn't want to explain to customers why she used Cary or because they didn't include last names on McCready's name tags.

Margot took the little tag from her great-aunt's wrinkled grasp and pinned it to her chest. "Thank you."

"Now, don't be nervous," Tootie said. "Most everybody knows this is new territory for you."

"I'm not nervous," Margot lied breezily, giving her a little smile.

"If you say so, honey. Now, I wanted to talk to you about your daddy. I know he wanted to come with Duffy yesterday to see to you at the airport, but there was a problem with the body he was drivin' and he couldn't get away."

"I'm sure," Margot said, running a cotton swab under her eye to remove the misplaced eyeliner.

"I know you have every reason to be pissed off as a sack full of wet cats at your daddy, and I know this is none of my business. But Stan, he's a complicated man, Margot. He's been through a lot. And he's missed you something awful. Just give him a chance and I'm sure the two of you will find some common ground."

"You're right." Margot nodded. "This is none of your business."

"Oh, I'm gonna like you, I can tell," Tootie said. "Be sure to use that frosty 'eat wheat grass and die' tone when Kay McComber calls to try to renegotiate the bill for her husband's funeral again. Fool woman would use a coupon for his casket if we'd let her."

"Is she struggling financially?"

"No. Asa hasn't even died yet. He's healthy as a horse. She's just cheap. Frankly, I hope she goes first, just to give Asa a break from dollar-store toilet paper."

Margot grimaced. A soft knock preceded a gracefully aging matinee idol lookalike sticking his head through her partially open door. "Hello?"

"Come on in, Bob!" Tootie exclaimed.

"Mornin', Tootie." The salt-and-pepper fox grinned at Margot. "Well, aren't you pretty as a picture? I'm your uncle Bob, your daddy's brother."

"It's nice to meet you." Again, she stretched her hand out for a shake, because she did not like the way Bob's arms were starting to spread. What was with these people and hugging strangers? Had they not heard of personal space?

Bob looked a bit startled to have a hug preemptively thwarted but shook her hand with enthusiasm. "You, too, sweetheart. I'm gonna be drivin' you to work this morning. Ready to go?"

Margot took a deep breath and picked up her shoulder bag. "Ready as I'll ever be. Thanks, Tootie."

Tootie patted Margot's cheek. "You have a nice first day, hon. I'll see you later on."

Bob opened the passenger side of his green McCready Family Funeral Home and Bait Shop truck and helped Margot climb up. Margot lifted her ponytail off the back of her neck, where a ring of sweat was already making the hairs stick to her skin. She could feel the wet heat soaking through her clothes, like she was sliding into a bath while wearing her suit. "It's only nine. How is it already this hot?"

Bob snorted. "Aw, heck, hon. This is nothin'. On the Fourth of July, you'd swear your face would melt right off. Now, don't worry, I'm not going to just throw you in the deep end on your own," he assured her. "We'll start you off with paperwork, a few casket catalogues, how to pull a widow out of the grave she just swan-dived into."

"Beg pardon?"

"It only happens every once in a while, but you need to know how to pull somebody out safely, because if you don't lift with your legs, you can really hurt your back."

Margot paused for the laugh she was sure would come. It did not.

"Is that for me?" She pointed to the oversize travel mug in the nearest cup holder.

"Yeah, I thought you might be a mornin' grump like my daughter, Frankie," he said as she took a sniff of the coffee. "She will spring up and poke you in the eye if you try to wake her before nine and she's not on call."

"What if you call her to wake her up?"

"She'll wait until the next time she sees you, and when you least expect it, she will spring up and poke you in the eye. And she'll yell, 'Let that be a lesson to you!' while doin' it," he said. "She's small, sneaky, and has a profound sense of retaliation. Like God's little angel of vengeance."

She snorted as she raised the mug to her lips. It struck her that despite the fact that he was describing his child's antisocial behavior, Uncle Bob sounded proud. Despite his conservative clothes and the JESUS IS MY COPILOT sticker on his dashboard, he didn't seem to have any problems with the fact that his daughter occasionally assaulted people. It would be nice to know that sort of unconditional love.

"Poison!" Margot gasped, spitting the coffee back into the lid of the travel mug. It was so bitter and acidic, she ran her tongue over her teeth to make sure they hadn't dissolved. "This is a mug full of poison."

"Yeah, we take our coffee pretty strong."

"It's chewy," Margot said, taking the handkerchief Bob offered and wiping her chin. And her teeth.

"Well, we work odd hours," he said. "And my wife, your aunt Leslie, she's at the Snack Shack making coffee for fishermen at five in the morning. So she makes it strong enough they could strip their outboard with it, if they wanted to."

"Does she make the coffee for the funeral home, too?"

"Oh, sure."

"Of course," she said, nodding. "So Leslie is the opposite of cousin Frankie, in terms of the morning person thing."

"Yeah, Les is a little ray of sunshine, no matter what time of day," he said, tapping the small plastic-framed picture of his smiling wife mounted near his steering wheel. "She bounces up out of bed at four and runs down to the shack to find new things to deep-fry, happy as a pup with two tails."

"Finding new things to deep-fry?"

"Oh, yeah, she loves breakin' new ground in deep-fryin'—ice cream, cookies, oatmeal. She runs a booth at the state fair every year just to show off her new discovery. This year, she's found a way to roll up an entire Thanksgiving meal in a cornbread stuffing shell and deep-fry it. Turkey, mashed potatoes and gravy, cranberry sauce, the works."

"Wow."

"Maybe you can come with us this year! It's only a few months away. And E.J.J. has been thinking about entering his church barbecue team in the cookin' competitions."

"Churches have barbecue teams?"

"Oh, sure, the elders get together and barbecue pork shoulders for fund-raisers and such. Our team calls themselves the Holy Smokes, on account of the big smokers they use."

She smiled and made a noncommittal noise. In a few months, she wanted to be back in a city with more than one Starbucks. Or even one. One Starbucks would be nice, since Leslie's coffee could potentially melt her esophagus.

"By the way, why is Tootie being chased by a pack of wild dogs?" Margot asked.

"Tootie's always had a bit of an issue with taking in strays," Bob told her. "Now, don't get me wrong. She's not like one of those people you see on the hoarder shows. Her house is a show-place. The dogs all have their own little kennel behind her cabin and they're all in good health. But Dougie Hazard is keeping a really close eye on her."

"And Dougie Hazard is?"

"The local animal control officer, fancy name for dogcatcher. He spends most of his time gettin' possums out of folks' houses." Bob turned the truck into the parking lot for the McCready Family Funeral Home and Bait Shop. Margot leaned forward, eager for her first glimpse of her new workplace. But then she slumped back, a little frown on her face. She'd expected some cross between a church and a mini-golf course, but the funeral home was, if anything, understated, a plain, cream-colored fa-cade with brass accents. A black late-model hearse was parked off to the side, next to a brick sign displaying the business's logo in brass letters.

The building was open in the middle, in what she'd heard called a "dog run," with double doors opening to the chapel on the right and business office on the left. She could see all the way through to the lake and the huge dock extending behind the funeral home. Several bass boats had already docked and Margot could see them lining up at Sarah's Snack Shack.

"Tootie wanted to call it a 'marina' to make it sound a little more dignified. But some people thought we were puttin' on airs, so we went with 'bait shop.' Of course, the locals just call it the Bait and Bury," Bob said, grinning. "But there's not much you can do to stop that."

Bob pulled the truck into the staff parking lot behind the funeral home. Margot could see now that the dock was one of three, all offering slips for boats. Another neatly painted red shop—Jack's Tackle and Stuff—took up the dock on the left. Unlike in the town proper, everything was recently painted. The landscaping was neat and the gravel was free of trash. Margot sincerely hoped keeping the gravel pristine wasn't part of her job description.

"So here's the water side of things," Bob said. "Donna, Les, and Duffy keep things running out here. Donna and Duff—and Marianne's husband, Carl, when he has the time—they all take turns running the tackle shop, though they both hate it something awful. Dealin' with one or two members of the public at a time in their boats, they can handle. Dealin' with multiple random citizens at the same time? We have to reward Donna with a gift sampler from the jerky store every time she goes a month without tossin' a customer out on his ass."

Bob grimaced and opened the console between them, dropping a quarter in a little plastic container labeled SWEAR JAR. "Just in case you ever tick her off, her favorite jerky is alligator. I would say it's because she absorbs the gator's meanness through the meat, but I wouldn't say it to her face."

Margot managed not to visibly shudder and was proud of herself for it.

"I am not ashamed to say I'm afraid of that woman," he said. "Cousin Junior, God rest his soul, was a brave, brave man."

"What's that little hut there?" Margot asked, nodding toward the third dock, where people were lining up at a kiosk covered in enlarged photos of happy tourists holding fish.

"That's where guests sign up to take private fishing excursions with Duffy and Donna. They've got a solid reputation for finding the sweet spots no one else can find, which is getting harder and harder."

Bob turned the ignition and the truck almost immediately got about five degrees hotter. Feeling her hair fall flat in the exponentially growing humidity, Margot opened the door and hopped out.

"Duffy said something sort of ominous like that yesterday, but then didn't elaborate. Which I found to be strange, and off-putting."

Bob opened a door labeled OFFICE and let her in first. She waved the lapels of her jacket to let the air-conditioning under her arms. "Well, I don't know what that is, but I was referrin' to what people around here call the water dump."

Margot took a moment to stare at the white-painted wood paneling decorated with various paint-by-number Jesuses. (*Jesusi?*) Some of the eyes stared back. And they followed her when she moved.

"Your grandma Sarah loved her paint-by-number Jesuses," Bob told her, smirking a little as he watched her move back and forth in front of one particularly creepy piece involving a Day-Glo crown of thorns. "She must have painted two hundred of 'em before she passed on. They gave Duffy and Marianne nightmares when they were kids, but no one has the heart to throw them out."

Margot shuddered. "You were saying something about a 'water dump'?"

"Two years ago, some dumbass—" Bob grunted as they walked into a darkened office and he dropped another quarter in another plastic jerky container marked SWEAR JAR. Bob tossed his jacket on a brass clotheshorse in the corner. "Some *dummy* at the Army Corps of Engineers forgot to carry the one when he was measuring the depth of the lake and overestimated by a coupl'a million gallons. So he sent a report to the guys runnin' the dam at Sackett

Point to let out about ten times the water they should have. The lake feeds the rivers, so the towns below the dam flooded. The lake dropped to record lows just as we hit a two-year drought. So we haven't had nearly enough rain to replace the water lost. When the water dropped, we saw parts of the county nobody had seen since the Corps made the lake sixty years ago. Discovered a few people we didn't know were missin', but that's beside the point."

Bob picked up a clipboard and walked Margot down the Jesus-lined hallway. "People were mad about it. There was a town meetin', where people mostly made jokes at the government's expense. The *Ledger* printed some pretty pointed editorial cartoons. But nobody really thought of how it was going to hit us long term. The fishing spots dried up. Boaters ran aground because they didn't know where the shallows were. And a couple of them ran into each other because they had less space and it got crowded. And the boatin'. community is pretty small. The word spread and our tourism numbers dropped like a hot rock. It's hurt the whole town, because the economy depends on tourist dollars. Jobs are dryin' up. We've had two restaurants shut down in the last year, and a gas station. Families that have lived here for generations are movin' away."

"Oh, that's awful."

"It's hurt us, here at the marina. But fortunately, funeral homes are a recession-proof business."

Margot nodded. "Because everybody dies."

"Exactly," Bob said. "Frankie wrote that at the top of our mission statement the last time E.J.J. made us have a board meeting. He swore it was the last time he would invite her."

"Did the townsfolk track down the guy who messed up the water math?"

"We tried," Bob grumbled. "Believe me, we tried."

Bob showed her the reception room, a welcoming area decorated in soft green and ivory. There was a private viewing room, four "chapels" for full visitations and funerals, a "retreat" room where bereaved families could get away from the other mourners and get something to eat. Again, it was all very comfortable and subtly furnished.

"Embalmin' and processin' happen downstairs and we move the caskets with a very quiet elevator system at the end of that hallway," Bob said. "I don't think you're ready to go downstairs yet."

"You would be correct," she said.

"Frankie's down there workin' on Mrs. Grady now, but she said she'd be upstairs to say hi later," Bob said, opening a pair of double doors to reveal a display of several shiny caskets and a wall of burial urns. A beautiful antique cherry table was situated in the far corner, flanked by two comfortable wingback chairs.

"This is the showroom and sales office," he said. "You wouldn't be able to handle that just yet because you're not licensed, but as soon as you're ready, I can help you through that process."

"Is that a dolphin urn? For ashes?" she asked, pointing at a cremation container fashioned to look like a cresting wave topped by leaping sea creatures.

"Yeah, we ordered it when Frankie was going through her dolphin phase as a teenager. She thought it was pretty. But it's been there for ten years, and no one has bought it."

"Of course not, it's like putting an ankle tattoo on cremains," Margot said, lifting a brow and making Bob snicker.

"That's a new one!" he cackled. "You'll have to share that one with Les. Now we just use it to store extra tissues. And as a conversation piece."

She nodded to a door at the rear of the salesroom. "What's back there?"

"Oh, uh . . . that's a sleepin' cubby. It's a sort of mini-apartment, a bedroom and bathroom and not much else. It's between this room and the break room, so it's convenient," he said. When Margot pulled a face, he added, "Well, it's tradition for an apprentice mortician to have an apartment on site when they're learnin' the ropes, so they can be on call for body pickups. With us, that's not really necessary, since everybody lives so close. So, really, it's just there for when we get called out late at night and don't feel steady enough to drive back home. At least, it was until your da— Stan moved in. Pretty much full-time, since your mom left. Said it was too quiet at his place."

"As opposed to the hustle and bustle of a funeral home?"

Bob's answer was interrupted by the appearance of a pale, slender woman just a few years younger than Margot, wearing ripped jeans, purple Converse, and a bright blue shirt with van Gogh's TARDIS spiraling across the front, under a long white lab coat. Her dark, almost black hair bore matching blue and purple highlights. "Hi, Daddy. I thought I heard you up here."

"And this is my Frankie," Bob said proudly, kissing her cheek. "Frankie, darlin', this is your cousin Margot. Margot, my daughter, Frankie."

"I tried to get everybody to wear name tags, but Mama said they would insult your intelligence," Frankie told her. Unlike most of the family, Frankie extended her hand for a shake instead of wrapping Margot up in a hug. Margot decided that despite the odd clothes and neon hair, she was going to like Frankie.

"I would be open to it," Margot said.

Frankie grinned. "Dad, I've got Miss Barbara downstairs. Uncle Stan said her sister should be comin' in soon."

Bob nodded. Margot swallowed a growing lump in her throat. She tried to clear it away. "Downstairs as in . . ." Margot glanced at the floor, as if she thought it might give way and drop her into a basement filled with nightmares. She stared at Frankie's lab coat. "So you . . ."

"I'm the undertaker, yes," Frankie said. "Fourth generation. And don't worry, I wear gloves."

Margot's gaze dropped. She hadn't even realized she'd been rubbing the hand that touched Frankie's against her slacks. "I'm sorry. That was rude."

"Eh, it's less offensive than a lot of people's reactions."

Margot cleared her throat again, fighting to find a way out of this awkward conversational lull. "Had Miss Barbara been ill for very long?"

Bob blushed to the roots of his silver hair. "Oh, no. She was in her late sixties and healthy as a horse until the end. And I suppose she died the way she lived."

Frankie added cheekily, "Under a thirty-year-old."

Margot clamped her jaw to trap the guffaw that wanted to burst out of her mouth.

"And a thirty-two-year-old," Bob added, pursing his lips.

Frankie snickered. "It was a real mess at the scene. Both of Miss Barbara's companions were trying to claim next of kin, which complicated transport. So Stan was out pretty late."

"Sounds like Miss Barbara kept a lot of people out late," Margot muttered.

"See?" Bob hooted. "You're already getting to know the community! Let's go get you acquainted with the forms and the filing system."

"I'd rather make a thousand Y incisions than fill out one form. Back to the basement," Frankie said. "I'll be downstairs if you need anything, Daddy. Nice to meet you, Cousin Margot."

"You too. Sorry about the hand thing."

"No problem. We'll talk after your shift." She winked at Margot and made for the stairway door marked EMPLOYEES ONLY.

A little fireplug-shaped woman with brassy blond hair and a bright pink leatherette Bible clutched in her hands waddled through the front door. Frankie walked that much faster to the employees-only area. Margot's brow lifted. Did Frankie avoid customers as a rule, or this woman in particular?

Margot watched as the easy humor seemed to slide right off Bob's face. His back went stiff and he started tugging at his blue-and-red-striped tie.

"M-Miss Justine," Bob stammered. "So glad to see you. I mean, not that we're glad that you're here. I mean, we're not glad that your sister died, but we're glad that we can help."

"Well, my sister wouldn't have wanted anybody else handlin' her services," Miss Justine said, staring at Margot through watery red eyes. A flush of unease swept through Margot's belly, with nowhere to run from this stranger's grief. But she plastered on her most pleasant, though not inappropriately cheerful, expression. She could do this. This was part of her job. She hadn't blinked in the face of hostile florists or hysterical knife-wielding omelet chefs. She wouldn't be scared off by a little old lady with a pink Bible.

"Margot, sweetheart, this is Justine Phillips, she's Barbara Lynn Grady's next of kin," Bob said. "Miss Justine, this is Margot, you remember? Stan's girl?"

Miss Justine's beady brown eyes went wide and this strange, greedy sort of glow shone through that mist of tears. "Of course I remember. You were such a pretty little thing. And we all remember when your mama, bless her heart, just up and left poor Stan. We always wondered if you'd ever come back."

Margot's expression went from pleasant to blank. "Um, yes, well, I'm glad to see you here. Er, not *here*, as in I'm happy you've lost a loved one, but glad to see you again."

Margot pinched her nose. She was off to a *wonderful* start.

Miss Justine dabbed at her eyes with a lacy white handkerchief. "I just can't believe she's gone."

"At least she passed peacefully," Bob added. Margot's brows lifted as she remembered Frankie's comment about Miss Barbara dying sandwiched between two thirtysomethings. Her head whipped toward Bob just as his face flushed red. "I mean, she went the way she would have wanted. I mean—"

Uncle Bob really did say the worst possible thing when confronted with non–family members. That was even worse than Margot's comment. Margot stared at Bob, who seemed to be at a loss for words. And whatever words he could come up with probably wouldn't help. The silence was a palpable thing, filling the room like infernal Jell-O. Margot's mouth seemed to flap open and shut. And for the first time in years, she couldn't come up with something clever to say to smooth the awkwardness away.

They both sagged with relief when an adorable old man in a navy suit walked through the door.

"E.J.J." Bob sighed. "Miss Justine is here to discuss her sister's service."

"Oh, Justine, we are so sorry for your loss," he said, his tone just the right balance of welcoming and respectful. He winked at Margot and took Miss Justine's hands in his.

"Miss Justine, you come on in here and we'll get ya taken care of," E.J.J. continued, guiding her toward the sales desk. "Bob here will bring you the paperwork your sister left behind for her preplanned service. Now, is there anything you need?"

"Some coffee would be much appreciated," Justine said with a sniff. "Light and sweet."

"I'll get it!" Eager for any task that would remove her from the awkward scene, Margot moved toward the break room on swift, quiet feet. As she walked out, he heard Justine ask, "Barbara didn't ask for her granddaughter to sing 'Amazing Grace,' now, did she? I love Carly like my own, but she couldn't carry a tune in a brass bucket."

⁓

MARGOT LEARNED A lot of things about her family that first day. Uncle Bob kept swear jars stashed all over the funeral home because he had the dirtiest mouth of any family member on the premises. He'd tried to kick the habit since his daughter was a little girl, but his wife had installed the jars six months before, after he challenged her to give up biting her nails. Aunt Leslie'd had a beautiful manicure since spring, while Bob was still dropping F-bombs at the dinner table. So Leslie was using his swear jar contributions to pay for her trailer rental for the state fair this year.

Duffy waved at her through the window of the office she would share with Bob. It was a welcome rest for eyes overworked by the tiny print on the various forms and procedure manuals. But as soon as a trio of pale men in expensive-looking fishing ensembles joined Duffy, he was all business, escorting them down the dock to their pontoon boat in manly, efficient fashion. Frankie spent most of her day in the basement but popped upstairs at lunchtime to share a sandwich with her father. They were a well-oiled machine, her family, and they were trying their hardest to make her into one of the little cogs. And Margot wasn't sure how she felt about that yet.

By five, the Allanson service was in full swing. As the funeral home's chief accompanist, Tootie had arrived earlier to plink gentle hymns on the piano as background music to the mourning. She'd stopped by the office to drop off a Tupperware container full of fried chicken and mashed potatoes and a pat on Margot's head.

For someone who was not used to casual affection or home-cooked meals, this was a bewildering gesture that made Margot close the office door and hide—work, she was *working*. She was being highly productive, studying a program that would allow her to launch an online tribute wall for the funeral home. She'd found the program while she was still in Chicago, researching ways she could be effective in this new job. She was *not* hiding like a little girl afraid of grandmotherly affection.

Margot took off her reading glasses and rubbed her hands over her eyes, fully aware that she'd sweated off her makeup hours before. She'd shed the suit jacket and her shoes and was drinking water because she didn't think her kidneys could stand much more of Leslie's coffee.

She was exhausted, but she felt like she'd put in a good day's work. She'd averted most of Bob's verbal disasters. She'd learned the scheduling process and the paperwork she was allowed to file with the state. She'd only contributed fifty cents to the swear jar.

A rough baritone sounded from the doorway. "You favor your mama. I always figured you would. You looked just like her, even when you were a baby."

Margot wasn't sure what she expected in Stan McCready. Maybe some hungover Bible-salesman type in a slick black suit and a gold cross tie tack, talking widows into more expensive caskets than they could afford. But Stan McCready was wearing navy dress pants and a blue button-down that looked fresh out of the package. He had the same look as the haunted lumberjack, that down-to-the-quick hurt that shaped his whole frame. Up close, he was basically a human basset hound. Big, sad brown eyes bracketed by puffy bags and a mouth that naturally turned down. She recognized the square chin and the bow shape of his lips as her own, and for the first time in her life she disliked her own face.

"I brought ya some sweet tea. Used to love it when you were little. Ya'd pitch a fit if I didn't stick a second straw in my glass at restaurants so we could share. I used to call you my little Sweet Tea." He quietly set a tall glass, already wet with condensation, on her desk. "Drove your mama crazy."

His speech was clear, she noted, and he didn't smell like booze, new or stale. So Duffy's tales of sobriety rang true. Good for him, she supposed, though it seemed to hurt a little more, knowing he'd sobered up after her mother left and *still* hadn't reached out to Margot. It almost made it worse.

Margot would not avert her eyes. She would not show distress. She was fine. She would show him that she was fine. She cleared her throat and reached her hand out, clenching her forearm to keep it from shaking. "It's nice to meet you."

Stan frowned at her outstretched limb as if she were offering him a dead fish. "Well, it's not like we've never seen each other before."

"Not that I can remember," she said, not intending that edge of accusation to color her voice.

"Yeah, well, that's how things worked out, I guess," Stan grumbled. "I was sorry to hear your mama passed. Nobody told me, or I might have come up for the service."

"I didn't know how to contact you," she said honestly.

There was a considerable effort rippling over his face, a fight to try to keep his expression neutral. "Well, you're here now, I suppose that's what counts."

"Not for long, though," she said, smiling that polite but cold public smile that didn't involve any teeth. "As much as I appreciate the opportunity to work here, I'm lining up interviews in other cities."

And then she took a drink of the iced tea to wet her parched throat and immediately spat it back into the glass. It was so thick and sickly sweet that for a second she thought she'd drunk maple syrup.

"Why?" Margot wheezed, gagging.

"What's wrong?" Stan demanded. "Ya have one of them food allergies?"

"No! I have functioning taste buds." Margot reached into her purse and swiped her mouth with a tissue. "You gave this to a child?"

"You loved it!" he protested. "What did your mama give you, growin' up? French spring water?"

"No, it's fine. I didn't know you could make diabetes in liq-uid form, but now I do, so . . . learning experiences all around." Margot shuddered. So much for dignity and reserve.

Stan lost the fight and his frown lines deepened. "So, Tootie said you got yourself crosswise with your job. I wouldn't let it worry ya. It happens to everybody."

"Unless you work with your family, of course," Margot re-torted, and she immediately regretted the bitter tone of her voice. She didn't want to lose her grip on the indifference she was trying so hard to exude. She didn't want him to know she was bitter or angry. She didn't want him to know how much she still hurt. She wanted him to know that her stepfather had taken care of her, for the most part. That she'd been just fine without Stan, thank you very much, and she didn't need him now.

Glancing at the clock, she stood, slipping into her jacket. "Yes, I lost my job. And, again, I appreciate your family allowing me to come here to work until I can find something else. It's very kind of you all."

"It's not kindness to take care of your family," he spluttered. "That's what families do."

Margot's sharp hazel eyes cut right through him. What would he know about taking care of a family? He'd given her away, signed away his rights to her. He'd just let her mother leave without a fight. How had Stan McCready slept at night, not knowing where his baby girl was, whether she was happy or safe or being raised well? How did he just go on living like she had never been there?

Margot felt an unexpected tide of angry words rising in her throat like bile. She gritted her teeth to keep them down, until she thought she heard her molars crack. Unfortunately, clamping down on her verbal pyrotechnics meant she'd completely lost control over that polite, distant smile and was full-on glaring at Stan. She shook her head, tamping down the anger and focusing on the calming visuals that had helped her through meetings with Dianne Deschanel, who changed the theme of her anniversary gala twice in one martini-soaked afternoon three days before the party.

"I'd like to schedule a lunch with you, sometime soon, if you have the time," she said, careful to keep her tone even and professional. She wasn't a little girl begging for her father's attention. She was a grown woman, damn it, and she would handle this like one.

Stan's already furrowed brow wrinkled. "Well, you don't have to talk about it like it's a business meetin'. If you don't want to have lunch with me, you don't have to."

"I never said I didn't want to," she said, an iron grip on her facial muscles to keep her expression neutral. "I invited you for a reason."

"And what reason is that?" he asked.

"Hey there, Uncle Stan!" Frankie bounded into the office without her lab coat and perched on Bob's desk, swinging her Converse-clad feet. "Dad says he needs you upstairs. Something about avoiding uncomfortable confrontations between Miss Barbara's boyfriends at the viewing. They're blamin' each other for her early demise."

Stan bit out a curse, stopping it short with a guilty look at Frankie. Frankie smiled beatifically.

"I'll meet ya here, tomorrow around noon," Stan told Margot. "We'll go to the Rise and Shine."

Margot made a noncommittal noise. As her father walked

away, she pinched the bridge of her nose and willed away the tension headache gathering behind her eyes.

"Well, that was the world's most awkward lunch invitation," Frankie said, biting her lip and nodding.

"I don't think I was handling my introduction very well," Margot said, closing her eyes so she didn't have to see Frankie's wide blue peepers all sad and sympathetic.

"Eh, it wasn't that bad, compared to some of the hissy fits we've had thrown in this place," Frankie said. "That's why the walls are soundproofed. But not the air vents. If you're going to have an argument in here, close the vents."

Margot glanced up to find that the air vents above her desk were indeed closed, despite the heat. "That is an important piece of information, thank you."

"So how about we go home, wash off the funeral smell, and I take you to meet our cousin Marianne for a 'you survived your first day' beer?" Frankie offered brightly.

"I don't know," Margot said. "I'm really very tired. And I don't know if I can handle meeting more new relatives. And I don't drink beer."

"Yeah, if my mama asks, I don't drink beer, either," Frankie said with a snort. "Come on. Dad says you've busted your butt today. You deserve a break. And you should meet Marianne on her own, when her boys aren't around. The poor thing never has a hot meal or a completed sentence when her youngest is on a tear. Besides, the Dirty Deer is the hottest nightspot in town! It will be fun!"

Margot pulled a face that was glorious in its skepticism.

"Okay, so it's the only nightspot in town since they closed down the Shoreline Restaurant," Frankie admitted. "It was the first place to go when the water started droppin'. The rich folks couldn't moor their boats up at the dock anymore. But the Deer has great appetizers and it's basically the only place in town for people our age to get together and try to match up our parts."

"Ew."

"Come on, it will be a bonding experience," Frankie said, tugging at her sleeve. "I'll buy you all the possum eggs you can eat."

"Is that a food?"

Frankie waggled her eyebrows and dashed out of the office.

"Frankie. That's not an answer. Frankie!" Margot called after her.

4

$\mathcal{M}$UCH TO MARGOT'S relief, possum eggs were just potato skins stuffed with smoked pulled pork, cheese, and bacon.
And deep-fried. Because Georgia.

The Dirty Deer was one of the few brick buildings in town,
low-slung with a leering neon-blue deer leaping over its sign.
The dim interior smelled of smoked meat and cigarettes. It was
crowded with high, scarred wood cocktail tables, all occupied by
locals chowing down on barbecue and drinking brew. Frankie
was dressed in a more subtle after-work ensemble of dark jeans
and a *Pacific Rim* kaiju T-shirt, with rhinestone T-Rex clips in
her pigtails. Margot felt overdressed in her little red print wrap
dress, but it was the first thing she'd laid her hands on when
she'd reached into her closet, and Frankie hadn't given her
much time to change before throwing her into the car.

The smoky haze took on the bright red of the neon beer signs,
giving the barroom a surprisingly cheerful glow. A small figure
waved frantically from across the crowd. Frankie laughed and
waved back. Marianne was built like an old-school Vargas pinup.
She was all lush curves, except for her tiny waist—downright

unfair, considering she'd had two kids. For what Margot assumed was a rare night out with the girls, her cousin had kept the makeup on her heart-shaped face simple, playing up bee-stung lips with a bit of coral gloss and wide blue eyes with a touch of mascara.

"Hey!" Marianne gave Frankie a quick cheek kiss and turned to Margot, taking her hand and pumping it like a Shake Weight. "I'm so glad to meet you!"

Margot smiled, the sort of warm, genuine smile you could offer only when given such a greeting. But before she could answer, a tall brunette in a bright blue Dirty Deer T-shirt sidled up to the table with an order pad in hand. "Hey, girls! What can I get ya?"

"Hey there, Sierra. We'll take a round of iced teas to start and then get down to the serious drinkin' when you bring our food." Frankie jerked her thumb toward Margot. "And this one needs to try some possum eggs before she dies. It's on the bucket list that she didn't even know she had."

"Will do," Sierra said, nodding. She glanced at Margot. "Sweet or unsweet?"

"Beg pardon?"

"Do you want sweet tea or unsweetened?" Sierra asked kindly.

"Oh, actually, I think I'll stick with water."

"Suit yourself." Sierra shrugged, then pointed at Marianne and Frankie, respectively. "Half-sweet and insanely sweet, right?"

The McCready girls nodded, pleased that the waitress remembered. Sierra shouted out a warning to a girl in her twenties who should have known better than to crawl on top of a pool table to make a difficult shot, and bustled across the room to stop her.

"What is the deal with 'sweet or unsweet'?" Margot asked. "Why can't they just bring you unsweetened iced tea and let you add sweeteners yourself?"

"For proper Southern sweet tea, you have to add the sugar to the brew while it's still hot. It lets the sugar dissolve evenly and you get a better-tasting drink," Marianne told her. "You can't do that at the table with a couple of packets of Splenda."

Margot nodded. "All right. Can we talk about the fact that all women here, regardless of marital status, are called 'Miss'?"

"It means that you recognize that you're younger than the person you're talkin' to, or that you're not familiar enough to be on a completely first-name basis," Frankie said. "It's a mark of respect. If you jump right to a first-name basis without permission, it's a sign you weren't raised right. Y'all don't do that up north?"

"No. And I am now sure I have offended ninety percent of the people I've met since I arrived in town," Margot said, pursing her lips.

"So, Margot," Marianne said. "It's nice to meet you. Again. Sort of. My mama says we were thick as thieves when we were little."

"I'm sorry, I don't remember anything from my time here."

"Not your fault," Marianne said. "Besides, we're here now and it gives us a chance to talk away from the rest of the family. Because, well . . ."

"We don't know a damn thing about you," Frankie interjected.

Marianne shushed her. "Frankie!"

"What? You're the one relative we have that we know nothing about, and in our family, that feels like a pretty big hole. So we wanted to ask you a bunch of questions, but Marianne here was afraid you'd feel like you were in a job interview or something."

Sierra delivered the drinks and Frankie picked up a menu and wordlessly pointed to a couple of items. Sierra nodded and sauntered away.

"Actually, considering the fact that I'm trying to get job interviews, this could be good practice."

"So, basic stuff: Where'd you grow up? Where'd you go to school? What did you study? What kind of music did you favor? Are you a reader or a movie girl? Romantic history—boring or completely sordid and nastier than I would expect of someone who dresses like a newscaster?" Frankie ticked the subjects off on her fingers. "And, most important, because this will determine whether we can truly be close friends or just cousins who tolerate each other—do you like mutant-sea-creature movies, yes or no?"

"Not everyone has to like *Sharktopus* as much as you do, Frances!" Marianne groaned, rolling her eyes.

Margot frowned. "I dress like a newscaster?"

"A really classy one," Frankie assured her. "Like the kind who would interview Michelle Obama on a morning show."

"Um, I'll get to your many, many . . . many questions in a minute, but I've just got to say—you seem really upbeat for someone who . . ."

"Works with corpses all day?" Frankie supplied.

Margot pursed her carefully glossed lips. "I'm trying to think of a nicer way to phrase it."

Frankie snorted. "When I was around eight, I got really sick. Leukemia, a scary, rare form of it. I went through chemo, went bald by age ten. I had to go to St. Jude's for treatment and everything. I was lucky, though. Uncle Stan was able to donate bone marrow. And then Duffy a couple of years later. Uncle Stan would have done it again, but the first procedure was too hard on him."

"Really? Stan?" Margot frowned. A bone marrow transplant for a sick kid? This did not match up with the wrung-out, selfish drunk narrative.

Frankie nodded, her purple highlights flashing in the harsh light. "He was one of the first people to get tested. We were lucky I got matched up so easily. And now, I've got triple the McCready runnin' around in my veins, which makes me extra terrifyin'."

"It really does," Marianne deadpanned, subtly touching her temple and grimacing. Frankie didn't even look over at her cousin while she slapped her arm. "She has all of the stubbornness of Uncle Stan and the creative stupidity of my brother, with none of the self-preservation instincts."

"Anyway, I spent a good part of my formative years staring my mortality in the face. And when I was twelve or so, I decided that I had to stop being scared of it, because otherwise I was gonna spend my life too scared to live it. So I went downstairs to the prep rooms and spent a lot of time with Uncle Junior, Duff and Marianne's daddy. He served as the undertaker before me. He taught me everything I know about takin' proper care of the bodies, givin' them dignity, makin' them look like themselves, so their loved ones have something to comfort them before the burial. Death spent too much time scarin' me when I was a kid, so I'm gonna spend my adult years giving it the finger."

"And the clothes and hair?" Margot asked. "Is that part of your 'finger' strategy?"

"The clothes are chosen to mess with the locals," Marianne said. Frankie opened her mouth to protest, but Marianne countered, "You have bookmarks in your Internet browser marked 'clothing vendors to piss off the locals.'"

Frankie shrugged. "They call me Dr. Frankenstein, I might as well dress the part of the town weirdo. And as for the hair, after spending a couple of years without hair, I promised myself that I would never limit myself to one style or color. If I want purple hair, damn it, I'm gonna have it."

"Kids can be really mean," Margot said sympathetically.

"Oh, it's not the kids. The adults are the ones callin' her Dr. Frankenstein," Marianne said. "Admit it, you enjoy provokin' them."

"Fine, I'm provokin' them, but they deserve it."

"Do your parents ever feel bad? Naming you Frankie when, you know, you work with dead bodies?"

"Well, technically, I'm named Frances for my grandma on my mom's side. It was a happy accident."

Margot pursed her lips. "Was it? Happy?"

Marianne snorted and Frankie gave Margot's arm a friendly smack.

"Triple the McCready stubbornness, hmm?" Margot laughed as Marianne rolled her big blue eyes. Conversation paused as Sierra delivered mason jars filled with an orange-red liquid on ice, the potato skins, and what appeared to be nachos covered in pulled pork.

"What's this?" Margot asked as Frankie handed her a jar. She sniffed the drink, which smelled pleasantly of peaches and mint. She took a sip and puckered her mouth at the sharp bite of alcohol. "Well, it's still less dangerous than Leslie's coffee."

"This, darlin' cousin, is a Georgia Peach—locally made moonshine, peach schnapps, and a couple of other secret ingredients," Marianne said as Margot took a longer pull on her jar. The second sip went down much smoother than the first and Margot smiled at the pleasant burn of liquor spreading to her belly. "You might want to take it slow. I know it tastes amazin', but moonshine will mess you up quick if you've never tangled with it before."

"Oh, I'm sure I'll be fine as long as I eat something," Margot said, forking a possum egg onto her plate. She grimaced at the sheer amount of heavy carbs and pork in front of her, but gamely took a bite. It was delicious, which meant it was terrible for her. "So, Marianne, tell me about yourself. Frankie says you have children?"

"I'm sure she politely described them as 'children' and not 'hyperactive demon monkeys,'" Marianne said with a snort.

"Actually, for once, I restrained myself," Frankie said. "I didn't wanna scare her."

"Well, you'll meet Nate and Aiden soon enough and decide for yourself. And my husband, Carl. He's been pretty busy lately. His towin' traffic always spikes during the last weeks of tourist season. Too many people who have no business drivin' big vehicles over hills those vehicles weren't designed for in the first place."

"Carl and Marianne are disgustingly happy together," Frankie said. "Honestly, you'd think after twenty years they'd run out of hormones or something."

"Twenty years?" Margot exclaimed over the rim of her jar. "What, did you hook up when you were twelve?"

"Sixteen. We're high school sweethearts. And remember, I'm

a couple of years older than you," Marianne said, shrugging, with a happy little quirk to her full lips. "Classic story of boy meets girl at a family barbecue, boy dates girl, girl runs away to a faraway college because she's afraid of bein' trapped in her tiny town, girl graduates and finds job in big city only to return to tiny town for the summer and realize that she's actually miserable in the big city and missin' the boy something awful, girl abandons life in city to marry boy, gets immediately knocked up, and joins the PTA."

"I keep telling you that's not a classic 'boy meets girl' story," Frankie chided, sipping her own cocktail.

Margot grimaced. "A family barbecue?"

"Oh, we aren't related," Marianne assured her. "He's a friend of Duffy's and got dragged along on the promise of free food. Carl's family didn't have much growing up, so a bellyful of pulled pork was a strong attraction for a teenage boy."

"And you don't work for the funeral home?"

Marianne shook her head. "I work for the law office here in town. It's better for me and my relationship with my mother."

"There's only one law office in town?"

"Marianne's only a couple of credits away from being a lawyer," Frankie said. "She does most of George Pritchett's work for him while he naps."

"I'm a paralegal. And I really enjoy being a paralegal. I realized after working at a prestigious law firm and applying to law schools that I didn't really enjoy the long hours or the stress."

"I will keep that in mind," Margot said. "There may be some legal action still pending from the flamingo incident."

Frankie raised her jar and pointed at her. "One day, we will

get the full story from you, Margot, and on that day, the teasin'
will be legendary."

Margot nodded and clinked her jar against Frankie's. Her
cousin grinned happily at her and inhaled nachos with gusto.
Margot relaxed against the table. This was easier than she'd
expected it to be, and certainly a lot more fun. She'd had girl-
friends in the city she'd met for decompression drinks. But they
hadn't returned her calls or e-mails before she left Chicago. And
her dynamics with other young, upwardly mobile professional
women had been biting and competitive. Every brunch felt like
a poker game, a contest to see who could subtly drop word of
their most recent triumph while keeping their disappointments
close to the vest.

Margot had come home from those outings feeling exhausted
and uneasy rather than relaxed. How different might her life
have been if she'd grown up close with Marianne and Frankie?
Would she have been able to count on them for a sympathetic
ear and easy camaraderie? Or would her mother have even allowed that? Linda had never valued social connections unless
they paid off in some material way—invitations to important
events or exclusive clubs. Margot doubted very much that Linda
would have let her run "thick as thieves" with her cousins. Her
mother would have found some excuse as to why Margot didn't
have time to spend with them, or assure her in private that her
cousins really didn't like her in the first place. So really, it might
have been worse, knowing the relationship she could have had
with them but being kept from it by her mother's resentments.

Singularly depressed, Margot finished off her jar and sig-
naled Sierra for another.

"Hey, there's Duffy," Marianne said. Margot turned to see

that her cousin had cleaned up for the occasion, wearing jeans and a freshly pressed blue dress shirt. He'd even made an attempt to slick back his curly hair. Margot was about to raise her arm to greet him, but Marianne caught her wrist and pressed it gently to the tabletop.

"Hold on a minute," Frankie said softly, neither she nor Marianne peeling their eyes away from Duffy to look at Margot.

"What is happening?" Margot asked, watching as a short blonde with naturally narrowed green cat's eyes sauntered up to Duffy and hooked her fingers into his belt loops.

"Wait for it . . ." Frankie whispered.

At first, Duffy didn't seem to want anything to do with the blonde, leaning away from her with the only frown Margot had ever seen on his face. The blonde tilted her head and walked her fingers up Duffy's chest while giving him this knowing grin that, frankly, made Margot's skin crawl.

"Wait for it . . ." Marianne said.

Duffy rolled his eyes and his face broke into a smile as the blonde dragged him out of the bar. Marianne groaned and pulled a twenty out of her pocket, handing it to a smirking Frankie.

"Again, I ask, what is happening?"

"My brother does not learn." Marianne sighed.

"It's human nature," Frankie told Margot. "That was Lana, Duffy's ex-wife."

"They seemed . . ." Margot paused to search for a word that didn't translate to *attached at the tongue*. "Friendly."

"That's because Duffy, as much as I love him, forgets that Lana is a bein' of pure evil with a Hellmouth between her thighs," Marianne grumbled, biting into a possum egg. "Every time she's been dumped and needs a self-esteem pick-me-up, Duffy lets her crawl into his bed."

"Is the Hellmouth why he divorced her?" Margot asked, grinning at Sierra as she delivered a fresh mason jar. "Because that is illustrative."

"No, she divorced him, bless her heart," Marianne said.

"Um, that didn't sound like you were wishing any form of happiness on your former sister-in-law," Margot said.

"I wasn't," Marianne said. "But I'm just Southern enough and polite enough to say 'bless her heart' instead of 'screw that knock-kneed bitch.'"

"The sweeter you bless somebody, the more you hate them. But nobody can get mad at you, because you're just being a good Christian lady," Frankie said, her eyes wide and guileless.

Margot shuddered. "I'm just glad women in Chicago didn't know about this."

"Anyway, Duffy held out hope that despite her sleepin' with two of his friends, concurrently, they could save the marriage," Frankie said, shrugging. "She was convinced that his best friend, Paul Dabney, was gonna marry her and take her to that big old house in Southern Oaks. So she dumped Duffy right quick and let Paul know she was available."

"And because Paul is and always has been an insufferable jackass," Marianne interjected, "he decided Lana wasn't all that interestin' when she wasn't married to Duffy. I'm only thankful that Duffy wised up enough not to let her back in the house."

"Sure, wise enough not to let her move back in. Wise enough not to prop her ego up with no-strings-attached rebound sex? Not so much," Frankie noted.

Marianne drawled, "I live in hope."

~

MARGOT WAS DRUNK.

She'd taken care, most of her life, to avoid this condition. Her mother's reminders of Stan's "bad habits" left little appeal to sloppy drunkenness. Plus, drinking equaled loose lips and poor judgment and the kind of talk that could sink careers and social standing. She held a club soda as a prop at parties to keep her wits about her while her mother's circle schemed. And now, here she was with unsteady feet and a head that felt floaty. She was sprawled against the edge of the table and laughing at stories that weren't really that funny, though at this point, she thought her cousins were downright delightful. She still felt together enough to try to straighten her posture every few minutes and appear sober, only to slump back against the table.

Margot didn't know why she'd avoided it for so long, really; it was kind of awesome. She felt awesome. Her cousins were awesome. This bar was awesome. Lake Sackett was awesome.

"Back in a minute," Margot said, carefully placing her wedge-clad feet on the concrete floor and putting one in front of the other in a manner that screamed "tragic first-time moonshine consumer."

"Don't break the seal!" Frankie called after her. "It's science!"

Margot teetered down the barely lit corridor toward the bathroom doors marked BUCKS and DOES. She was glancing over her shoulder, waving at Frankie and hoping she remembered deer genders correctly, when she collided with a warm, solid object.

"Oh! I'm so sorry," she exclaimed as two strong hands shot out to steady her on her wobbly legs.

"You again."

Her head shot up at the source of the gruff voice, so quickly it made her dizzy. Sandy hair, thick dark-blond beard, big sad brown eyes. It was the troubled lumberjack. He wasn't wearing his serial killer utility coat, but he was right there in front of her, keeping her from falling off her shoes.

Margot stared up at him. All the hurt in the world was contained in those eyes. And she wanted to hug him. She normally didn't go for beards with broken wings, but something in this man made her want to reach out and tell him that everything was going to be okay.

No, wait, she was *actually* reaching out to him. Physically. With her hands.

Not good.

And he didn't seem very pleased about it, either. He pulled back and frowned at her as she stretched her fingers toward his face.

She rose up on her toes to press a featherlight kiss to his cheek. He froze, his hands contracting at her arms. "It's going to be okay," she whispered, kissing his cheek again.

All the tension in his frame seemed to melt, curving his body around hers. She bobbed a bit, bracing herself against a nice solid chest. And her incorrigible hands were sliding down his T-shirt to a narrow waist. His hands contracted again, pulling her closer. She felt her cheek dragged against his whiskers as she pulled back and then the softness of his lips brushing her jaw.

Fireworks. Electricity. Heat blossoming from her belly and rolling heavy between her thighs. Every explosive and magical sensation she'd been promised by romance novels and Julia Roberts movies swelled inside her in one dizzying rush.

He braced her elbows in his hands as he felt her drop, pulling his face toward hers. With a confidence born of already having hit rock bottom, she pressed her mouth against his. He froze up again, but this time he relaxed against her just a little faster, pulling her against him, moaning into her mouth, tentatively sliding his tongue across the seam of her lips. He didn't taste like booze or even smoke. He tasted like Dr Pepper. She fucking loved Dr Pepper.

Her errant fingertips slid up his side, stroking over corded muscle hidden by soft cotton, making him jerk and bark out a rusty-sounding laugh when she reached his ribs. She grinned against his mouth.

Ticklish. She could work with that.

His hand slid to the small of her back, securing her against him. She combed her fingers through his thick hair and found it softer than she expected. No product. Some people were just lucky.

Except, he wasn't lucky. He was clearly hurting—at least, he had been until she came along with her lips and her wandering hands that seemed to make him somewhat happier. She was over-freaking-joyed to have provoked that rusty barking laugh. Sure, she was still sort of miserable about her current work-life-family-chaos imbalance, but helping someone else escape for just a few moments? That was a heady thing.

Her hands slid from his hair to his earlobes, rubbing lightly at the spot some ladies' magazine had described as a happy acupressure point. But for the haunted lumberjack, the earlobes seemed to be another ticklish spot because he huffed out another laugh into her mouth. He turned his head, the scratchy-soft texture of his beard tickling her palm as he pressed a kiss to the center of her palm . . . which did nothing for the stability of her knees.

He eased her arm around his neck and slanted his mouth across hers. His own hands—huge, by the way, enormous— splayed across her waist, his fingers resting just above the curve of her ass. His tongue lapped delicately against hers, as if he wasn't sure he had the right. And she welcomed him with firm, excited strokes of her own.

Never breaking from her mouth, he urged her toward the emergency exit, a stumbling, awkward waltz out into the cooling Georgia night. Her shoes snagged on the gravel of the bar's parking lot and he caught her, pinning her against him and almost carrying her toward what she hoped was his truck.

This was insane. Margot had never done anything like this before, enthusiastic petting with a total stranger in a parking lot. She'd been too well supervised during her student years and too professionally paranoid as a young adult. She didn't do messy or complicated or awkward. But she knew if she stopped now, she would die. All the nerve and spine she'd managed to build in the last few days would be sapped out of her, and she would be a complete mess again. This was crazy. But so far, crazy had worked for her.

He fumbled in his pocket and clicked the key fob to unlock his truck. He opened the passenger door and slid into the cab, pulling her with him. There was a second row of seats, and for a moment, Margot considered dragging him back there. Sure, there were things she couldn't do, considering her "delicate condition," but she was a creative girl with a *Cosmo* subscription. She could improvise. He guided her into his lap, so she straddled his thighs and pressed his lips to hers and the front seat felt just fine. Her hair fell in a gold curtain around their faces as she wrapped her arms around his neck.

"Are you sure you're okay with this?" he asked, his breath puffing in cola-flavored whispers over her lips.

She nodded, stroking her fingers along his throat, ringing her fingertips around the hollow. She spread those hands over his chest, caressing down his flat belly.

Okay, she was just petting him now, to a ridiculous degree.

Margot bit down gently on his bottom lip and he groaned, rolling his hips up. He was warm and solid against her, rubbing with just enough insistence to make her legs weak.

She'd done that to him. And she was sinfully proud of it. This was so much more than polite, no-strings frottage with a reasonably qualified partner, sought out when she needed to scratch an itch. This was raw, throbbing need and the heady fog of bad decisions.

His fingers curved around her waist and almost met in the middle, guiding her down against him as he rolled up. She moaned, not remotely ashamed when her back instinctively arched and thrust her breasts in his face. He nuzzled his forehead against the smooth warm skin above her neckline. Warm— she was so warm and stupidly pleased with herself that absolutely everything seemed possible.

He kept one hand at the small of her back, anchoring her to him while he reached down to recline the seat. She let loose a little squeak as they dropped back, sighing as her sensitive skin collided with his shirt. But his hot fingers at the base of her spine kept her from pulling away from him.

"You have really big hands," she mumbled against his lips as those long fingers cupped her ass through her dress. She moaned softly as he kneaded the flesh, moving up along her back, teasing the tension from her muscles.

"I do?"

She nodded, enjoying the way her lips brushed over his bristly upper lip. "You know what they say about men with big hands. They have big . . . gloves."

He laughed, the vibrations of that sound echoing through his chest to hers, and she moaned. And she'd made that happen. She grinned against his mouth, that wicked pride warming her through to her thighs.

He skimmed those big hands up her arms to the straps of her dress, and then her phone buzzed in her purse.

She tried to pull away from him, but his mouth followed her like a magnet. He grumbled softly as she leaned over and pulled her phone out.

"What?" he panted against her neck.

"I'm sorry," she whispered, dialing in her access code.

Frankly, she was sort of amazed she was getting enough reception to receive a text, but there it was, a message from Marianne blinking on her screen. **M, are you OK? Couldn't find you in the ladies room.**

Marianne and Frankie. She'd just left them in the bar. She'd been gone for at least fifteen minutes. Guilt splashed through her middle like rainwater from a bucket. She'd abandoned her cousins to make out with a strange man, like some teenager at a kegger. She sat back and took in the kiss-drunk face of a stranger, pupils blown, an impressive erection tenting his jeans as he stared up at her, caressing her neck.

Disgraceful.

She shivered as her mother's disapproving voice echoed in

her head. And Mother was especially disapproving at the moment. Margot's stomach dropped. What the hell was she doing? She didn't even know this guy. She didn't know his name. What if he was some sort of psycho? What if he knew her family? What if he *was* her family? For all she knew, they were cousins.

"Ohmygod," she whispered, climbing out of his lap.

"What, are you okay?" He sat up suddenly, his expression alarmed.

"I'm so sorry." She reached for the door handle, throwing her weight against the door.

"Are you going to be sick?"

"No, no, I'm just—I'm so sorry."

Margot opened the truck door, suddenly very sober, and booked it across the gravel without looking back. The muggy Georgia air seemed to leave a clammy sheen on her skin, making her rub her hands over her upper arms. She walked into the front entrance of the Dirty Deer and found her cousins there, talking to the manager with concerned expressions on their faces.

"Honey, where were you?" Marianne cried, throwing her arms around Margot's neck.

"I just stepped outside for some air. The liquor got to me a little quicker than I expected. But I think I'm ready to go. Don't you think we should go? Yeah, let's go. Now. Please."

Frankie lifted a dark brow, skimming her eyes over hair Margot knew was disheveled and a dress that seemed to be sticking to her sweaty thighs. But much to Margot's eternal gratitude, her cousin said nothing.

"That's okay, just don't go wandering off again. Uncle Stan would kill us if we lost you," Marianne said.

Margot tried not to snort. "Did I ruin the evening?"

"No, it's all right. Aunt Donna is our designated driver and she's supposed to pick us up in a few minutes anyway. Be warned, when you're drunk, she thinks it's hilarious to speed up over the sharp drops so it feels like you're on a roller coaster."

Marianne nodded. "It's her way of making us pay the piper."

"No chance of Uncle Bob picking us up?"

"No, my dad also wants us to pay the piper." Frankie snorted. "He recognizes that I'm physically an adult, but still feels the need to parent me in a passive-aggressive fashion."

"Well, that's kind of sweet," Margot said, glancing over her shoulder at the door, praying that her brooding lumberjack wouldn't storm through it and demand answers.

"You say that because you haven't ridden with Aunt Donna yet."

5

MARGOT SAT SLUMPED against the outside wall of her cabin, letting the heat absorbed into the porch soak through her suit jacket and soothe her aching . . . everything. The price for this comfort was exposure to the evil sun, but she fought the unwelcome blast of light to her corneas with huge Jackie O sunglasses. She was just grateful that the possum eggs stayed down.

She hadn't been this hungover—ever—and vowed she would never touch moonshine again as long as she lived. She was actually looking forward to a big mug of Aunt Leslie's chewy coffee. Despite her drunkenness, the physical exhaustion of white-knuckling through her aunt Donna's driving, and the emotional exhaustion from fighting off post-truck-make-out regret and mortification, she'd had trouble falling asleep. She'd tossed and turned in her narrow bed, kept awake by the sound of rocks being banged together. She'd gone to her window, searching her yard for drunken cousins or bearded locals who might think this was a funny prank, but she couldn't see anything but trees.

She'd finally drifted off around three and woken up to a text from Frankie, promising to pick her up for work. But instead of the tires-over-gravel crunch she expected, her ears were assaulted by the baying of Tootie's pack of hounds. Margot winced and slumped forward, clapping her hands over her ears.

"Rough night, huh, honey?" Tootie called as the dogs clamored around her legs, sniffing and licking despite Margot's feeble attempts to bat them away. "I told Frankie to take it easy on you. The first time you tangle with moonshine is like dancin' with a good-looking carnie. Sure, it feels great at first, but you wake up sore and soaked in regret."

Margot blanched. Aunt Tootie shooed the dogs away and pressed a Tupperware container—the vintage turquoise brand—and a travel mug into her hands. She poked her head through Margot's unlocked cabin door.

"Aw, it looks like you're gettin' comfortable. That little bird you hung up looks so nice! And the candles. I'm so glad you're settlin' in."

"It's just a piece of window art; it's not like I'm signing a five-year lease," Margot grumbled, opening the Tupperware. Inside, wrapped in wax paper, was a flaky golden biscuit the size of her fist, soaked in melted butter, with thick slabs of bacon, scrambled eggs, and melted Velveeta oozing out the sides. She quickly snapped the lid back on the container, breathing through her mouth to avoid the smell of food. "What the . . . ?"

"Best cure for hangover is a big greasy breakfast," Tootie told her. "The bacon fights off the booze."

"Is there any food available in this town that isn't soaked in pork fat?"

"Nope," Tootie said, shaking her snowy head. "It's in the

bylaws. If we're not feedin' someone pork products, we get all twitchy and just start throwin' biscuits at innocent bystanders."

"Is it in the same bylaws that command you all to carry Tupperware with you at all times?"

"What do y'all carry your food in up north? Your bare hands?"

A little beagle mix trotted up to Margot and balanced his chin on her knee. He whimpered and eyed her sandwich with his hopeful doggy eyes. "I will not share," she told him.

More whimpering. The big brown eyes seemed to get even bigger.

"Fine," she huffed, opening the container again and breaking off a little piece of biscuit. He snapped it from her fingers and gobbled it down.

Margot sniffed at the travel mug and blanched. Was that oranges and . . . garlic?

Tootie hooted. "And that's my special secret cure."

"What's in it?"

"You don't want to know," Tootie told her. "Just down most of it in the first gulp or you'll lose your nerve."

Margot grimaced but gamely pinched her nose shut and downed most of the mug in one long gulp. "That's not so bad," she said, smacking her lips against the flavor of citrus. It tasted like a Flintstones vitamin with a chunk of habanero-flavored tuna for flavor.

"Wait for it," Tootie said. Margot recoiled at a combination of fish and fiery spice battling it out on her tongue. "There you go."

"Why are all the beverages here trying to kill me?" Margot spat, wiping her tongue with one of the many napkins Tootie had supplied with the biscuit. "Sorry, I'm usually more of a morning person. I didn't get much sleep last night."

"Really? When I drink my own weight in moonshine, I usually conk right out."

"No, I couldn't sleep because some animal was building a nest out of rocks or something right outside my window. I heard this weird clacking noise all night, which made sleep difficult, even with the moonshine," she said.

Tootie waved her hand dismissively. "Oh, that's just the Sasquatch."

Margot laughed, but Tootie's expression remained completely serious. "Oh, come on."

"No, really, the Sasquatch have lived in these woods since before we even dreamed of climbing the mountains. They're harmless, really, as long as you stay out of their way. They just like to bang the rocks together to remind us that they're out there."

"So, you're telling me that Sasquatch is loitering behind my house, clapping rocks together?"

Tootie nodded. "That's why we told you to stay inside at night. Sasquatch don't appreciate it when you try to spy on them. There's a reason no one's ever seen one."

"No one has ever seen one because they don't exist."

"You tell that to the cryptid-hunting teams that come through town trying to spot one. It's been the one area of tourism that's expanded for us over the last few years. We've been featured in three of those cable shows."

"I would argue with you, but I'm just too damn weak," Margot said.

Donna's big red truck roared around the corner and skidded to a stop in front of Margot's cabin, riling up all the dogs. The barking alone was enough to make Margot want to knock herself unconscious with a moonshine jug. Donna, the roller-coaster driver with the long, angular face and messy auburn curls, rolled down her passenger window and yelled, "How ya doin' there, Big City?" over the loud purr of her engine.

"I'm fine," Margot insisted, waving at her. Donna had hit every bump in the road between the bar and the McCready compound the night before. She'd stopped short. Hell, at one point, she'd turned a corner so hard all three of her passengers' heads whacked together. "Just recovering from a driving-related concussion."

"I'll bet." Donna snorted. "Next time don't wake me up to come get your drunk asses in the middle of the night and maybe I'll give you the kid glove treatment."

"Frankie said you told her to call you!" Margot exclaimed.

"Doesn't mean I have to be nice about it!" Donna called, gunning her engine and waving before speeding off.

"She's just delightful," Margot muttered, peering into the Tupperware once more. Though the smell of bacon and cheese still made her stomach roll, she took a big bite and forced herself to chew. She groaned, letting the combination of comfort flavors coat her tongue. Her diet had been completely wrecked by her move to Georgia. She was going to have to rein in her carb consumption or she wasn't going to be able to zip her pants.

Still, it might be worth it.

"Don't mind Donna," Tootie told her. "She's been a little . . . prickly since her husband died."

Margot thought Donna was more aggressive than prickly, but she figured that note wouldn't be well received. The beagle made a huffing noise and tried to nose at her container again. She rolled her eyes and broke off some of the bacon. He snapped it out of her fingers before she could even offer it, making her wipe her hands on another napkin. The dog put his paws on her legs, sniffing and attempting to lick at her hands. "No. That's all you get. Don't be greedy. This doesn't make us friends."

The dog grumbled and put his chin back on her knee.

"I don't recognize him from the great closet raid," Margot said, giving him an arch look.

"No, this here's a new addition," Tootie said, leaning down and scratching under the dog's chin. "I'm calling him Arlo. Found him rollin' around in the mud at the Food Carnival parking lot. But he cleaned up nice."

Margot thought Arlo's face, framed by the new blue collar Tootie had given him, was perfectly sweet. But she had no desire to form an attachment to a creature who could endanger her shoes. She loved her shoes.

"Go on," Margot told him. "I've got to go to work. And I don't need to do that with dog hair all over my pants. So . . . shoo."

Arlo grumbled again, but Margot would not be moved. "Shoo."

Arlo huffed and sat back but didn't move away.

"Oh, no, you gave Arlo food," Tootie said. "You're his buddy for life."

"Just what I always wanted," Margot muttered.

"Come on, hon. I told Frankie I'd drive you into work," Tootie said. "Eventually we'll get you your own car so you don't have to depend on us for transportation."

"I don't think that will be necessary," Margot said, opening the passenger door of Tootie's impeccably clean early-model Cadillac. "I won't be here long enough to need my own car."

Tootie made a little noise of disapproval before settling in behind the wheel and starting the engine.

"Y'all get goin' now," she called to the dogs. "Go on home!"

Though the pack dispersed, Arlo remained on Margot's porch, his little dog chin resting on his forelegs. Margot would have to deal with that later.

Tootie was oddly quiet on the drive to the funeral home. Margot wondered if she should stop referring to her eventual departure from Lake Sackett. She'd thought she was doing her family a favor, keeping them from having false hope that she would stay. She would have appreciated someone squashing her false hope when she was a child. But she could see that she was only upsetting Tootie.

When Tootie turned the car into the McCready's parking lot, a van labeled BONNIE'S BLOSSOMS was parked next to the building and Margot watched as someone carried a huge princess phone composed entirely of bright pink carnations toward the back door. The phone was wound with a white sateen ribbon reading JESUS CALLED HER HOME in magenta script.

"That'll be the floral centerpiece for Elsie Mayhew's visitation. Bless her heart."

"I have so many questions," Margot marveled.

"Oh, yes, the Heavenly Connection is very popular among the older ladies," Tootie told her. "The brighter the carnations, the better."

Margot shuddered. "I had an easier time believing in Sasquatch."

She balled up her napkin. "Thanks for the disgusting curative smoothie and the pork products, Tootie. I feel almost ready to face my day."

"Aw, that's no problem, hon." Tootie patted Margot's arm. "Now, I don't judge someone tyin' it on every once in a while, and I'm glad you're gettin' to know your cousins, but it's best not to make a habit of this. That's not why you're down here."

The note of unease in Tootie's normally cheerful voice, underscored by the tiniest hint of judgment, made Margot's stomach turn. And between the hangover and the sunlight and the tang of oranges and tuna lingering at the back of her palate, the tight lid she normally kept on her emotions had loosened just enough. "So are you going to give Marianne and Frankie the same hand-pat and mini lecture, or is this just because I'm Stan's daughter?"

Tootie's eyes went wide. "What do you mean by that?"

"I can assure you that I have never had a drinking problem. Last night was an anomaly. I joined in what I thought would be bonding activity with the cousins you want me to get to know so badly."

"I'm not sayin' that, Margot. I would never throw Stan's problem in your face like that. I'm just sayin' that spendin' time with your cousins is well and good, but goin' out drinkin' is not exactly how I hoped you'd spend your time with the family."

"I've barely had any time to spend with any of you," she said.

"Yes, that's what I'm sayin'," Tootie said. "I was hopin' that when I moved you here, you would make more of an effort to get to know your daddy, but you've barely spoken to him."

"And I hoped that when you contacted me, it was to help me. But you seem to have some very definite ideas about why you did and didn't bring me down here." Before Tootie could reply, Margot climbed out of the car with more speed than she thought possible, given the condition of her head. She slammed the car door behind her and instantly regretted it, not just for the noise but also the insult to Tootie.

Margot's position here was precarious, she knew that. And she'd just antagonized the matriarch of the family. If she wasn't careful, she would be booted out of her last resort before she'd had a chance to rebuild her life into something acceptable.

She opened the funeral home's office door and was confronted by the walls lined with paint-by-numbers Jesusi.

This was not going to be a good day.

~

MARGOT ROLLED HER shoulders, dislodging the sleeveless silk shell where dried sweat had adhered it to her skin. Though she'd ruthlessly rehydrated herself with bottled water, she felt like the walking dead . . . which was an uncomfortable position, considering her current location.

Between Frankie's wincing at every sound and Margot's snippy mood, Uncle Bob figured neither of them was fit for public interaction. He kept Margot busy with paperwork in the office all morning. Today's Sisyphean task included learning the antiquated accepted style for newspaper obituaries. Apparently people took it very seriously if their step-grandmother's cousin's second wife's uncle wasn't included in their loved one's death notice. But at least she hadn't been saddled with some of the more bitter "Ding Dong, the Witch Is Dead" obituaries she'd come across in her research. People really enjoyed getting the last word in family arguments.

Margot had proposed an alternative that morning, showing Bob the program that would allow her to establish an online memorial wall for the funeral home, but Bob had rejected her idea before she'd even finished showing him the features.

"People around here don't want their business put online, hon," he'd told her.

"But they're fine with airing all of their dirty laundry in the local rag?" Margot asked, lifting a copy of the *Ledger*. "And as a follow-up question, do people in this town still read newspapers?"

"I know it doesn't make any sense, but it's just different," Bob said. "There's a real distrust of technology around here. Hank Mason hooked his son's iPod into the church's PA system to play a hymn he found on the Internet and one of the seniors smashed the 'devil's rectangle' with her shoe. It's your second day on the job, sweetie, just slow down. Learn the ropes. And then you can make some changes. Why don't you just focus on learning to write the obits?"

Bob gave her a pat on the head—what was with this family and head pats?—and walked out of the office. Margot thought he was out of hearing range when she muttered, "It's not like it's that hard."

But he was not. He heard. And that was when he put her in paperwork time-out, leaving her in the office largely unsupervised. It gave her plenty of time to think about the lunch scheduled with her father and how that was going to play out. She had so many things she wanted to say to him, but she knew she wouldn't have time during one lunch. And she couldn't exactly fulfill her teenage fantasy of telling him off and throwing a napkin in his face. That would make staying in Lake Sackett too uncomfortable. She'd accepted that she probably wasn't going to get the answers she wanted that day. She was going to have to settle for collecting basic information about Stan McCready and hope that they could work up to her more complicated questions.

At ten till noon, Margot combed her hair and slicked on another coat of lip gloss. Stan wouldn't care about her grooming habits, she was sure, but it would settle her to know she looked her best. She waited, completing a few last-minute tasks that she could walk away from easily. She ignored the condor-size butterflies in her belly.

It surprised her how unprepared she felt for this type of relationship. She'd thought she'd been close with her mother and stepfather, but she realized, watching the casual affection the McCreadys showed one another, that her family had been guarded even in their relaxed moments. Margot was reserved with Bob, uncomfortable with the encouragement he offered her at almost every turn. And she was even more politely distant with Tootie, who was a lot to handle even without a hangover.

What if she wasn't capable of being a daughter to a father? What if she found that Stan was a horrible person? Or Stan decided he didn't like her after all?

No. This was just lunch, she told herself. She had nothing to lose. This would not change her life. She was fine either way.

So why did the two minutes after 11:58 seem to take so damn long?

Margot's foot jiggled under her desk in time with the fingers tapping against the surface.

The digits finally crept to noon and . . . nothing. He was late, that was all, just running a little late. Margot was sure he was going to be there any minute with an explanation involving work, and in the spirit of cooperation, she would graciously shrug it off.

As the minutes ticked by, her inclination to be generous eroded like Cousin Duffy's truck bumper. Margot stood, slipped on her jacket, and walked a lap through the funeral home. She offered a polite but muted smile to the Akemans, who were discussing their mother's service with E.J.J. Stan was nowhere to be found.

Returning to her office—just in case Stan showed up after all—Margot pulled out her phone and texted Frankie down on the morgue level.

Have you seen Stan?

Frankie replied, **U're texting me from 1 floor away? Just come dwnstrs.**

That's not happening.

Fraidy cat.

OK, but have you seen my Margot stopped typing and backspaced to replace *my* with **Stan?**

Nope. Haven't seen him for about an hr.

Did he have to go pick up a body? Margot asked.

Nope. My dad took pickups this afternoon because of your lunch plans.

Margot breathed deeply and counted to ten. Stan didn't have a work-related excuse for being late. She rubbed a hand over her sternum, willing the acidic burn there to fade away. She would not get upset over this. She would stay calm. She would be fine.

A memory bubbled to the surface of her mind, of a very small Margot, waiting at the window of their first little apartment in Chicago, watching the street. *She just knew her Daddy would be coming down the street at any minute. His big green truck would make that roaring noise, like a tiger, and she would know he was getting close, just like back home. She didn't care what Mama said, this little room on the second floor of the moldy-smelling building wasn't home. Home was the lake and Tootie's house and the dogs. Daddy would be here any minute to take her home. She knew it.*

Margot shook her head. No. That memory couldn't have been real. She'd spent years in therapy and never come close to any recollection like that. That was just a weirdly real daydream brought on by a few emotionally intense days and the remnants of moonshine in her brain.

She was fine. This was disappointing but hardly surprising. Stan had spent her whole life avoiding contact with her; why would he suddenly want to schedule a one-on-one meeting just because Aunt Tootie had wedged Margot into the family's life again? Margot had set herself up for this. Now she knew better than to reach out to Stan again. Lesson learned.

Her head rose when she heard a light knock at the office door. She refused to let her disappointment show when she saw that it was Frankie.

"It's twelve nineteen," Frankie said, her red mouth turning down at the corners. "That's why you were textin', right? Uncle Stan didn't show up?"

"No, he did not." Margot opened a new file on the computer and started another obituary.

"Dammit, Stan," Frankie grumbled, whipping out her phone with its Avengers-themed cover. "I texted him, but he hasn't responded, the doofus. I can't believe he did this."

"It's nothing, really." Margot smiled, even though it made her face ache.

"It *is* somethin'," Frankie insisted, her cheeks red and flushed. "I've told him—well, never mind what I told him. But I told him what would happen if he pulled somethin' like this."

"You two talk about me?" Margot asked.

"He was nervous about today," Frankie said. "He needed a pep talk."

Margot pinched her lips together and didn't respond. Frankie tapped out messages on her phone while Margot typed out the names of Mrs. Akeman's grandchildren.

"He's still not respondin' even though my text messages are showing up as 'read,'" Frankie seethed, shoving her phone in her pocket. "Do you want his cell number? Maybe he'll answer if he knows it's from you."

"No. If he wanted to be here, he would be here. I'm not going to beg him."

"There has to be a good reason for him not being here," Frankie protested.

"Then he can answer for himself. Frankie, I appreciate how concerned you are, really, I do. But you can't do the work for Stan in this situation. Let this go."

"Well, at least go get something to eat. Just because Uncle Stan is bein' a jackass doesn't mean you have to starve."

"I have a protein bar in my purse for days like this. I'll be fine."

"That is the saddest damn thing I've ever heard," Frankie said. "A 'bar' is not a meal, sweetie."

"I'm fine."

"So you keep sayin'," Frankie said. "If you need anything, let me know."

"I will, thank you."

Margot dropped her head, breathing deeply as Frankie's sneakers thunked down the hall. Nothing had changed since this morning. Her father was still unreliable and unavailable.

She'd lost nothing. Nothing about her life had changed. And when she went to the bathroom to check her makeup, she told herself it was the humidity that had smeared her mascara.

Hours later, Uncle Bob stuck his head in the office door to find Margot still at the desk, updating preplanned service files. His expression was uncertain, as if he expected her to snap at him after that morning's irritability.

"Hey, Margot, I just got a call from Marianne. She's stuck over at the elementary school. She took the boys there for Back to School Night and her car's dead. Something about an angry 'check engine' light. I would go, but I have about thirty pounds of King Ranch potatoes arrivin' any minute for Miss Elsie's visitation dinner. Do you mind wrappin' up and takin' the van over there to pick them up? Cail can go get the car later."

"Sure, no problem," she said, not bothering to ask what King Ranch potatoes were, because the answer would inevitably be "something carby seasoned with pig."

"Thanks, hon. You're a lifesaver."

Walking out the employee door, Margot swigged the last of her water and prayed she could make it to the van before the sweat rolled down her back. Across the lot, she spied Aunt Donna. She was standing on the dock, arguing with a tall African American man while waving what looked like a large hook in his face. Margot thought about intervening, but Duffy was standing right there, and when he saw Margot, he waved cheerfully, like there wasn't a battle royale going down on their dock. If Duffy wasn't alarmed, she wasn't going to risk life and limb to help.

The more frightening question was *why* Duffy wasn't alarmed. Was this "normal" behavior from Donna?

As the van cooled, Margot took advantage of the stronger cell signal and checked her phone. There were three increasingly urgent voice messages from Carrington, her former boss, asking her to call back right away. An inadvisable thrill of hope blossomed in Margot's middle.

Could this be the end of her exile? Was it possible that Carrington and the partners realized they couldn't run the company without her and were asking her to come back? Or maybe Carrington was just trying to give her a tip on a good job in another city. That would be just as welcome. Margot plugged her earbuds into her phone jack and hit the CALL BACK button so quickly she almost dropped the phone on the van's floor.

Margot rolled the van out of the parking lot. Carrington picked up on the first ring. "Margot! Sweetie, how *are* you? Did you really move to Georgia or is Cecily in HR drinking again? Is it dirty and awful there? Tell me everything."

"I did move to Georgia," Margot said, a bit stiffly. "It's not dirty or awful. It's actually very nice here. It's warm, but I'm living in my family's lakefront property. I'm very comfortable."

It wasn't a lie, exactly.

"Ugh, that means I owe Cecily ten dollars. I told her there was no way you'd move that far away from civilization. But she said you left a forwarding address for somewhere called Lake Sackett. I guess she wasn't exaggerating."

Margot rolled her eyes. Had Carrington phoned to gloat over her situation or was there a point to this call? She'd thought they were friends, before she left Chicago. And just for her ego's sake, she'd hoped that someone from her old life would call. It was possible she was still feeling residual anger at her father, but she found that she was annoyed with Carrington and her condescending tone.

"Is there something I can help you with, Carrington?" she asked. "I'm on my way to meet some friends."

"Really? Well, I needed to ask you about the florist you used for the Hopmann Enterprises executive dinner last year. Franz simply refuses to follow the color schemes I'm giving him. He always seemed so cooperative when he worked with you. What's your secret?"

Margot huffed, "You fired me; that means you lose my secrets. I'm not super inclined to help you, especially since you've probably given Mandy my job by now."

"Of course we didn't promote Mandy to your job! We promoted Natasha."

"Natasha? The intern?" Margot exclaimed.

"It's nothing personal, darling. Natasha's put in her time. It's only fair to give her a chance. Besides, I was only calling to see how you were doing down there in the sticks. I know it has to be awfully hard, but think of it like those boot camps where they send teenagers into the woods for character development. You're going to come out of this stronger and better for it."

"I'm going to go now, Carrington."

"If you change your mind and decide to be a team player, you can—"

"Good-bye, Carrington."

Once she managed to shake off Carrington's "concern," Margot found the elementary school pretty easily. It was at the end of Main Street, located right next to the Lake Sackett Middle and High School. Dozens of families were milling around the parking lot while a screen-printed WELCOME TO BACK TO SCHOOL NIGHT banner flapped over the main entrance.

Margot could only hope that Marianne's parent-teacher conferences had gone well. She didn't want to be stuck in the car while her cousin dressed her children down for whatever kids got into trouble for in the middle of nowhere. Her own parent-teacher conferences always seemed to end with some sort of lecture at home about how she could be trying harder, doing more to bring her As to A-plusses.

She parked the funeral home's van in the lot and noticed the uncomfortable looks she got from the parents, like her presence at the school was somehow wrong. She wondered if Marianne's older son had reached the age where he would be embarrassed by being picked up in a funeral home vehicle.

She walked through the front entrance, narrowly avoiding collision with the kids darting around the construction-paper-bedecked lobby. If she'd known that her suit would be in danger of contact with gummy, glitter-covered hands, she would have worn the emergency poncho stashed in the back of the van. That mothering instinct that made women decide that sleepless nights and perpetual yoga pants were a fair trade for tiny, cute people? She did not have it. She valued quiet. She valued her time. She didn't judge the people who had kids. She understood the necessity of children. She did. Someone had to run the retirement community where she would inevitably end up. She just had no desire for her own.

The sight of a boy running down the hall with his shirt pulled over his head, his belly painted with a neon-green smiley face, confirmed that she'd made the right choice.

Marianne dashed past Margot without looking at her, yelling, "Nate!"

So that was what Frankie meant by it being better to meet Marianne without her boys around as a distraction. Marianne had clearly birthed hellspawn.

"I'll just wait here, Marianne!" Margot called down the hall. She pursed her lips. "She didn't hear me."

Margot scanned the lobby, looking for a place to sit among the homemade posters and display dioramas of dinosaurs. But the school seemed to have some sort of policy against sitting— no benches, no chairs, nothing. She glanced toward the office; maybe they had a waiting room or something. A place where she could protect her clothes from the thin layer of sticky substances that seemed to coat every surface in this building. Her eyes landed on a familiar face and she gasped.

It was the haunted lumberjack, he of the comfortable truck seat and agile tongue.

He'd cleaned up considerably, wearing khakis and a crisp white button-down shirt. His hair was neatly combed. He was smiling, talking with other parents, but the smile didn't quite reach his eyes. He barely had a grip on it.

That grip slipped entirely when he saw her. His eyes went wide and his mouth dropped. She wasn't sure whether it would be more awkward if he didn't recognize her. Her face flushed hot. Why was he here? He was supposed to be off smoldering in the forest somewhere, staring pensively into the distance.

Oh, no, was he a parent? Had she climbed into a truck with a married man? She couldn't see his ring finger, as his left hand was curved around the shoulder of a nearby woman. Was Margot going to have her ass handed to her by some backwoods bottle blonde for him violating their marriage vows?

No, wait, he was wearing a name tag. Maybe he worked here. Which would be better . . . right?

And he was making eye contact. So much eye contact. Because the whole "I know the exact texture and circumference of your tongue" element of this interaction wasn't uncomfortable enough. He wiped his hands on his khakis as he crossed the lobby, again preventing her from seeing his ring finger. And he didn't reach out to shake her hand as he asked, "Hi, um, are you a new parent here?"

"A parent? Me? Oh, no no no no no *no*."

His brown eyes went wide at her tone and she stammered, "I—I mean, it's not that I don't like children. I like them just fine . . . when they belong to other people."

His lips pinched together, but a snicker escaped. And then his lips parted into a dazzling smile, hesitantly, as if he hadn't done it in a while. Margot shook her head and returned the smile, hoping it was half as stunning as his. "Never mind. What are you doing here?"

She glanced down at his engraved metal name tag, which read KYLE ARCHER, PRINCIPAL.

"You're the *principal*? At an *elementary* school?"

Kyle frowned. "Yes? Why does that seem to upset you?"

"Oh, I'm not upset. I just didn't expect it," she said. "You don't seem like the educator type."

She couldn't help but notice—now that she wasn't completely addled by moonshine—the lack of an accent. Unlike the molten-sugar twang of most of Lake Sackett's residents, Kyle's speech had the quick, sharper tones of the northeast. And there was the smile again, slow to bloom but sweetly sincere. "What type do I seem like?"

Lumberjack. Underemployed poet. Spokesman for paper towels.

Margot managed to keep those answers to herself and changed the subject. "Aren't you kind of young to be a principal?"

"There were very few candidates when I applied. It was between me and the guy who wanted to remove prepositions from all of the grammar textbooks."

"Well, then I'm glad they hired you."

"Me too."

He lowered his voice and stepped so close she could smell that clean, crisp fabric-softener smell. She could feel sweat gathering behind her knees. That was a new reaction to a man. "So, you've made it very clear you're not a parent. Why are you here?"

Margot scoffed. This man was not good for her. Despite seeming somewhat reluctant about his flirting with her, he made her feel things that were reckless and do things that were just plain stupid. Kyle Archer and his soulful beard were dangerous. And yet she leaned closer, too. Then she leaned a little closer because if he happened to get a glance down her blouse, that was just the blessing of good tailoring. "Family. I'm picking up my cousin and her sons."

"Really? Who are they? Maybe I could at least figure out your last name, which you haven't bothered to share with me. Or your first name, actually. It was pretty sexy at first, but it's getting weird."

"Margot Cary," she told him, glancing to his name tag. "Nice to meet you, Mr. Archer."

Kyle raised a sandy eyebrow. "Oh, I think we're on a first-name basis by now. But I don't have any students named Cary."

"Oh, well, it's not my local family's name."

"Margot!"

They turned to find Marianne showing considerable upper body strength for a petite woman, tucking her struggling seven-year-old child under her arm like a football. "You okay, hon? You're a little . . . what's a name for a color between pink and red?"

"Blush," Kyle said, the smirk still in place. "So you're related to Nate and Aiden?"

"Margot is my cousin, through Stan," Marianne supplied. "Sweetie, are you sure you're okay? Maybe the heat is getting to you."

"I'm fine. Everything is fine, absolutely and totally normal," she said, looping her arm through Marianne's. An older boy—possibly nine? Margot was not a good judge of these things—with Marianne's big blue eyes and dark hair, followed them out the door, his nose stuck in a Goosebumps book.

"Okay, we'll pretend I buy that," Marianne said. "Mr. Archer, thank you for your time earlier. Carl and I appreciate your patience with Nate."

"Hey, we want progress, not perfect, right, Nate?" Kyle held his fist out for a bump, which Nate stopped squirming long enough to return.

"Yep!"

"Bye, Aiden, try not to run into anything," Kyle said, snickering as even an admonishment from his principal didn't raise Aiden's head from his book. He leveled Margot with those bitter-chocolate eyes. "It was interesting to see you again, Margot."

"I'm sure we'll run into each other again very soon, Kyle," she said, her lips twitching into a smile.

Kyle's brow creased, but he nodded slowly. "Looking forward to it."

Margot followed Marianne's hustling form out the school door.

"That was weird. Mr. Archer never talks to the moms in that tone of voice," Aiden said, still not looking up from his book.

"What tone of voice?"

"Like the way my dad talks to my mom when it's almost bedtime."

Margot's jaw dropped open.

"Come on, Aiden, keep up, hon," Marianne said, bouncing Nate on her hip. "Margot, Frankie texted and said you didn't have lunch. Let's go get the boys something to eat while we wait for Carl to fix the car. Nate gets a little out of sorts when his blood sugar gets low."

"Really?" Margot asked. She looked to Aiden, who shrugged. "What's that like?"

Aiden sighed. "You don't want to know."

6

THE RISE AND Shine was a cozy traditional diner with worn red vinyl booths and a shiny black-and-white tile floor. Hank Williams Sr. blasted through the jukebox in the corner. The race car–themed pinball machines looked like they might have been original to the building construction in the 1960s. And when Marianne and Margot herded the boys through the door, Margot couldn't help but notice that people stopped talking.

A lot of people.

They weren't even subtle about staring at her. Margot was being weighed and measured, and based on some of the sneers she saw on the other customers' faces, she was not making a great impression—which was weird, considering she hadn't spoken or even moved yet.

"Sorry," Marianne murmured. "You were a little less visible at the Dirty Deer."

"Let's just get a table," Margot whispered as Nate tugged her toward a booth in the back. "Tell me honestly, is it the way I dress? Is that why people stare?"

"Nah, people around here don't take much notice of tourist

types. But, uh, your mama didn't leave a great impression when she took off. I don't want to speak ill of the dead, but my mama says that Linda never let someone's feelings get in the way of her sharin' an opinion. And she had a lot of opinions. She gets a *lot* of 'bless her hearts.'"

"That I believe," Margot muttered.

The diner served breakfast food, and only breakfast food, all day long because as the mustachioed owner, Ike Grandy, said right on the front of the menu, "This is America and I'll serve any damn food I want." There was a whole panel of the menu devoted to grits. But Margot was determined to order the Rabbit Food Special—a fruit plate and a veggie egg-white omelet—to try to counteract some of the fried food she'd eaten over the last few days.

She was also determined to avoid sweet tea, asking for a Coke instead. Their waitress, Marla, smiled warmly, her teeth showing stark and bright against smooth teak-colored skin, and asked, "What kind of Coke would you like? We've got regular, diet, Sprite, root beer, and Fanta."

"Just a diet Coke, please," Margot said. Marla nodded and made for the kitchen. Margot turned to Marianne. "You know, I've been ordering half-caf nonfat lattes from Starbucks for years and never had the complications I've had here."

"You're in Georgia, sweetie, home of 'Co-Cola.' Folks call all sodas Coke, no matter what brand they are. And then it's up to you to get specific." Marianne leveled Margot with her blue eyes and asked, "So, what was that with Kyle Archer earlier?"

"Nothing," Margot lied smoothly as her cousin lifted an imperious dark brow.

"Principal Archer is nice most of the time, unless you take

things off his desk and build towers with them," Nate told her as he constructed a tower from tiny square butter containers. "And then he makes you write 'I'm sorry' sentences."

"Have you done this more than once?" Margot asked.

Nate's bright blue eyes darted toward his mother, as if he was mentally reviewing his Fifth Amendment rights.

"He's okay," Aiden said, his little face serious as he set his book aside. "He doesn't take any bullcrap—" He paused to sneak a look at his mother, who frowned. "Any trouble from anybody, but he's fair about it. And when he says he's gonna do something, he does it, which is more than I can say for some of the grown-ups at the school."

"Aiden, honey, why don't you and Nate go play some pin-ball?" Marianne said, giving them each an equal stack of quarters. "No rockin' the machine!"

The boys promised solemnly as they swept their change off the table and ran to the bank of video games across the diner.

"Okay, seriously, what's going on?" Marianne asked.

Margot shrugged and restacked the sweetener packets in the table caddy. "I may have met up with your kids' principal at the Dirty Deer last night and made out with him a little," she said quietly, well aware that people at the surrounding tables could be listening. "There was some grinding and groping involved. In the front seat of his truck."

"That's where you disappeared to last night?" she cried. "I didn't even see you! Or hear about it. Do you know how hard that is to pull off in this town?"

"Well, clearly, I didn't pull it off, because now you know about me and my throbbing id."

"Still, you had twenty-four hours," Marianne told her. "That's an accomplishment. You should be proud. Around here, everybody sees everything. And just in case you forget something stupid that you did, there will always be someone who's known you since birth to remind you."

Margot's face went hot. As much as she wanted the information, she couldn't bring herself to ask about Kyle's background, not just because she was embarrassed but because she didn't want to give the impression that she was attaching herself to someone local. She didn't know if she would ever feel the kind of instant connection with anyone, certainly not in the way Marianne and Carl shared. And she didn't want to give Marianne the wrong impression about her commitment to Lake Sackett.

"That sounds claustrophobic."

"It can be. So, throbbin' id, huh?"

Margot nodded.

"Do you think that you and Kyle might be a thing?"

"I don't think so. I didn't even know his name was Kyle until I saw his name tag at the school. That's probably not a foundation for a lasting relationship."

"Well, just so you know, he's a really nice guy. And not one of those 'nice guys' you read about on the Internet, but a truly sweet person. Really good with the kids at school, very understanding of Nate and his special brand of 'creative chaos.' Just one thing—"

Ike, the owner, interrupted, delivering the food himself, carefully spinning the plates heaped with waffles and bacon and eggs into their correct spots without being told who had ordered what. As the boys gave warrior whoops and stampeded back to the table, Ike leveled Margot with a long, speculative stare.

"I want you to know I am serving this plate under protest,"

he said as the Rabbit Food Special came to a stop in front of her. "No one ever orders the Rabbit. It's there for profiling purposes. But you're Stan's girl, so I'm gonna let it slide, just this once."

Margot managed to refrain from the "you have disappointed me" stare she normally gave mouthy servers. She did not appreciate the reminder of her absentee father at the moment.

"Next time, you're getting the Smokehouse Breakfast with a side of hash browns, and you're gonna eat the whole thing," Ike told her sternly. "I won't be responsible for you blowin' away in a stiff wind."

"I appreciate your concern."

Ike nodded and grumbled. "Boys, remember, no throwing the jellies. Marianne, my mama would like to pass along to Miss Tootie that she's bringing seven-layer salad to the card game this week."

"I'll let her know," Marianne promised as the boys dug into their pecan waffles.

Adult conversation was impossible while Marianne tried to get her children through a meal without a maple syrup explosion. Nate needed help cutting his waffles. Aiden had trouble opening up the ketchup bottle for his hash browns and then elbowed his water over onto the table while handing it to Margot. As soon as Marianne got them settled and raised a fork to her lips, Nate had to go to the restroom, and due to an incident involving the hand dryer, he wasn't allowed to go alone.

"Is it always like this?" Margot asked Aiden as Marianne led his brother to the bathrooms. "Does your mom ever get a hot meal?"

"Nah, sometimes we spill more," Aiden mumbled around a mouthful of waffle.

Margot shuddered.

The door to the diner opened with a peal of bells. Margot glanced up and her fork stopped midway to her mouth.

A scruffy-looking man with dishwater-brown hair hanging over his eyes stalked through the door. While handsome in a lean, unrefined sort of way, he also had the hardened look of someone who'd never quite had a break in life. He wore a Dawson Towing T-shirt with the sleeves ripped off and jeans streaked with grease. The muscles of his arms were sharply defined in a way that spoke of capability, not gym hours. He glanced around the diner, scanning, frowning. Margot put her arm around Aiden in a protective sweep.

Oh, no. Margot had not spent nearly thirty years successfully avoiding victimhood in Chicago to be killed in a diner robbery in Georgia. She slipped her hand into her purse and dialed 9 and 1 before Marianne and Nate emerged from the restrooms.

The scruffy man spotted Marianne and the natural scowl seemed to slide right off his face. Margot had never seen someone light up before, but this man's sharp features softened to anime levels of adorableness. His eyes brightened to an emerald green. His smile was wide and dazzling.

"Hey, baby!" he exclaimed.

Margot frowned and glanced around. Was he calling for one of the other customers?

Marianne turned and melted at the sight of the man while Margot was trying to remember wanted posters from her last trip to the post office. She pointed to their table. "Hey, sweetie, we're over here."

Margot lifted a brow. "Sweetie?"

Marianne giggled like a tiny, tiny schoolgirl as the man wrapped an arm around her waist and kissed her soundly. "Got your van all fixed up with a new battery. Jeeter dropped me off so I could drive you home."

"Aw, thanks, baby. Cousin Margot, this is my husband, Carl Dawson. Carl, this is my cousin Margot." The boys started talking a mile a minute and leaped up to climb all over him, which he greeted with hugs and unabashed kisses to both.

And then he turned that devastating smile on Margot and suddenly she understood why her cousin had given up a comfortable life in Atlanta to come home to her high school sweetheart. To have someone look at her the way Carl was looking at Marianne, like she'd personally hung the moon and stars and then threw the sun up in the air just for bragging rights, Margot could see how Marianne would sacrifice quite a bit. She didn't know if she could ever do the same, but she saw the benefits.

"Well, it's nice to meet ya, Margot. My Marianne has told me all about you," Carl rasped in a bourbon-soaked drawl that should not have been sexy.

"Nice to meet you, too," Margot said. The *sorry I thought you were going to rob us because I'm a classist, judgmental cliché* was silent.

Ike delivered a plate of ham, bacon, sausage, scrambled eggs, and biscuits to the table. "Hey, there, Carl, I brought your usual."

"I 'ppreciate it, Ike," Carl said, shaking Ike's hand.

Ike leveled a stern look at Margot while he pointed to Carl's gravy-laden plate. "The Smokehouse Breakfast. This is a proper meal."

"Noted," Margot said.

Ike nodded and backed away from the table. Aiden took a seat at the end of the table to make room at the four-top. The boys began chattering about their school day and who had thrown what at lunch. Carl listened patiently, nodding and asking enough questions to show that he was paying attention. Margot just watched the volley of conversation bounce around the table, with her heart clenching inside her chest. She was glad her cousin was happy. She was glad the boys had a doting father. But it only served to remind her of what she didn't have. Margot wondered if this was how Marianne's family dinners usually went, or if the excitement of Back to School Night and dinner out was making them especially lively. She couldn't remember a single meal in her home being so loud or relaxed.

Mother had insisted on playing classical music while the three of them ate at the dining table. Conversation was always polite but distant and cool, barely heard over the Chopin. And her mother had never craned over the table to give her full attention to Margot's stories from school. Margot frowned, wondering again how different life would have been if she'd grown up in Lake Sackett. She couldn't picture Mother and Stan having animated, cheerful meals together, but at least watching a happy family eating wouldn't feel like something out of *National Geographic*.

"So how was the school meetin'?" Carl asked.

Marianne groaned and dropped her head nearly to her plate. Margot's eyes cut toward their youngest. "Um, I can leave, if you don't want me around for this. I mean, parent-teacher conferences are sort of like medical records, in terms of none of my business."

"Oh, no!" Marianne assured her. "Both the parent-teacher

conferences went really well. Aiden's already ten points ahead of his Accelerated Reader goals. Nate's math proficiency has shot up to the ninety-second percentile and his trips to the office are down by twenty percent."

Carl offered both boys silent fist bumps.

"The meeting Carl's talking about is the parent committee for the Founders' Festival," Marianne said, looking to her husband. "And it was exactly what I expected it to be."

Carl grimaced and tucked into his bacon.

"I'm assuming the festival is a really big deal around here?" Margot asked.

Marianne sighed. "Yes, it's coming up in early October. We've been planning for months, but nothing has actually been accomplished because every time the committee makes a decision and presents it to the PTA president, Sara Lee Bolton, she rejects it and does whatever she wants, while Mr. Archer tries to keep up. Meanwhile, the rest of us have already made plans and reservations and payments based on what we thought were the plans, and everything gets undone and confused and I have to count to a hundred so I don't end up shoutin' profanities in a children's school."

Margot shuddered. "So why is the Founders' Festival so important?"

"Well, after the water dump, we have less to draw tourists to the town," Carl said. "For Founders' Day, we do up a farmers' market and a craft fair and games and rides. People come down and make a real family trip out of it. And with fewer people coming into town for fishing and boating and the like, we have to draw even more people in to make up for the loss. We've stretched it out to more of a Founders' Week."

"And why is Mr. Archer involved?" Margot asked, ignoring the smirk Marianne tried and failed to hide behind her hash browns.

"The elementary school kids do a play and a concert and presentations about the town's history. Plus the rides are all set up on the school grounds. And the retired principal always made a big point of being part of the planning," Marianne said.

Carl's green eyes narrowed at Margot and she felt herself swallowing in a noisy *gulp*. "You know, you probably wouldn't be half as crazy as Sara Lee when it comes to all this planning stuff."

Margot bit her plump bottom lip. "Was that a compliment?"

"I'm just saying that if we have this all-powerful, fancy-pants event planner, who better to plan it than her?" Carl said, nodding to his wife's cousin. "You could do some good for the town. And build a little goodwill for McCready's as you go."

Marianne stood up and lunged across the table to grab Carl's work shirt, pulling him into a fierce kiss. Margot imagined it tasted like gravy. "You are freakin' brilliant sometimes, you know that?"

Though his cheeks flushed pink, Carl jerked his shoulders and casually returned to his food. "Course I am."

"What do you say, Margot?"

"What? A hostile takeover of planning for an event that I'm completely unfamiliar with that's only about two months away, in a place where I have no connections or vendor pull? That's insanity. Why don't you do it?" Margot asked. "You're the one with children at the school."

"My name is mud when it comes to workin' with the community and anything involving children or charity or the public.

It's a long story," Marianne said, turning to her youngest. "Nate, puppy face."

Nate wiped his mouth with the back of his hand and very carefully poked out his bottom lip, angled his chin down, and widened his eyes to the point that Margot feared for his eyelids. "Please, Cousin Margot, won't you please help run the Founders' Festival and save our town?"

Margot pursed her lips. "That's playing dirty," she told Marianne.

"I'm a desperate woman."

"I don't even know if I'm going to be here in October," Margot exclaimed. "I could get a job offer in the next few weeks and move, and then where would you be? Even more confused and unproductive."

Marianne frowned as if she'd forgotten that Margot wasn't a permanent resident of Lake Sackett. "Oh, right. Sure."

"I'm sure it will work out just fine," Margot said. "This always happens with big community events. Egos and chaos and details that don't get addressed until the last minute. But it will come together, trust me."

"Sure." Marianne looked down at her plate and poked a bit of egg around with her fork. "So, Aiden, tell me about this new book you're readin'. No scary ventriloquist dummies this time, right? That one gave you nightmares for a month."

"Nope, this time it's garden gnomes, thirstin' for revenge!" Aiden said, grinning viciously.

Carl gave an exaggerated shiver and ruffled Aiden's hair. "That's creepier than the dummies. I don't trust anything that tries that hard to be cute."

Margot glanced at Nate, who was still using the puppy face while reaching for the strawberries on her fruit plate. "Exactly."

~

MARGOT WAS RELIEVED and disappointed that Stan wasn't waiting for her with an explanation when she arrived at work the next morning. She buried herself in details and busywork. She faxed. She filed. She even vacuumed flower petals out of the west chapel when Eunice Woodson's grandson knocked over a vase full of daisies.

And that nauseating mix of anxiety and irritation hadn't ebbed out of her stomach. It was still there, hovering under her diaphragm, when Uncle Bob poked his head in the door, his expression uncertain. "Margot, are you done with the Branson file?"

"Yes," she said, handing him the manila folder from the neat stack on her desk.

While Bob had handled the planning and sale portion of the process, the Branson service was the first set of paperwork that Margot had completed on her own. It had not been easy, given all the customs and niceties—not to mention state laws—she'd had to remember while talking to Mrs. Branson. And it had given her an odd sense of accomplishment to finally slide the file into the outbox.

"Mrs. Branson called to double-check some details and I talked her into upgrading to the Buchanan casket with the bronze fittings, rather than just the brass-plated," Margot said proudly. "And the bronze-lined burial vault, plus the waterproofing, which I don't think anyone has ever ordered here, given the way the supplier reacted when I requested it. Mrs. Branson agreed with me that it was a much more fitting tribute to her husband, and if it happened to add another four thousand dollars to her total bill, so be it." She offered her uncle a cheeky smile . . . which he did not return.

In fact, Uncle Bob looked downright horrified.

"Margot, what were you thinking?"

"I was thinking that if Mrs. Branson wanted to make herself feel better by spending a little extra on her husband's funeral and the business happens to make a little extra money, what's the harm? I took Mr. Branson from a Toyota Tercel funeral to a nice respectable Cadillac."

Bob's voice dropped to a stern level she'd never heard out of her cheerful uncle. "The harm is that Arlene Branson can't afford to spend a little extra on her husband's funeral. Her George's cancer treatments ate up most of their retirement funds. She's havin' to move in with her daughter as it is. To play on her grief like that, to make her spend more, that's not how we do things, Margot."

Margot's brow wrinkled. Upselling was one of her main skill sets at Elite Elegance. She was known for her ability to talk clients into premium catering orders, bigger floral arrangements, better linens. It was what she did. The idea that this talent might not be appreciated at McCready's left her unsteady. She wasn't sure what else she had to offer.

"I'm sorry. I didn't know we were running a nonprofit," she said crisply.

"That's not what I meant and you know it. We're not runnin' a charity, but we are runnin' a company that has stayed in business for almost a hundred years because we don't treat our neighbors like sheep for the fleecin'. We're part of the community, Margot. And we take that seriously."

"Fine," Margot said. "I'll keep that in mind."

Bob's lips pinched into an unhappy expression. "I'm going to call Mrs. Branson back and explain to her that the suppliers didn't have those upgraded features after all, but we can give her a deal on a package somewhere in the middle. Give Mr. Branson a comfortable Ford Taurus funeral."

Margot knew he was trying to soften the blow with a joke, but she couldn't find it in her to smile. She prided herself on her work ethic and talent. Flamingos aside, she'd never been chastised for how she handled events. And at this stage, she didn't need the knock to her confidence.

"I'll leave you to do that." Margot stood and grabbed her purse. "I'm going to go into town and grab some lunch. Would you like something?"

"No, Leslie's got me covered. Why don't you just let her fix you something at the Snack Shack?"

"Because I need to eat something green that doesn't involve gummy candy," Margot shot back. "I'll be back in an hour."

"All right, then." Bob sounded disappointed in more ways than one as he sat at her desk and picked up the phone.

Margot sped down the hall and outside into the stifling heat. This was manageable. A little fruit, some lean protein, and she would be back on track. Everybody has bad mornings at work, and it wasn't as if Tootie was going to let Bob fire her. Of course, she'd had a bit of a spat with Tootie the last time she'd spoken to her, too. Maybe there was a reason she'd grown up without an extended family. She didn't seem to be very good at it.

Margot rooted around in her purse for the set of truck keys

Duffy had graciously shared with her. And when she looked up, she realized she was walking toward Stan, who was waiting for her by the truck. He looked more rumpled than the first time she'd met him, more worn. The bags under his eyes were even more pronounced now that those eyes were infinitely sadder. But his eyes were clear and his hands were steady.

"Just what I need," she muttered under her breath.

Stan chewed on his lip as she approached, as if he was still trying to figure out what to say to his daughter. Margot made it very easy for him.

"Whatever excuse you have for standing me up yesterday, I don't want to hear it," she said, clipping past him. She still couldn't find the damn keys. How did giant pre–keyless entry metal monstrosities like that get lost in her relatively small purse?

"Margot, I'm sorry," Stan said.

"Sorry for what, exactly?" she asked, her voice icy as she pawed through makeup, tissues, her phone. "Missing a lunch you agreed to, the first commitment you'd made to me in thirty years? Or being absent for those thirty years? Because if it's the former, don't worry, I'm used to it."

"I don't know what your mother told you about me—"

"She told me you were a drunk. That you weren't the sort of man she wanted raising her daughter, that you were unreliable and unstable. She wasn't wrong. She's still not." Her fingers closed around the keys and she pulled them free.

"About the drinking, no, not at the time. She was right about that," he agreed. "But I'm dried out now. Got my twenty-year chip, even though I never got to make my amends to you. Your mama was right to—"

"I don't want to hear it," she said, unlocking the door and

yanking it open. "I really don't. I was wrong to reach out to you. I was setting myself up for disappointment. I don't want your excuses. I don't want a dramatic apology. I don't want to hear about your feelings. I just want to come to work, earn my keep, and get out of this town and far from you."

"Margot, please. I didn't mean to hurt you. I never did."

Margot wedged her foot into the truck and hurdled into the driver's seat. "And yet you have, over and over. You had a choice yesterday. You chose not to show up."

"I wanted to, but—"

She slammed the door, but unfortunately, Duffy had left the window down, so this conversation continued. "Was there a work-related emergency that couldn't have been handled by anyone else?"

He shook his head, swallowing thickly. "No."

"A mechanical failure affecting every vehicle in town that prevented you from keeping your appointment with me?"

Stan's big sad eyes narrowed a bit, like he didn't appreciate her frigid tone of voice. "No."

"A cell phone tower outage that kept you from being able to call me to tell me you weren't coming?"

"No."

"So you chose not to show up, you let me sit here in my office waiting for you, wondering where you were. And you didn't think that maybe that would hurt me?" Margot slid the keys into the ignition.

"No, I knew it would, but I thought it would be better than hurting you some other way."

"That's bullshit. It's emotionally lazy bullshit," she snapped. "Look, when someone shows me who they are, I believe them.

You've shown me every day, since before I can remember, who you are. I believe it. Now, please, just let me work. Nothing's changed. We don't know each other and we don't have to know each other. We are two strangers who happen to work in the same office. And that's fine. I'm *fine*."

Stan stiffened, staring at her for a long time. "If that's what you want."

"It is." Margot nodded, turning the key. The engine roared to life and Stan's response was drowned out. Margot gunned the engine, whipping her head forward and speeding off.

7

$\mathcal{M}$ARGOT COULDN'T BRING herself to go to the diner and face people, so she went home to forage in her fridge. As the truck bumped over the gravel drive of the McCready compound, she spotted Arlo waiting for her on her front porch. His ears perked forward and he hopped to his feet as she climbed out of the truck.

"Oh, no," she said. "You just go home to Aunt Tootie. I don't have time to lint-roll away dog hair. I only have an hour for lunch."

Arlo whimpered and cocked his head to the side.

"Seriously, go," Margot said, shooing him away with her hands. "Now."

Arlo darted to the door and plunked his butt in the center of the frame.

"I will wait you out," she said, leaning down and pointing a finger in his face. "I outlasted a shoe model who threatened not to walk in the Ladies Charity League Spring Fashion Show until she got a hyper-dry triple-shot soy cappuccino, because there's no such thing. I can outlast a rescue mutt."

Arlo yipped and licked at her finger.

Sighing, Margot turned her back on the dog and stared out at the sunlight flickering across the expanse of the lake. She hated to admit it, but her view was one of the things she enjoyed about living in Lake Sackett. In the mornings, she got up a few minutes early just to drink her coffee while watching the dragonflies dart across the surface. After dinner, she'd spent the evening on her porch, just staring out at still water purpled by twilight.

Margot glanced down the drive. She still didn't know who had once lived in the yellow house with the dilapidated green roof. She hadn't had time to ask anyone. She'd thought she would feel crowded and put-upon, living so close to the family. But Margot found it was a lot like living in her apartment building. She knew her family was close by, but everybody seemed to respect each other's privacy. And there were times she was absolutely unnerved by the silence. She was used to the constant rumble of traffic and the wail of sirens—even in her relatively nice neighborhood. The lack of noise made her feel like her cabin was surrounded by a layer of Styrofoam.

But now, the noise in her head felt overwhelming, like she had an ocean between her ears, roaring and crashing. She couldn't believe a simple lunch invitation had turned out so badly. It was a nightmare, all of her childhood insecurities, every question she'd asked herself about her father, all dredged up at once. She sank to the porch step, not caring when the seat of her pants suit landed on the dusty wood. Her mother had been right. Her father wasn't a father. He wasn't capable of that kind of responsibility, even sober. Linda was not a mother who hugged or even showed approval that often, but she'd done a loving thing in taking Margot away from here.

Arlo padded over to Margot and slipped his head under her

arm and into her chest. She sighed, forgetting about dog hair, and combed her fingers against his neck. The warmth of his fur and his heartbeat under her hand, even with the doggy smell, were comforting. She relaxed around him, letting her face drop against the top of his head. For a brief moment, she let her eyes burn and water. She took a wobbly breath.

Why did missing one stupid lunch hurt so much? She'd had worse done to her by people she liked more. Why was she giving so much power to someone she barely knew? And why was she burying her face against dog fur?

"No," she said, gently easing Arlo out of her lap. "No offense, Arlo, but no."

She stood, shoving her door open. Arlo yipped and dashed into the house. "No! Arlo!"

Arlo hopped on the couch, made a couple of circles, and burrowed into a throw pillow. "You're not staying."

Arlo made a whining noise that sounded like a canine version of "That's what you think."

Margot crossed to the fridge, which had nothing green in it. Nothing. Not even mold. She groaned. "That's it. I'm taking the rest of the day off."

~

MARGOT DROVE DUFFY'S truck to the Food Carnival at the end of town. While Leslie and Tootie had been diligent about delivering casseroles to her door, Margot really needed to start stocking her own pantry. She couldn't keep living on a diet entirely based on Velveeta and cream of chicken soup.

As she pulled into the parking lot, she reminded herself that she'd shopped in tiny bodegas while living in the city and she could make do with whatever she found on the shelves. And then she walked into the cheerfully lit shop, saw motor oil displayed right next to fresh fruit, and almost lost her nerve.

While there were huge pallets of sunblock, beer, and pool noodles, there were no ethnic foods beyond the pasta aisle. There was no organic produce. And when she asked for the health food section, the clerk directed her to a display of Flint-stones vitamins. She was a little discouraged by these developments, but they weren't nearly as concerning as the store's use of Snacky the Clown as its mascot.

She stocked up on produce, almonds, and oatmeal and with apprehension turned toward the toiletries section. She'd brought half-full bottles of her prestige-brand toiletries to Lake Sackett, expecting them to hold out until she found a new job and moved on. But she was running low on basically everything, as the ridiculous heat had her showering twice a day. Between her dwindling funds and spotty Internet access, she was going to have to break down and buy . . . bargain brands. She fully expected her pampered blond locks to rebel and detach themselves on principle.

Margot was considering which overscented fruity body wash would offend her sensibilities the least when a girl around age five with a honey-blond ponytail ran full-tilt into her legs. The girl bounced off Margot and went sprawling across the floor and started crying. Margot glanced around, searching for a parent who would fix this. But most of the other shoppers were just staring at her as if she'd knocked a child to the floor on purpose.

"I don't know what to do here," Margot said, helping the girl to her feet. The little girl leaned her head back, opened her mouth, and let loose sobs that could have shattered the store's front windows. Margot couldn't help but notice the girl's windblown hair and a very *interesting* outfit consisting of khaki shorts, a purple-and-orange-striped sweater, and pink rain boots with little green whales on them. Maybe she was one of those feral children you saw on the news? It would explain the fashion choices and the lack of a parent to soothe her out of her sobs. Margot awkwardly patted the little girl's arms. "I don't know how to deal with crying kids. Do I give you a Band-Aid? A hug? What's going to make you feel better?"

Suddenly the girl stopped crying and her huge brown eyes popped open. "Candy."

Margot's own eyes narrowed, but there was a little quirk to her lips as she said, "Oh, you're good."

The little girl grinned and did not look one bit sorry. There was something familiar about that expression.

"June?"

"Daddy?" The girl's head snapped left as Kyle Archer rounded the corner of the body wash display. He sagged with relief when he saw Margot crouched in front of his daughter. Margot quickly released June's shoulders and stood, taking a step back from the girl.

Damn it. This was just not her day for uncomfortable inter-actions with fathers. *Fathers.* The little girl had called her truck-seat paramour "Daddy." Margot's stomach dropped. Where was the mother? She glanced down at Kyle's ring finger, which was bare but still showed the faintest of tan lines. Not married, then. That was a relief.

Margot took a step back, staring at Kyle's open smile. How could he look so happy, with his daughter in his arms, but so miserable when he was away from her? Was it a custody thing? Was he only cheerful when his daughter was around?

Kyle lifted the girl into his arms and leveled her with serious but not angry eyes. "Juniper Grace Archer, we've talked about this. You can't run off on your own at the store."

"Sorry, Daddy, I was boooooored," June said, as if that explained abandoning her father in the grocery store and giving him a minor cardiac incident. Kyle turned his attention to Margot and lifted a dark-blond eyebrow.

Margot raised her hands in surrender. "I swear, I am not stalking you."

He smirked. "That's what the last girl who stalked me said."

"I didn't knock her down or anything. She ran around the corner and bounced off of me."

"June, we've talked about that, too," Kyle scolded.

Juniper shrugged. "It gets me around faster."

Margot tried to back away slowly from the little domestic scene, but Kyle turned to her. "I'm sorry, I'm usually better at supervising my own kids. But my other daughter was picking out a shampoo, which is sort of a 'wisdom of Solomon' thing, and June got away from me."

"Oh," she said, nodding and trying to back away down the aisle. "All right, then, see you around."

"Um, actually, I could use your help," he said. "With the shampoo thing. You're a woman."

"Thank you for noticing," she deadpanned.

"And you're probably better at picking out this stuff than I am," he said, his cheeks flushing under his beard.

"Why is it so hard to pick a shampoo?" she asked.

Kyle cleared his throat. "Well."

An older girl, maybe seven or eight, stepped around the end display and into the aisle, looking highly disgruntled. Her hair was several shades darker than her sister's. It was also several times larger than her sister's, forming a sort of unintentional cloud of frizz around her head.

Margot flinched. "Oh."

"Hazel tried a new shampoo this week because it smelled like One Direction is supposed to smell. Don't ask me why that makes sense. It's a girl thing and I can't possibly understand. And it made her hair all flat and stringy-looking. So I got her a volumizing shampoo, which was obviously a mistake because she has naturally curly hair and the chemicals awoke something evil in it. We tried defrizzing shampoo and dry shampoo and it just keeps getting bigger. And then at school today, the static electricity from the other kids just made it angry . . ."

June tugged on Margot's shirt. "We're afraid it's going to start sucking people in, like the Blob."

Hazel made an indignant noise but moved behind her father, out of sight. Margot turned to Kyle, brows lifted.

"I should not have let them watch that vintage horror movie marathon," he admitted.

Margot sighed. She felt deeply underqualified to handle this. But Hazel looked so miserable with her giant cloud of hair. And she just couldn't let Kyle make this worse for his daughter before she went back to school. Hazel was already the principal's kid, which probably made life at school hard enough.

"This is not a problem that can be solved with more shampoo," Margot told him, leading the little family back into the shampoo-and-conditioner aisle. June climbed down from her father's arms and tugged on Margot's jean pocket as she walked.

Margot carefully peeled her hand away and tucked it back into Kyle's.

It was unsettling how quickly kids attached themselves to people they barely knew. She needed to help poor Hazel with her follicle emergency and then get away from Kyle and his kids and his soft, teasing lips as quickly as possible. Surely there had to be some nice local lady who could decipher Kyle's dual personality and his girls' personal hygiene issues. She just needed to make some sort of dignified exit and never leave work or home again, so these awkward encounters would stop.

Reasonable solution.

Margot searched for the best brand among the value labels and started handing Kyle products. "Deep conditioning, spray detangler, and a Wet Brush. And if that doesn't work . . ."

Margot turned to Kyle with a hesitant expression on her face.

"I'm scared," Kyle whispered.

"Do you have olive oil at home?"

Margot separated from the little family as soon as Hazel's hair care regimen was selected. She didn't even say good-bye. She just said, "All right, then! Good luck!" and disappeared like fog. She felt a little guilty being rude to children, but this breakdown of the sexy, brooding image she'd had of Kyle to the responsible school administrator to the guy picking out no-tears shampoo was too much for her to handle. Not because it destroyed her unreasonable expectations, but because she could picture that very easily—Kyle standing at the stove while the girls ran around the kitchen, waving their sticky hands near all the available surfaces. She shook that image out of her head. As adorable as Kyle's baggage might have been, she was in no way prepared to deal with them. All she'd wanted was a nice, simple romp with the hot broody local. She didn't want to know about his home life. She didn't want to meet his adorable, follically challenged children.

The lump of unease in her belly turned to ice-cold disappointment as she grasped the full implications of Kyle having kids. It felt like a death of possibilities. She was not prepared for this kind of complication in her life. She was going to be leaving Lake Sackett in a few weeks, God willing. She did not have time to form any sort of attachment to a single father of two girls.

Unfortunately, that father of two girls managed to catch up to her as she was loading her groceries into the truck. Over his shoulder, she could see that June was already strapped into the booster seat inside what she realized now was a sensible, *family friendly* four-door truck. Hazel was climbing in after her.

Margot moved toward the driver's-side door but couldn't unlock it without being obvious about dodging him.

"Hey, I didn't have a chance to say thank-you properly," he said. "I really appreciate the help. Every time I think I have a handle on this whole 'parenting daughters' thing, something pops up and bites me on my ass. And Hazel struggles without her mom."

"As someone with challenging hair, I sympathize with her plight," Margot said.

Kyle cleared his throat. "So, um, this is . . ."

"Uncomfortable to the point of pain?"

"I was going to go with 'a little awkward,' and end it there," Kyle countered, pursing his lips. There was a pause in the conversation. With the way Kyle was looking her over, his gaze appreciative, Margot thought that he might ask her out. And she was already coming up with a list of reasons why she couldn't accept. But she didn't have the opportunity to use any of them, because he just smiled, said, "Well, I'll see you around!" and pushed his empty cart toward the corral.

Margot couldn't help but bite back some discontent. Clearly the connection she'd felt with him in that brief moment of madness hadn't meant nearly as much to him as it had to her. And that was a good thing, right? She didn't need to get all tangled up with this man and his kids. It was already going to be messy enough leaving her own family behind in Lake Sackett.

Margot palmed her keys. Right. Good life choices. Minimal complications.

She yanked open her door and called over her shoulder, "So if you see me sometime in the next twenty-four hours, it's not stalking. It's a coincidence. An embarrassing and ill-timed coincidence."

Kyle opened his driver's-side door and smirked. "That's what the last girl who stalked me said."

~

AFTER THE MISSED lunch debacle, Margot had planned to avoid her father. Stan had made his priorities clear. She needed to do the same. She just wanted to do her work, stay away from charming single fathers, then find a job and get out of town before she had to deal with Stan again. She got really good at tailoring her schedule to avoid seeing him at work, orbiting around the funeral home on a "Stan free" track.

Of course, her scruffy cousin blew that plan all to hell at the earliest possible opportunity just a few days later. Duffy insisted on showing her the "other side" of the business by taking her fishing. She'd pictured waking up around nine, going to the Rise and Shine, and then spending an hour flicking some bait over the water just to say they did it. She did *not* expect him to show up at her cabin before dawn, throw some worn boots at her, and drag her into his truck.

In most cases, being dragged from bed into anyone's truck would be problematic.

"I'm reporting this as a kidnapping as soon as I'm awake," she said through a yawn, leaning her forehead against his cool passenger window. "I have memorized the number for the Georgia State Patrol."

"You'll never get a cell signal out here," he reminded her.

"I'll mail them a letter," she countered, her face smashed against the glass. "On very official-looking paper."

But when she woke up she didn't have time or stationery with which to report her cousin for multiple felonies, because she was sitting on a bench against the weathered red exterior of the Snack Shack. The water lapped loudly against the dock, occasionally splashing hard enough that droplets launched up from the surface and landed near her feet. She started, shrieking a little bit, grateful that she hadn't rolled off the bench and into the water. "Duffy! Did you carry me down the dock while I was asleep? That is wrong!"

But Duffy didn't answer. She couldn't even see him, only the peachy orange of sunrise peeking over the horizon. The water lapped gently under the dock, its glittering surface making Margot squint even behind her sunglasses. Margot groaned and rubbed her hand over her face. "I'm going to shave his head while he sleeps."

"Here, hon, this will perk you right up."

Margot jerked again. Her eyes flew open and she found the

tiny form of Bob's wife, Leslie, blocking the rising sun. "Aunt Leslie? What are you doing here so early? Did Duffy kidnap you, too?"

A compact pixie with fading blond hair and a penchant for floppy straw hats, Leslie passed her an enormous thermal mug. "You have to wake up pretty early to beat the fishermen to the water. And I have to have the food ready for them. Now, you take a big swig of that. Bob told me the brew was hard on your system, so I mixed in some milk and sugar, like we fix for the kids."

Margot rolled the oversweet substance on her tongue and winced. "You give this to children?"

"Well, not Nate," Les said, shaking her head. She pressed a grease-spotted paper bag into Margot's hands. "I've gotta get to work. Here, hon, you tell Duffy I made these for your breakfast."

Margot sniffed the bag. It smelled like at least two hours on an elliptical. "What is it?"

"Bacon wrapped around a sausage, stuffed with cheese, dipped in egg batter and deep-fried. I call it a Breakfast Stick."

"I don't know how to respond to that."

"The gravy's in the spare thermos!" Les called brightly, walking back into the shack.

Margot heard a rumbling and turned to see Duffy guiding what looked like a floating front porch toward her. According to the bright red paint scrawled across the bow, it was called *Sarah Jane*. He waved cheerfully. "Hello, the dock!"

"Hello, wide flat boat thing!" she called back.

"This is a pontoon boat," he told her as he deftly steered it parallel to the dock without colliding with it. "I figured it would be a little bit more your speed than one of our bass rigs."

"You would be correct," she said as he helped her step on

board. She was pleased that the boat didn't give under her feet. It was a nice stable surface, not at all tippy. "Here, Aunt Leslie gave us breakfast."

Duffy looked into the bag and grinned. He called over Margot's shoulder, "Oh, um, hey, Les? We're gonna need enough for two more."

"Is Frankie coming with us?" Margot asked, stowing her purse under one of the seat cushions and flopping onto the wide, couchlike seats.

"Not exactly," Duffy said, flushing behind his gingery beard.

"Duffy, what did you do?" Margot turned to follow his eye line and saw her father walking on the dock with Aunt Donna at his side.

Aunt Donna looked ready for camping in the outback, wearing a khaki tank top with a green bandanna knotted around her neck. Her frizzled reddish hair blew in a curly cloud around her face, occasionally falling over a pair of black aviator sunglasses. She was sun-burnished and blowsy but looked perfectly at ease as she jumped onto the boat.

Seeing the uncomfortable expression on Margot's face, Stan dropped the large Coleman cooler gently to the dock. A chubby Jack Russell terrier with gray-white hairs streaking out from its muzzle trotted down the dock, wearing a little doggy life vest.

Huffing at Stan until he stepped aside, the dog leaped gracefully onto the boat and hopped up on the seat nearest Donna. It turned in a circle until it found the best napping-in-the-sunshine position and dropped to its stomach.

"Look, I can just stay here," Stan said as Donna tossed a bag full of gear to her son. "Don't feel much like fishing anyway."

"No, no, you stay, I'll go," Margot said, grabbing at the cushion that hid her bag. "You'll probably get more out of this trip than I would."

"No, the whole point of going out this morning was to teach you about fishing," Stan protested as Leslie dropped a grease-spotted bag into Duffy's waiting hands. "And I don't want to mess that—"

"Really, it's no trouble, I'll just head back to the cabin and catch up on chores."

"Now, listen here, if your cousin wants to take you fishing, I'm not gonna interfere."

Donna turned, hands on hips. "Get your ass on the boat, Stan."

"But—"

Donna lowered her sunglasses and glared at Stan. He threw his arms into the air. "Fine!"

While Margot sat, feeling pretty useless, the other three moved about the boat with practiced ease, securing the canvas screen overhead, prepping fishing rods, and most important, distributing the Breakfast Sticks. The terrier popped its head up, sniffing with hopeful eyes, but Donna scratched behind its ears and dug a treat out of her fishing vest.

"No Breakfast Sticks for you, Willie," she said, though Margot noted her no-nonsense aunt didn't have a cutesy dog voice. Her dog voice was just as exasperated as her people voice. "I'm not gonna have the vet fussing at me over your cholesterol again."

"Willie's been fishing with Mom and her charters for more than ten years," Duffy told her. "He's enjoyed a fair share of Breakfast Sticks in his lifetime."

"Do the charter clients mind sharing their boat with a dog?" Margot asked.

"Anybody who does mind gets tossed off my boat," Donna said, peering over her aviators at her niece.

Margot raised her hands in surrender. "Understood."

Duffy revved the engine while Stan cast off a line. Margot just sat there and smeared SPF 30 sunscreen on her face and throat. Leslie stuck her head out of the Snack Shack and waved them off with a big grin on her face. Behind her, trucks were already pulling into the marina lot, eager for coffee and bait and deep-fried breakfast.

"Here you go." Donna plopped a floppy canvas fisherman's hat on top of Margot's head. "You're gonna need more than sunscreen to protect that fair skin of yours, Big City."

"Actually, I've always tanned pretty easily," Margot said. "I just haven't been outdoors much lately, so I'm kind of fish-belly pale."

Donna scoffed. "Stan's the same way. Get him near a strong lightbulb and he's brown as a walnut."

Margot glanced at her father's craggy face. He nodded and shrugged, seeming pleased that Donna had noted a similarity between him and his daughter. Margot cleared her throat. "So where are you taking me?"

"One of my favorite spots," Donna assured her as Duffy glided the boat easily across the water. "Crappie galore. You'll love it."

Donna handed her one of the rods she'd brought, with the McCready Family Funeral Home and Bait Shop logo printed on the reel. She explained the mechanics of casting, when to release the tab on the reel, how to know when to start turning the spinning handle, and then dropped it into Margot's palms. "Trust me, any fool can use this."

Margot grimaced. She had a feeling Donna would have no problem telling her when she was being a fool. Donna slapped a plastic container of minnows on the seat next to her. "If you want to fish on my boat, you're gonna have to bait your own hook. Put that college education of yours to good use."

Margot lifted the lid of the minnow container and blanched at the poor, defenseless feeder fish. "Oddly enough, fish murder was not covered in my major."

Margot was well aware of her own disgusted expression as she struggled to slip the hook through the bait. She didn't even look up as she felt her father's weight settle next to her.

"Don'tcha know anything about baitin' a hook?" Stan asked, glancing up to make sure Donna wasn't watching while he demonstrated the proper skewering technique.

"Well, I didn't spend a lot of time fishing as a kid. Or any time, really," she said, subtly shifting away from him on the seat. At least, she hoped it was subtle.

"Well, what *did* ya do?"

Margot stared at him. After the lunch debacle, he didn't deserve to know anything about her childhood. She wasn't going to answer. But then Donna started giving *her* the scary, pointed glare and Margot said, "Piano, which I was terrible at. Ballet, at which I was a bit better. French lessons. Horseback riding, though I never got to a competition level beyond our country club."

"It figures you'd have that sort of thing up there in Chicago."

"I was lucky. Gerald wanted to make sure I had all the same extracurricular opportunities as my classmates."

"Was that your mom's husband?"

Margot nodded. "They married when I was still very young."

"Was he good to ya?" Stan asked. "This Gerald, was he decent to ya?"

"He's a very decent man. A doctor. He's in England right now, doing a teaching fellowship at a medical school there. We haven't spoken in a long time, but when we do, it's very civil."

"Well, at least there's that," Stan said.

Margot swallowed, suddenly uncomfortable. She didn't want to compare and contrast father figures. She didn't appreciate Duffy's meddling. She didn't appreciate being trapped on a boat with her estranged father. Surely this was some sort of scenario designed by Alfred Hitchcock. Maybe she could swim to shore.

She tried to focus on the passing scenery. She didn't know much about lakes, despite growing up near one of the largest in the world. But she recognized signs of drought when she saw them. The shore was marked by at least two feet of baked earth. Mud-coated trash lay exposed in the shallows. It was like seeing a body of water without its toupee, sad and lesser and sort of desperate.

"Shouldn't you have a tour booked this morning?" she asked Duffy over the noise of the engine.

Duffy flushed again, glancing at his mom. "Yeah, well, the doctor I had booked backed out at the last minute."

"Duff, it wasn't your fault." Aunt Donna's voice softened for the first time since Margot had arrived in Lake Sackett. "The doctor canceled his whole weekend when he saw the 'cabin' he booked. That idiot Maybelline Mathis has been renting out the pottin' shed behind her house and calling it a guest cabin. She puts fake pictures on the rental web site. It was bound to catch up to her eventually."

"It's been happenin' a lot," Duffy grumped. "It's the fourth cancellation I've had in the last couple of weeks. People are losing their patience with the town. The water's too low and the rental cabins are gettin' shabby. And the owners can't afford to fix 'em up again because the renters cancel. I don't know how much longer we're gonna be able to keep this up."

"Well, that's a real cheerful sentiment for this early in the morning, son," Donna retorted, her flinty tone restored. "Moanin' over loomin' financial disaster is just what I wanted as a side for my Breakfast Stick."

Duffy jerked his shoulders as he slowed the boat and anchored it about twenty yards from the shore of a little alcove surrounded by fallen trees. Stan was largely unaffected by this exchange, his big basset-hound eyes focused on his daughter. "And your mama, was she finally happy in the big city?"

"What do you mean by that?" Margot asked, standing on steady legs and moving to the starboard side of the boat. Watching Duffy's and Donna's movements, she plopped her minnowed hook into the water.

"I mean, she was never happy here. I just want to know was she finally happy, movin' to a big city, marryin' a doctor. Being away from this place. Was she happy?"

Margot frowned. Her mother hadn't been built for happiness. Surely, having been married to her, Stan knew that. Resentment rose up in her throat, hot and bitter. She noticed her father hadn't mentioned his drinking this time. What was Stan looking for? Did he want her to take away his guilt? Was she supposed to convince him he'd done the right thing by doing nothing to get Margot back? What gave him the right to ask these things?

"Margot?" Stan said, following her to the side of the boat. Margot stared across the water, determined to ignore him.

In the distance, she saw the silhouette of a beautiful wooden sailboat, the old-fashioned kind you saw in aftershave commercials. It slipped smoothly across the water, and Margot was struck with a sort of envious longing. Stan was still standing next to her, asking her questions, but she managed to block him out, focusing on the distant ship.

What would it be like to move so quickly and quietly? She'd known plenty of people with yachts on Lake Michigan, but they'd been more mini cruise ships, used for parties and not much else. This boat looked like it was flying. She longed to stand on that deck and slide so easily into the wind. But then again, anyplace seemed preferable to where she was standing, being interrogated by her father.

The sailboat veered closer, and suddenly Margot pulled her fishing hat over her face and slumped down. Kyle Archer, windblown and handsome, was sitting at the rudder and wearing a life vest that should have made him as dumpy as she felt in her floppy hat and flotation device. But it didn't. He was gorgeous. Damn it. And he was smiling, his face angled down as he talked to someone slumped against the hull. A long brown ponytail flapped in the breeze over the edge of the highly polished wood.

Her first thought was *girlfriend*, and she was surprised by the spike of jealousy that flared in her belly. She didn't get jealous. A man proved himself unworthy or unavailable, she moved on. But the idea of Kyle sailing around with that happy expression on his face because of another woman, it made—

The brunette head popped over the hull and Margot saw that it was his daughter Hazel, she of the challenged follicles. Somehow, that was worse. This was a man with a family. His attention would always be divided. He would never have time for spontaneous moments together because he would have to deal with babysitters and pickup schedules. His daughters would always come first, as they should. She didn't think she would want him as much as she did if he put them second.

A little puttering motor in the distance drew Margot's attention away from the sailboat and its baffling owner. She was struck by the image of an African American man in his fifties aiming for their boat at what seemed to be ramming speed. He wore a Braves cap that looked like he'd had it since boyhood, but his boat looked showroom new. As he drew closer, Margot recognized him as the man Donna had been yelling at on the dock days before. He turned the boat just as he killed the engine, meaning he splashed their pontoon as he skidded to a drifting halt.

"Donna McCready!" he yelled. "I know you're not poachin' my territory."

"I don't see your name on it, Fred Dodge!" she yelled back.

Margot was grateful for the interruption of her less loud but more awkward conversation. She would much rather watch her aunt Donna yell at someone who was not her.

Stan and Duffy seemed more exasperated than worried by the exchange, sitting back on the cushions of the pontoon and crossing their arms. So Margot sat back, too—in a spot as far away from Stan as possible—to enjoy the show as Fred yelped, "Woman, you know I've been fishin' that spot since we were in high school!"

Margot watched the verbal fencing between her aunt and Mr. Dodge with a little smile on her lips. She couldn't help but notice the way Donna's face flushed as she parried and shouted.

Mr. Dodge's wide brown eyes blazed as he wagged his finger at her aunt. They were into each other. In a big way.

"She's right," Duffy said dryly. "I signed the territory agreement as a witness. Your exclusive spot is over on Deer Tick Bay."

Fred pursed his lips. "Oh . . . right. Well, that doesn't change the fact that you're in my spot here, Donna!"

"Fine," Donna bit out. She stomped over and started the motor, then moved the boat ten yards down the shore. "Happy now?"

"Overjoyed!" Fred shouted back. He started his engine and guided his boat away. But he glanced over his shoulder to see if Donna was watching.

Margot grinned. Fred had it bad for Donna—scary, loud Donna. They would be the most prickly, adorable couple, if they ever stopped yelling at each other.

Triumphant in clinging to her favorite fishing spot, Donna dropped her hook in the water and stretched across her seat, long legs propped on the bow. Stan had turned his back on everybody and commenced fishing. Duffy occupied himself with eating his Breakfast Stick. Margot watched her bobber, well, bobbing, for almost an hour, with no change. And she realized that she'd missed very little, not going on fishing trips as a child. It was hot and too sunny and too quiet and everything smelled like dirt and pennies and frustration. And she'd forgotten her cell phone on her nightstand when Duffy abducted her, so this was basically her nightmare.

Margot huffed out a breath and pulled her hat over her face, hoping it would muffle her frustrated groan.

"What are you doin', girl?" She pulled her hat back to see Stan staring at her, his brow furrowed.

She cleared her throat. "Um, nothing, just trying to keep the sun out of my eyes,"

"Well, that's no way to do it." Stan set his root beer aside and reached up to shape the brim over her face. He tapped her nose with his index finger. "And you should put some zinc on that nose before ya get burnt. You couldn't stand having a sunburn when you were little. Used to carry a jar of Noxzema around the house, telling everybody you were dyin'."

Margot glanced up into her father's face. He was gazing down at her, a little smile playing on his lips as he relived this memory. Out of the corner of her eyes, she saw the sailboat pass. She tipped her head down to avoid eye contact. And Stan's hands froze, millimeters from her cheeks.

"Sorry," he mumbled, and shuffled away to the other side of the boat.

And that tension that had been building up inside Margot snapped. "Look, I don't know what you want from me. You had a chance to get to know me and you left me hanging. How am I supposed to trust you enough to try now? These memories that you have of me that you keep bringing up? I don't remember anything like that. And you asking me all of these questions, it's not going to make me remember. And I can't change it. It is what it is. I can't tiptoe around your feelings because I have no idea what happened between you and my mother. And it's not my job to make you feel better about it, either way."

"Well, what am I supposed to think?" he demanded. "Your mama ran off without a word. I don't hear from you for years—tens of years! And then you show up out of the blue after all this time and I'm supposed to, what? Say 'Thank you for deciding to show up'? I didn't expect to see you again. And you don't get why I would be too intimidated to just go to lunch with you the other day?"

"Oh, I have a lot of things to say to you on the subject of showing up, if you'd like to start a dialogue," she said, smiling with so much acid, it could dissolve the bottom of the boat.

"See, that's why I can't even have a conversation with you. You talk like a damn robot."

"Don't curse at me!" she shot back.

He crossed his arms over his chest, eyes narrowed. "Yep, there's your mama in you."

Margot yelled, "You do *not* talk about my mother!"

"Don't tell me what I can and can't say! I'm your father!"

"You haven't done *anything* to deserve the title of father! You might as well have been a sperm donor for all I knew from you!"

For a moment, Margot didn't know whether Stan was going to slap her or burst into tears. Having been raised by two passive-aggressive cold fish, she couldn't remember seeing such strong emotions fighting it out on a person's face. No one in the family had ever mentioned Stan having a nasty temper, even when he drank. But had she pushed him so far that he would lash out like that? Was it sick that she wanted to know? Maybe she was just some giant psychological cliché, pushing at her parent's boundaries to see what she could get away with. Therapy would probably be a good idea, once she was living outside of the Lake Sackett gossip zone.

Stan glanced down at his clenched hands and seemed horrified, backing away from her and putting several feet of space between them. A tiny flicker of guilt fluttered to life inside her, and she told herself it was natural to feel bad about making anyone hurt that much. It had nothing to do with who Stan was or any feelings she had about him. Not wanting to hurt another human being only proved Margot wasn't a complete sociopath.

"Well, this is fun." Donna spat, making a sour face at Duffy. "'Take 'em fishing,' you said. 'Put 'em on a boat where they can't get away from each other,' you said. 'They'll have to bond eventually,' you said."

Duffy threw his hands up in the air in a helpless gesture. Stan crossed the boat, sitting as far away from Margot as possible. The baleful silence between them lasted for hours, until Donna and Duffy caught their fill. Stan was clearly off his game, catching only a handful. Margot, predictably, caught nothing.

Seriously, why did people put themselves through this and call it a hobby? Why were there so many movies, books, magazines, TV shows dedicated to sitting still and staring at water? She resorted to making lists in her head to keep herself sane—groceries she needed to shop for, contacts she still needed to make in her job search, excuses to give to Duffy so she never had to go fishing again. She almost wept with relief when her cousin yanked the anchor from the mucky bottom and motored the pontoon boat back toward the family marina. Stan kept his back to her up until the moment the boat bumped against the dock, and frankly, that was the only bright spot to her morning.

"Well, that was fun," Donna said dryly as Stan moved with more speed than anyone could have expected from him and leaped onto the dock. He stormed toward the parking lot without a word, gear in hand. "Damn fool."

"Aunt Donna, thank you for taking me fishing," Margot said politely as Duffy helped her step off the boat. She whirled on her cousin and pointed a finger in Duffy's face. "You. Dead to me."

Duffy poked his bottom lip out in a pout so pathetic, she added, "For at least two days."

The pout turned into a smile, so she felt compelled to smack the back of his fluffy head and snatch the truck key from the carabiner that secured it to his fishing vest. "And you're riding home with your mother."

"I deserve that," Duffy conceded.

8

MARGOT BOBBLED THE plastic storage containers as she knocked on the door of the "main house." The biggest and oldest of the cabins on the compound, Tootie and E.J.J.'s place had a sort of White House feel to it, with its pristine white flower boxes and the little leaping concrete fish that flanked the front door. Margot felt like she should be curtsying instead of smacking the trout-shaped door knocker against the aging wood.

A handful of unfamiliar cars were parked in the semicircular drive, all with local plates. She could hear people—well, women—inside laughing and talking. It sounded like there were dozens of them. It was oddly soothing, the sounds of a party, like slipping into old comfortable slippers. She stopped and smiled. Her hands itched for a clipboard and her earpiece. Her brain switched into full party mode, timing food platters and composing a pleasant toast in her head. She could almost feel the tray of empty champagne flutes in her hand.

She had to get a real job soon.

No one had answered her knock. Surely, even in the South, even when you were related to your nearest neighbors, it was rude to just walk into someone's house without permission. Maybe it would be better for her to drop Tootie's Tupperware by her front door and run back to her own cabin. She hadn't spoken directly to Tootie since the argument in her car. She didn't want to cause a scene if her great-aunt had guests. What if this was a private family thing? She didn't want to interrupt that. Sure, it didn't make sense that they would have a party without inviting her when they'd insistently included her in every remotely interesting moment since she'd arrived. But because her family had been so welcoming—aside from Stan—she didn't want to intrude on the few things they'd kept for themselves.

Dropping the containers gently on the porch swing, Margot tiptoed toward the steps.

"Margot, honey, where're you heading?"

Margot froze and turned to find E.J.J. standing in the doorway, frowning at her.

So much for a graceful exit.

"Hi," she said. "I was just dropping off Tootie's containers . . . I knocked, but no one answered."

"Aw, honey, you don't have to knock. You're family, you just come on in."

"I'm really not comfortable with that," Margot said, shaking her head.

"Welp, you might as well come in. Tootie's card night just started up. You're gonna want to get some food before it gets in full swing."

"Oh, I don't want to interrupt."

"Sweetheart, I understand that you're trying to use your best company manners. But it doesn't feel polite. It feels like you're keepin' us at a distance. I'm not sayin' let us run roughshod all over you. I've only known you for a short while and I know that's not your nature. You need to relax, just a little bit."

"I'm relaxed."

"Right now, you're wearing your shoulders as earrings," E.J.J. noted. Margot glanced at her shoulders, which were indeed tensed up around her ears. She frowned and forced them down into a slightly less intense posture. "There you go."

"Has anyone ever told you that this level of insight is annoying, even in an adorable old man?"

E.J.J. grinned, his impossibly white false teeth winking in the dying afternoon light. "Your granpda would have gotten such a kick out of you. Now go on in there. I'm headin' to Bob and Leslie's cabin, where it's safe."

"That doesn't give me a lot of confidence about going inside," Margot told him, though she let him shove her inside the door. "You are surprisingly strong for an old guy."

The voices got even louder as she got closer to the kitchen. Margot had expected the house to be decorated in kitschy Americana and reproduction antiques. But it was subtly done in creamy whites and slate blue. A comfortable rocker stood by a river-stone fireplace. A blue-and-white quilt was thrown over an overstuffed navy couch. The hardwood floors were painstakingly restored and polished. It wasn't magazine perfect, but it was cozy and clean. Margot's eyes caught on her mother's face, staring out at her from a framed family portrait on the mantel. She stepped closer. The photo was taken in the mid-eighties, judging by the hair. The family was *mostly* recognizable as the one she'd just met. Donna was smiling sweetly, tucked into the side of a big, burly man with Duffy's eyes. Tootie was sitting next to E.J.J., who had his arm wrapped around her, pulling her close to him. And Linda stood out like a sore blond thumb, her body angled away from Stan and Margot. Linda stared straight into the camera, her dark eyes flat and bored. Her face was unlined but unsmiling. Margot had always thought her mother had grown into her unhappiness as she got older, but it seemed to be a lifelong trait. How could someone smiling as easily as Stan seemed to be want to make a life with someone so dour? How could the other McCreadys see this photo and not notice how dissatisfied she was?

Stan, on the other hand, looked pretty pleased with his life. He was grinning at the little girl in his arms, the toddler with golden curls who had her hands pressed against his sunburned cheeks. In fact, everybody but her mother looked perfectly content.

Every other photo in the room was up-to-date. Why had Tootie held on to this old one, displaying it in such a central location? Given Margot's age, this may have been the last family photo taken before Linda ran off. Was Tootie passive-aggressively trying to remind Stan of the family he'd given up?

"Hey, sweetie, whatcha doin' in there?" Tootie called from the kitchen. She was dressed in a purple velour tracksuit, but she was wearing a green poker visor on her head and shuffling a deck of cards between her hands like a street magician . . . which was different.

Margot cleared her throat. "Hi, Tootie, I brought the Tupperware back. Thanks again for the casseroles."

"Well, we have to keep ya fed, don't we?" Tootie motioned her closer with both hands. "Come on in and meet the girls."

"Oh, I don't want to impose," she said, shaking her head.

"Come on." Tootie dashed forward and looped her arm

through Margot's, practically dragging her past the enormous dining room and into the kitchen. The woman was awfully spry for a senior citizen.

Instead of the dozen women Margot expected, there were only three ladies sitting around the kitchen table, cackling and chatting. Aunt Leslie sat at the breakfast bar of Tootie's rooster-themed kitchen, slicing cornbread in a blackened cast-iron pan.

At the sound of Tootie's shuffling steps, the ladies' heads snapped up in unison, like blue-haired velociraptors. Tootie gestured to the bar stool next to Leslie and Margot climbed on. Arlo sat at her feet, gently pawing at her stool and looking up with hopeful eyes. She shook her head and scratched behind his ears. She was just happy to see him somewhere besides her porch.

"Girls, this is Stan's girl, Margot," Tootie cooed, giving Margot's hand a squeeze. "Margot, this is Lucille Bodine, Betsy Grandy, and Delilah Dawkins."

Margot smiled. She didn't curtsy, but it was a near thing. She watched as the three women, each sporting football-helmet-shaped coiffures and floral print dresses, scanned her from head to toe. Lucille, who had a little dashboard statue of Jesus standing guard in front of her chair, eyeballed Margot with a wary expression. There was audible sniffing. That didn't bode well.

"It's very nice to meet you all," Margot said.

Betsy's red-painted mouth popped open. "Well, don't you sound fancy! Do you work on the TV?"

"No," scolded Delilah, a reed-thin woman with cow-print reading glasses perched on the end of her nose. "Remember, Stan brought her in to work for the family business."

"Oh, actually, Tootie brought me in to work for the family

business," Margot said, while Tootie waved a pig-in-a-blanket in recognition. "She's quite the online recruiter."

Margot didn't mention that the position was only temporary. Somehow, she thought it would embarrass Tootie, and she didn't want to do that in front of her card friends.

"Leslie, you didn't put sugar in the cornbread, did you?" Tootie asked.

"One little teaspoon doesn't hurt anything, Tootie," Leslie said.

"You put sugar in it—it's cake, not cornbread!" Tootie said.

"Well, when you make the cornbread you can use your recipe! Otherwise, feel free not to burden yourself by eatin' my 'cake,'" Leslie shot back.

"What are you playing?" Margot asked in an attempt at a subject change. "Bridge? Canasta?"

"Texas Hold'em, jokers wild, minimum bet twenty dollars," Tootie said, spreading the cards in a broad fan across the table before sliding them back into her hand and shuffling them with speed unexpected in her arthritic hands. Delilah hauled a casino-style rack of poker chips out of her enormous shoulder bag and plopped it in the middle of the table. Lucille took a roll of bills out of her own handbag and counted out more than a hundred dollars in twenties.

"I did not see that coming," Margot said as Arlo shoved his head insistently against her palm.

"You wanna play a hand, honey?" Tootie offered, to almost immediate objections from the other players.

"It's bad luck to switch players!" Lucille protested.

Betsy cried, "You have to give us a chance to win our money back!"

"Is this some sort of hustle situation?" Delilah asked.

"I don't think I'm at your level of play," Margot said, raising her hands. "I'll just sit over here, where it's safe."

"Down, Arlo," Tootie called as he pawed at Margot's legs, his little doggy expression still hopeful as he sniffed the air. Margot took a tiny piece of cornbread and held it out for him. Arlo snarfed it up, licking at her hand. She wasn't sure whether it was a gesture of canine gratitude or he was searching for crumbs.

Leslie slid a plateful of sliced fruit and a bottle of water toward her.

"Thank you." Margot sighed, spearing an apple slice with a fork, and gagged the moment she put it to her tongue.

"Did you roll the fruit in sugar?" Margot asked.

"Well, yeah, what sort of flavor would you have without sugar?" Leslie scoffed.

"Fruit?" Margot guessed.

"Speaking of the Food Carnival," Tootie said, none too subtly, "Lucille here says she heard you were talking to Kyle Archer in the beauty section the other day."

Margot narrowly avoided doing a spit take with the water she was using to rinse her teeth of the fruit sugar. She dabbed delicately at her lips with a poker-themed party napkin. "Where did you hear that? *Why* would you hear that?"

"The whole town has been keeping an eye on poor Kyle ever since his wife passed." Lucille sniffed. Again with the sniffing.

Wait.

"Passed? As in 'passed away'?" Margot said, an unpleasant cold feeling fluttering through her belly. She'd assumed Kyle was divorced, that his girls struggled because their mother had left them behind when she blew out of this backwater. It had never occurred to Margot that she'd had no choice in the matter. An uncomfortable pressure bloomed around her heart, making her chest ache.

Tootie nodded as she dealt the hands. "About five years ago, the sweet little thing was just et up with cancer. She was carryin' their youngest at the time. Little Juniper? Maggie's mama, Rosie, she said Maggie and Kyle had been trying for another baby for months with no luck, but all of a sudden she was tired all the time and sick. They thought it was just the usual morning sickness, but the doctor did all the blood work that you do on pregnant women, and they found something off with her cell counts. Breast cancer, can you believe that? She was twenty-eight years old, havin' a baby, and dyin' of breast cancer. It had already spread up in her lymph nodes by the time they caught it. And she had the choice between chemo or keeping the baby safe, and she chose the baby. They started her on the treatments as soon as they could after the delivery, but it was too late. She passed when Juniper was a few months old, bless her heart, leaving Kyle behind with those poor babies. It was one of the saddest services E.J.J. has ever presided over. And after all these years, his heart is pretty hard to touch."

"He's not over her," Delilah said. "He was still wearing his wedding ring when I saw him at the church picnic last month."

Margot pursed her lips. Well, that explained the misery. Was that how Kyle spent his time away from his children? Wandering around town, mourning his lost wife? But if he was still in so much turmoil over her, what was he doing kissing Margot until her insides went to jelly?

"I've never cared for him," Betsy said, peering over her reading glasses at her cards.

Delilah shushed her.

"What? He's lived in town a few years, but he's hired on as the principal? Jimmy Greenway's barely out of the door and all of the sudden he's makin' all sorts of changes at the school?"

"Kyle Archer was overqualified to teach in the first place and we were lucky to get him. Jimmy hasn't quite managed to get out the door, if you'll recall," Tootie said. "And some of those changes he had to make because the state was going to slap some sort of sanction on the school. Kyle has every right to run the school as he sees fit. He's got all those degrees for a reason."

"Fancy degrees from some highfalutin school telling him every kid has to be wrapped in cotton wool and tricked into learnin'," Betsy said with a snort. "Whatever happened to readin', writin' and 'rithmetic?"

Leslie leaned close enough to whisper, "Betsy is Jimmy Greenway's cousin by marriage. She's loyal to a fault." When she was sure Betsy wasn't listening, she added, "That fault is willful blindness to the fact that Jimmy is a jackass."

Margot bit her lip to contain the laugh that bubbled up.

"He's a good man. We want to make sure that if he starts seeing someone, it's the right someone. Not a stranger who hasn't bothered showing up to a church service since she rolled into town. Not some big-city girl who's gonna up and leave without a word," Lucille sniped.

Tootie shot her the nice Southern old lady version of side eye, and then announced that she'd just beaten Lucille's flush and taken a lot of her money. Feeling somewhat vindicated by Tootie's strategic support, Margot offered Lucille a frosty smile. "I'm not seeing him. I had a conversation with him in a grocery store. Is there some city ordinance stating that I'm only allowed to speak to an unmarried man if I have a chaperone?"

Strong words from someone who had done a lot more than have a conversation with Kyle. In public.

Also, how many church services could she have missed so far? She'd only been there a week.

"I'm just saying that there's a couple of real nice girls around here who have set their caps for him. And if he's gonna end up with anybody, it's probably gonna be one of them."

Margot tilted her head. "Are you telling me that there's a dibs system?"

Lucille opened her mouth to answer, but Betsy demanded, "Are y'all gonna flap your lips or are we gonna play cards? Mamaw needs a new pair of shoes."

"Fine, fine," Lucille huffed, muttering under her breath, "Just like her mama."

Margot was prepared to ignore this statement entirely, but Tootie shuffled her cards around in her hands. "Now, Lucille, how is that son of yours? Is he gettin' along okay with his new parole officer?"

Margot watched Lucille's righteous indignation deflate just a little bit. "He likes her just fine."

"And your grandson?" Tootie asked casually. "Has he paid back Wally Simpson the money he owes for peeing in the drinks cooler at the Gas'N'Go?"

"Just about," Lucille mumbled.

Margot watched this interaction with horrified fascination. She'd seen this sort of viciously passive reestablishing of pack order in high-society circles, but she expected better from members of the church floral guild. Somehow, she thought they'd have a carefully cross-stitched sampler reminding them to behave better. She felt a little bad for Lucille, for being embarrassed in front of her friends, but Lucille *had* basically told her that she wasn't good enough for Kyle and besmirched her dead mother, so . . .

"Don't take it personal," Leslie told her. "Lucille's had her eye on young Kyle for her granddaughter, Darlene."

"Does Darlene feel that way about Kyle?"

"No, Lucille just wants Darlene to move out of what was supposed to be her guest room," she said. "If you're sparkin' on Kyle and he's sparkin' on you, I think y'all would do well together."

"Sparkin'?"

"You know, when you look at somebody and you just spark with 'em. Every time ya see 'em, you get flustered. Every conversation leaves ya all breathless and stupid. Your skin feels too tight and your chest aches."

"I think that what you're describing is a heart attack," Margot told her.

"And there's the Stan in you, remorseless smartasses the both of you. In particular, when you're uncomfortable and tryin' to change the subject." Leslie snickered. "You'll know sparkin' when ya feel it. I had it with my Bob, Lord knows. The man could take me from giddy to spittin' tacks and back again in a few seconds. But I wouldn't trade those years for anything."

"I don't think I have to worry about sparking anybody. I'm not going to be here long enough to . . . spark. And if I did, I think I would try for something a little less complicated than a widower with two small children."

"Complicated can be good, too," Leslie said absently, and then suddenly grinned when Tootie won another big pot. Leslie pulled out a little notebook and scribbled Tootie's winnings amid several carefully organized columns of numbers.

"What's that?" Margot asked.

"Tootie's bet book," Leslie whispered. "I keep track of her winnings and debts, so she doesn't lose sight of how much she's gambling."

"The pots are a bit richer than I expected," Margot murmured. "I thought nice little church ladies played for matches or pennies."

"Oh, no, Tootie hasn't played small since the kids moved out and her pin money got more plentiful," Leslie said. "She's been saving up to take E.J.J. on a fancy cruise to Aruba for nigh on ten years now. Of course, step one would be getting him to retire, which will take an act of God and Congress."

"I thought E.J.J. made a pretty good living at the funeral home," Margot said. "It's a recession-proof business."

"Of course he does," Leslie said. "But Tootie wants to pay for the cruise with her own money. And that means her poker winnings. Don't let her fool ya. She's a card shark."

"How close is she?"

"Close enough that she might kick us out for talkin' and splittin' her attention in a couple of minutes," Leslie said. "She's got enough saved for a concierge room for a weeklong cruise. Now she just wants to make enough to cover the spa treatments. She's hopin' that once she finally gets E.J.J. on that cruise ship, he'll finally retire. I keep trying to tell her that McCready men don't retire, they just keep workin' so long that they eventually fall into the newest grave they dug, but she's holdin' out hope."

"That is very dark, Aunt Leslie," Margot said, picking at her plate.

"Can't shine up the truth."

Margot blanched, tossing aside a carrot stick, which had been rolled in butter substitute. "I think I'm done."

～

MONDAY MORNING BEGAN with Bob and Margot pulling into the McCready's parking lot and finding Frankie loading embalming equipment into the funeral home van. Margot cast a sidelong glance at Bob, who didn't seem at all alarmed that his daughter was absconding with thousands of dollars' worth of sterilized stainless steel. Of course, Bob seemed to be ignoring the fact that their "upselling" argument had ever happened, so Bob was clearly pretty open to denial.

Margot hopped out of the truck, shuddering as her suit jacket seemed to vacuum seal around her body with the force of the humidity. It was a rare cloudy day on the lake, the water gunmetal gray and flat as a dime. Leslie called out from the Snack Shack, and Bob raised both hands to wave to her.

Shaking her head, Margot picked her way across the parking lot on her needle-thin heels. She was proud that she managed the gravel much more easily than she had when she'd first arrived.

"What are you doing, Frankie?" she called over the noise of several bass boat engines purring at the dock.

Just then, Frankie bobbled a heavy electrical appliance and Margot caught it before it hit the ground. Frankie turned and grinned at her. "Quick hands, cousin."

Bob bussed Frankie's temple. "Taking your show on the road, honey?"

"I'm going to the elementary school for Career Day. These are my visual aids."

Margot glanced down at the appliance in her hand, which she now saw was a wicked-looking saw. The blade was covered by a heavy protective plastic sleeve. Between that and Frankie's outfit, a black tiered square dance skirt and a black T-shirt covered in neon roller skates, Margot could only produce "What?"

"Mortuary sciences is a viable career option!" Frankie said. "I plan on luring the next generation into the fold with stories both horrific and whimsical."

"Doodlebug, I know you're gonna do a great job, but maybe you should leave the skull saw here. I'm sure the school has a 'no weapons' policy," Bob said. "Also, maybe you shouldn't use the word 'lure' when you're describin' a presentation for children. While you're drivin' a van."

"You use this on people's skulls?" Margot whispered. Frankie smiled and nodded. Margot tossed it back to her cousin and waved her hands in the air. "Gah!"

"Oh, take it easy, I've washed it since," Frankie said.

Margot shuddered. "Still."

"Doodlebug, the saw may be a little bit much for the third graders," Bob persisted.

"Fine," Frankie grumbled, dropping the saw into Uncle Bob's waiting hands. She carefully slid a big, colorfully illustrated foam-board poster labeled HOW A CREMATORY WORKS into the back of the van and closed the door. "Tie my hands."

"You'll thank me later! The parents will definitely thank me!" Bob called as Frankie rounded the van to climb into the driver's seat.

Bob chewed his lip as he watched his daughter fire up the engine.

"I should go with her," Margot said, her brow creased.

Bob nodded and patted Margot's shoulder. "Yeah, that would be a good idea."

~

THE SCHOOL WAS not quite the colorful riot of noise and germs that she remembered from Back to School Night, though there was a new screen-printed WELCOME TO CAREER DAY! banner hanging across the entrance to the school. Margot wondered how much time and money was devoted to specialty banners in this school district.

The children were moving in *mostly* organized lines down the hallway to their next classes. They were *mostly* quiet and well behaved, though they still wriggled and yapped like little puppies. And the surfaces were *mostly* clean, but Margot suspected that the janitor mopping the area in front of the little boys' room stayed in almost constant motion throughout the day trying to maintain even that underwhelming state.

It took Margot and Frankie two trips to unload all the props from the van, and that was with Margot forcing her cousin to leave the embalming needles behind.

"So, Aunt Donna said your fishing trip was a disaster," Frankie huffed as they lifted a rolling cart full of funeral show-and-tell onto the sidewalk.

"I don't want to talk about it," Margot said.

"Uncle Stan can be a puzzle," Frankie said. "I'm not making excuses for him. He has his moments when I'd gladly smack him over the head with a bedpan. But I think he's spent so much time being unhappy, it's like he doesn't trust himself to feel good. And any fool can see he doesn't know how to talk to you. It's like he tries to let out just a little bit of his feelin' but the spigot breaks and it all comes up at once as word vomit."

"Did you notice, earlier, when I said I didn't want to talk about it?" Margot asked. "That was what is politely called a 'hint.'"

Frankie waved her off. "Yeah, I usually get more information if I just ignore those. Just like I will ignore the fact that I found about ten copies of your resume in the office printer this morning. If you're gonna misuse the office equipment, hon, you're going to have to learn to be more subtle."

"I was up way too late last night tweaking my CV. I'm lucky I made it home with my purse and my pants."

"Well, that would have caused some talk, which would have added to the gossip already circulatin' about you and our dear principal. Mama said the church floral guild is all up in arms. Half of 'em are already planning out your wedding bouquet and the other half want to file some sort of appeal with the dating police on behalf of their single daughters."

"Do I need to explain 'hints' to you again?"

"Don't insult my intelligence and pretend you're not interested in— Kyle, how are you?" Frankie ended her sentence on a chirpy note, reaching out to pump the principal's hand as he stepped out of the school office.

Margot's hands wanted to smooth over her hair. She wanted to check her lipstick in the reflection on the office door. But she knew she looked good. She'd done her makeup less than an hour ago. Still, she stepped behind Frankie, because there were kids running around and her pants were Prada.

"Ms. Cary, good to see you again."

Margot smiled briefly and then looked to Frankie for help in escaping this conversational death trap. Frankie completely ignored the social cue and abandoned her.

"Well, I better get down to Ms. Rainey's classroom and set up."

"I'll come with you," Margot insisted.

"Oh, no, you stay here. I've got this," Frankie insisted. She cast a sly look toward Kyle. "I'm sure you have all sorts of things to talk about."

"No, Frankie, I came along to help you."

"Actually, if you could stay and chat for a minute, I'd appreciate it," Kyle said.

"See?" Frankie asked brightly. "He *needs* you."

"Traitor!" Margot whispered out of the corner of her mouth. Frankie didn't look sorry in the least.

Kyle's face became very serious very quickly. "You should know that I have the restraining order paperwork all filled out on my desk."

Margot's jaw dropped. Kyle grinned at her.

"That is not funny."

"It's a little bit funny," he told her.

"This time, I'm here in a professional capacity," she swore. "My uncle was worried when he saw Frankie's visual aids for Career Day. I'm here to minimize the emotional trauma to the children."

"No, Frankie's presentation is probably going to be the most popular one today," Kyle said. "I know she keeps up an . . . unconventional appearance compared to everybody else around here. But she really has a way of talking to kids. She was a huge hit during Health and Safety Week last year. Her speech was entitled 'The Many Stupid Ways You Could End Up on My Table.' Her list was alphabetical and it rhymed. She keeps them entertained, but for all her joking, she won't go too far. She knows where the line is."

"You know, I keep thinking my father's family can't surprise me any more, and then . . ." Margot shook her head. "So you said you needed to speak to me?"

"Please." Kyle nodded and motioned toward the door marked OFFICE.

"How is your daughter's hair?" Margot asked as they passed through a small reception area that smelled of peachy potpourri. The cheerful yellow-painted room was mostly occupied by a desk and a plump, gray-haired lady with narrow brown eyes. The nameplate on the desk read CLARICE YANCY—SECRETARY.

"We ended up having to use that olive oil concoction you recommended, but it's returned to its normal nonfrizzy state," Kyle said. "Miss Clarice, if you could hold my calls for about fifteen minutes, that would be great."

"The first graders are heading to lunch in eighteen minutes," Clarice said, glaring at Margot. "You know they'll cover the whole cafeteria in mashed potatoes if you're not there to keep an eye on them."

"Yes, ma'am, I'll keep that in mind," Kyle said, smiling winsomely. He took a big bite out of a cookie he grabbed from a decorative metal container. "Did you put nutmeg in these snickerdoodles, Miss Clarice?"

"I know you can't stand clove," Clarice said with a sniff.

"You take such good care of me, Miss Clarice," he said, winking at her. Clarice's lips twitched into a little smile. But when she realized Margot was still looking at her, Clarice cleared her throat and frowned again. Margot pursed her lips and followed Kyle into his office.

Kyle closed the office door while Margot scanned the space. Instead of the cheerful yellow, the walls were painted a soothing muted blue. The few decorations on the walls involved nature scenes with animals and open spaces. He didn't display his diplomas or awards. His desk was neat, but not rigidly so, and he kept a framed picture of his girls next to his phone. He'd designed his office to be comfortable for the kids and unintimidating for the parents. It showed a certain amount of awareness that she found endearing. But again, she had to wonder at the split sides to this man's personality, that the same guy who oversaw lunchtime behavior was the despondent man she'd met at the Dirty Deer.

"Did you just manipulate your secretary out of her bad mood by complimenting her cookies?" she asked, sitting in the comfy wingback chair across from his desk.

"I know it's a little misogynistic and heavy on the 'aw, shucks, ma'am,' charm," he admitted, dropping wearily into his own chair. "When I was first hired on as a teacher, I tried to be progressive and forthright with her and she got offended, then called me 'uppity.' Took me months to win her back over. And now that I'm her boss, there's a certain way things are handled around here. As I'm sure you're finding out, bucking the system is not well received."

"Yes, I have found that to be true," Margot agreed, nodding slowly. "I take it that you're not from Lake Sackett?"

He shook his head. "I'm from New York, originally."

"Really?" Margot said, trying and failing not to sound gobsmacked. "Why? I mean, how? I mean . . . There's no way to ask nicely. Why would you give up New York for this?"

"My wife," he said succinctly, and all the good humor seemed to be sucked out of the room. "So Marianne says you were an event planner before you moved down here. What kind of events?"

"Oh, society galas, corporate launches, charity functions, that sort of thing," she said.

"So . . . large-scale events," he said, nodding. "Involving a lot of moving pieces, and sometimes on a very small budget."

"This conversation is starting to feel pointed," Margot said. "I think I would feel more comfortable if you asked me for what you want instead of giving me cookie compliments."

Kyle nodded. "Straightforward. I like it. Marianne also mentioned that she's told you about the Founders' Day celebrations and how we're pretty much off in the weeds in terms of planning. We've got about seven weeks left and we need your kind of help to make the celebrations huge this year. And for me, it's personal."

Because she didn't want to bark no at him right off the bat, she asked, "How is it so personal if you're not even from Lake Sackett?"

"The former principal, Jimmy Greenway, he worked at this school for more than thirty years. He was a teacher at Sackett Elementary when my wife was a student here. The school library is named after him."

Margot nodded, pursing her lips, still unsure of what that had to do with anything.

"He announced his retirement years ago, when I was still teaching," Kyle said, leaning forward and propping his elbows on the desk. Margot couldn't help but notice how the blue dress shirt he was wearing strained across his chest, the chest she knew was toned and firm. This was not helping her keep her focus on the conversation. "Jimmy promised the school board he wouldn't leave until they found a replacement, which was nice of him. He stuck around for almost a year while they ran a search. I took the job and Jimmy said, 'Oh, well, I'll stick around for a few extra months to help you make the transition.' I thought, great, what a nice guy, caring enough about the school to put off his retirement and make sure I got off to a good start. Except he never left. He just kept showing up, day after day, checking up on me, making sure I was running bus procedures the way he taught me, making sure the Christmas pageant went smoothly, supervising the milk deliveries at the cafeteria, for God's sake. And it kept that line blurred as to who was really principal, me or him. The school board finally told him he had to retire or his pension was going to be at risk. So he retired and I thought that would be the end of it. No. He starts showing up at the school as a volunteer. Any time I try to change policies, the teachers go to him to complain and he tells them not to worry about it, just go back to his policies. Parents go to *him* with problems. It's like having the Ghost of Principal Past lurking around the hallways, undermining my authority with grandfatherly, passive-aggressive charm. And I can't tell him to stay home and keep his folksy wisdom to himself, because then I'm the ungrateful city boy who locked a beloved educator out of the school building."

Margot blinked, absorbing the sheer volume of his rant. "That is very unfortunate, but I fail to see how it connects to Founders' Day."

"If I can be seen organizing the kids' participation in the festival, making it successful, then maybe it will help secure a little authority," he said.

"You are grasping at some very thin straws."

"I know, it's a little far-fetched, but I'm trying to take the high road here. Community politics are very touchy in small towns like this, especially when it comes to schools. If I want to be able to do my job, I have to be seen as someone who's effective but still respectful of traditions, like Jimmy Greenway . . . and yet slowly undermine those traditions until they go away, unlike Jimmy Greenway."

"Did Marianne tell you how I lost my last job?"

"Yeah, I saw the news clips on YouTube. Don't care. I need you."

Margot sighed and sat back in her chair. Her first thought was that she didn't have time for this, but honestly, for the first time in her life, she had plenty of spare time. Her job search was basically at a standstill. If word spread that she'd sent out blanket coverage of résumés, she would come across as desperate. She had plenty of hours in the evening that she could devote to the festival, and honestly, the McCreadys would probably be so thrilled she was involved in local events that they would let her conduct festival business from her office at the funeral home. It would be nice to do something to repay their kindness, so at the very least she wouldn't leave town feeling indebted to them.

And then there was Kyle.

Kyle. Kyle. Kyle.

She'd moved beyond liking the *idea* of Kyle to actually liking the man with the frizzy-headed, opinionated children and the high-stress job. It would be so much easier to walk away, to prevent an attachment deeper than just liking. And her argument that she might not stay in Lake Sackett long enough to attend the festival herself still stood. But she found that she wanted to help him. Even with their strange, somewhat embarrassing history and the complications of his children, she wanted to spend more time with him. She wanted to help him see her as something besides a tragically manic woman with a tendency toward vehicular frottage.

Oh, who was she trying to fool? She was going to say yes anyway.

She moaned, pinching her nose. "All right, I'll help. Because I would hate for you to get fired for tossing an old man out of a library window in front of impressionable children."

He held his hands up as if he was going to cup her face or shout "Hallelujah!" But instead, he let out a long, relieved, cookie-scented breath and said, "Thank you. You are saving my dignity here."

"You say that because I haven't put you in a dunk tank—yet."

"Your attempts to intimidate me mean nothing. You said yes. You're committed. Now, our first grade class is particularly . . . energetic this year," he said, pulling on a rain poncho over his clothes. "And if I'm not out there to glower at them, they will launch the fourth great mashed potato war. So I have to go. If you want to meet sometime over the next few days, that would be great."

"I will call . . . the school," Margot said. "I will call the school to set that up."

"You don't think it would be better for you to just take my cell number?" he asked.

"No, I think it's better if I don't have that," she said. "I don't think that will look good for you on the restraining order paperwork."

"I deserved that," he said, glancing at the clock. "I don't

mean to be blunt, but you seem to appreciate honesty. I find you very attractive. I enjoy whatever this dynamic is, but I'm not looking for a relationship. I'm not ready for one right now, maybe not for a long time. And you strike me as a relationship kind of lady."

"You'd be surprised," she muttered, thinking of her last three lovers, who barely qualified for the title.

He opened the office door. The noise and bustle of hundreds of children came pouring through the doorway. Clarice was already staring at Margot as if the secretary was accusing her of *something* ill-bred and skanky, but she just couldn't figure out what it was yet.

"Probably should have kept the door open for your groveling," Margot whispered out the side of her mouth. "I think I just ruined your reputation."

"I didn't grovel," he protested.

Margot lifted a blond brow. "Dunk tank."

"I groveled a little bit."

9

As PREDICTED, THE McCreadys were overjoyed that Margot was going to take over the Founders' Festival. Almost as predictably, her introduction to the planning committee was a complete disaster—not flamingo level, but close.

Kyle wasted no time, scheduling a planning meeting the next evening. Following an afternoon of combative mourners and depressing organ music, Margot actually found herself eager for the cheerful noise and color of the school. She may have followed Kyle's lead and worn her raincoat to protect her clothes, despite the fact that the sky was blue and cloudless. This was her favorite DKNY suit and she wasn't risking a drive-by mashed potatoing.

Kyle had asked her to meet with the parent volunteers just after classes let out, during their regular weekly session. He'd apologized for not being able to get her an updated planning committee manual, but Sara Lee hadn't provided him with "this week's" draft. The way he emphasized *this week's* made a shudder of apprehension ripple down her spine.

Margot had almost convinced herself that she was going to

be able to work with Kyle and remain completely unaffected. She could push through her attraction to his big brown eyes and his adorable half smile and the little dimple on his left cheek with the power of professionalism and poise. At least, that's what she told herself right up until he put his hand on the small of her back to usher her safely through the children rampantly zigzagging down the hall.

And her resolve melted like Aunt Leslie's fried ice cream.

Margot followed Kyle into the library, where several adults sat around a small round table, poring over papers as a thin blond woman with a ruthlessly sharp pageboy said, "Just trust me on this, Sweet Johnnie. People aren't gonna want brownies at a cake walk. That's why it's called a *cake* walk. Just stick to the list of desserts I gave you."

Margot scanned the group quickly. A heavier woman balanced her round chin on her palm, frowning as she glanced over the papers in front of her. An older man wearing a frayed John Deere cap and overalls was glaring into the distance. A silver fox wearing a Lake Sackett Elementary Staff polo shirt was staring at the ceiling like it was his job.

Margot pursed her lips. She'd run across civic groups like this before, people serving because they hadn't been able to find a way out of being volunteered. They didn't want to stand in the way of tasks being accomplished. They just didn't want to be put out themselves. They wouldn't give her any trouble.

Margot's eyes narrowed at the blonde. She was the only one looking up, the only one shuffling through a binder filled with notes with any purpose. Clearly she was in charge. This had to be Sara Lee, the misguided but very committed leader. Margot could tell just from the sleek hair and the rigid posture that Sara

Lee was going to be a problem. Actually, the dessert microman-agement was the biggest clue, but the posture didn't help.

"Hey, folks, this is Margot Cary, E.J.J.'s great-niece. She's a fancy event planner and she's going to be helping us iron out some of the plans for the festival. Miss Margot, this is Sara Lee Bolton, Sweet Johnnie Reed." The heavyset lady refused to meet Margot's gaze, choosing to stare at the papers on the table in front of her. Margot wondered if Sweet Johnnie had been cho-sen for this committee because she was too quiet to do anything except what Sara Lee told her. Kyle continued the introductions. "And this is, ahem, Jimmy Greenway, and Dobb Cunningham."

"Just call me Dobb," the man in the John Deere cap rumbled.

Jimmy Greenway, the silver fox, stood and pumped Margot's hand firmly. "Nice to meet you, young lady, Principal Jimmy Greenway."

Margot feigned confusion. "But I thought Mr. Archer was principal."

Jimmy's face flushed red. "Uh, well, *retired* principal, but as I've told young Kyle here, you never really retire from a job like this. It's your lifelong Christian duty to stay close to make sure the children get the best possible education."

"Well, isn't it nice of you to hover so close," Margot said, smiling warmly. "It's so nice to meet you all. Ms. Reed, did I hear Mr. Archer call you 'Sweet Johnnie' before?"

"It's a nickname," Sweet Johnnie said, her voice quiet and melodic, like a music box under a pillow. "Nobody on my mama's side of the family birthed any boys, which was a big disappointment to my Grandpa John, so they tried to make up for it by naming all us cousins after him. And we all ended up being called Johnnie, when we were kids, so we had to have the nicknames so people could tell us apart in school. It's a little silly, but it's better than being called Toothless Johnnie or Jumbo Johnnie, like my cousins."

"You definitely got the best one," Margot told her, making Johnnie smile.

"If we could get back on track, I don't see why we'd need *outside* help," Sara Lee protested. "I have everything in hand."

"Well, with the festival coming up so quick, I thought it would be good to go over your plans so far. Miss Margot's experience is a real resource for us and it would be silly not to take advantage of that if she's willing to help."

"I'm just here to tie up some loose ends," Margot told her. "Put a pretty bow on it. I don't want to step on toes or take over."

Sara Lee's already thin lips pressed into a stubborn line across her face. "I still don't see the point in it. You're not from around here. You don't know anybody. You don't know any of our traditions. You don't know who to call or what to order. Do you even know what we're celebratin'? I don't want to waste time havin' to explain things to you. Maybe I should talk to my cousin on the county commission, see how he feels about some outsider bein' put in charge of the festival."

Margot stared at Sara Lee for a long moment, weighing, calculating. She didn't care that Sara Lee didn't want her help. She didn't care that Sara Lee didn't seem to like her. But she wasn't about to let this woman treat her like yesterday's Breakfast Stick. Private though it may have been, this was the sort of gossip that got passed around like collection plates on Sunday morning.

If she let a bully like Sara Lee push her around, Margot would get branded as a weakling, and the little respect she got from people beyond her family circle would evaporate. Even with her limited time left in Lake Sackett and her utter lack of giving a damn, she didn't like the idea of walking through the Food Carnival knowing the locals looked down on her. So she thought back to the time a financier's wife tried to get Margot fired for nixing her "European-inspired" puce and lime-green color scheme for the CEO's annual black-tie dinner for investors. She hadn't shrunk from that woman or her neon-tinged threats. And she wouldn't shrink from this small-town dictator.

She smiled, not quite as warmly as before. "And that's how I approached any of the events I was assigned for my company. I didn't know the hosts or their histories or their favorite vendors. But I learned. I learned quickly. For instance, I'm assuming that we're celebrating the founding of the town, considering that it's called the Founders' Festival."

Across the table, quiet Sweet Johnnie snorted and then covered it with a cough. Margot decided she was going to like Sweet Johnnie.

Kyle and Margot took the open seats at the table. Sweet Johnnie slid her copy of the planning committee manual across the tabletop to Margot. And Margot realized that most of the committee members looked uncomfortable, not just because of Sara Lee's attitude but because the chairs they were sitting in were designed to support elementary school students. This was going to be a long afternoon.

"Now, if we could just get started, I'll do everything I can to make this a painless process."

⁓

"IT'S GOING TO be a horribly painful process," Margot told Kyle long after the meeting ended and Kyle had finally convinced

Sara Lee to leave the school grounds. The meeting agenda had been deadlocked between Sara Lee's desire to change everything and Jimmy Greenway's desire to do everything "the way it has always been done."

Sara Lee seemed reluctant to leave Kyle and Margot unattended, as if they were going to plan a bunch of stuff behind her back the second she left. But Kyle reminded her that her son Austin's soccer practice was letting out soon and she needed to pick him up—a benefit of knowing the schedule for all the school's extracurricular activities—and she finally left, glancing over her shoulder all the way.

Kyle and Margot were still hunched in child-size chairs as Margot sorted the box of records she'd pried out of Sara Lee's hands into categorical piles.

"Oh, come on, it can't be that bad," Kyle protested.

"Who planned this before Sara Lee took over?"

"Margene Moffat," Kyle said. "She was head of the ladies' auxiliary. They handled the planning before the PTA took over."

"Is there any way I can talk to Margene to get a look at previous plans?"

"No, she's in the state penitentiary for embezzling more than fifty thousand dollars of the auxiliary's fund-raising money. And she burned all of her planning binders, along with the auxiliary's books, in an 'accidental' fire she set four years ago to try to throw the auditors off her trail. That's why the PTA took over the planning."

Kyle laughed when Margot's face drooped into an incredulous, exhausted expression. "So what's wrong with the plans?"

Margot sighed. "Okay, there's no layout for the booths and rides. Sara Lee hasn't booked the permits or asked the local police for help directing traffic and blocking off streets. But she did get a petition against an activity called 'punkin chunkin,' due to injuries sustained last year. And there's a little Post-it on the petition that says, 'Ignore this,' with a frowny face. I can't tell what she's done and what she's undone. I know that there have been *some* contributions from local businesses, but I can't tell who donated or how much they gave, which could be important for tax reasons. There are order slips, canceled order slips, contracts with vendors, canceled contracts with vendors. A lady who was contracted to do face-painting sent her a letter that basically says, 'Eff you, I can't put up with your constant contract changes. I'm out.' Do you know how hard it is to piss off someone who puts glitter paint on children's faces? Pretty damn difficult." Margot glanced around the library, feeling guilty for cursing in a room filled with children's books. "Sorry."

"It's okay," he said, scrubbing a hand over his face. "There are days when I have to play the school song at full blast on my computer speakers so I can yell the F-word at the top of my lungs. Usually it's after a parent conference. Also, we need the face-painting lady. Her line is always huge."

Margot's grimace deepened. "I know we told Sara Lee that we wouldn't make major changes, but I don't think we're going to have a choice. I don't know what planning strategy she's using, but unless her goal is 'frustrate people with long lines, boredom, and bad food,' this is not going to work out the way you hope."

"Planning strategy?"

"Every event has to have an end goal, yes? To raise money or show appreciation or make rich people feel even better about themselves for a couple of hours. And for the Founders' Festival, I assume that—beyond celebrating the anniversary of your town being established—the point is to convince visitors that they should eventually return to town and insert their tourist dollars into local pockets."

"Yes, but I think that would be tacky in terms of a slogan . . ."

Margot smirked. "I'm going to figure out a list of ways to keep people's attention on the many wonderful places to spend those tourism dollars while competing with the expected funnel cakes and bouncy castles. I should be able to get a list of strategies to you by tomorrow."

"So quickly?"

Margot scoffed. "This is nothing. I once planned a children's hospital carnival on a shoestring in twenty-four hours because it turned out the previous event planner spent the entire budget on—wait for it—luxury balloons. The entire budget. On balloons. Really nice balloons, but still, balloons."

"She must have really loved balloons."

"No, she really loved cocaine," Margot said. "The balloons just seemed like a good idea while she was on a bender."

"You know, that's one advantage of small-town living? Not a lot of stories end with 'because cocaine.' I mean, some stories end that way, but not a lot."

"Are there any drugs that explain Sara Lee's behavior? Because that was an unusual amount of hostility . . . and while she was sitting in front of a Curious George display, which was pretty shocking."

"That's just Sara Lee." Kyle sighed.

"Is she mad that her mother named her after pound cake?"

"No, she takes her authority as PTA president very seriously. She sees you as a threat to her power base."

"She realizes that the PTA president has no actual authority in the outside world, right? She knows that she can't order me to be shot by the PTA secret service . . ." When Kyle said nothing, Margot exclaimed, "Tell me she knows that!"

"I make no guarantees. She may use the punkin chunkin catapult to get rid of your body."

"That's what punkin chunkin is? Launching pumpkins with a catapult?"

"Well, it's really more of a trebuchet. Because it uses a counterweight instead of—" He paused when he saw the exasperated look on her face. "Not important."

"Again, this seems like an overreaction to someone trying to help with a small-town festival."

"Well, to Sara Lee, it's not just a little carnival, it's her way of showing everybody in town how smart and wonderful she is. She's a local girl, didn't go to college, doesn't work outside of the home. And she has more than a little crush on your cousin-in-law, Carl."

"Carl?" Margot pursed her lips. "No, I can't even say that with convincing surprise. I can see it very easily."

Margot was flattered by the flicker of irritation on Kyle's face before he said, "Yes, well, according to local lore, Sara Lee wanted Carl, but settled for Dougie Hazard back in high school."

"The animal control officer?" she said, remembering the story about Aunt Tootie's conflict over her dog pack.

"Yes. She dumped Dougie as soon as he took her to senior prom, and he never quite got over it. And Sara Lee never got over Carl."

"Since high school?"

"When you live in a small town and remain in that small

town, staying in contact with the people you went to high school with, it's hard to get away from those little disappointments. No one's immune. Even after living away for a few years and moving back, my wife still got irritated every time she went to the grocery store and saw the girl who hazed her at band camp."

Kyle frowned suddenly and the color drained out of his cheeks. Margot supposed it was still painful for him to talk about his late wife, especially when he was talking to someone he'd recently kissed. It didn't exactly make her feel free of moral confusion.

Kyle cleared his throat. "Anyway, showing up Marianne, who crashed and burned as PTA president two years ago, would go a long way to soothing the sting."

Margot gasped. "Marianne crashed and burned? But she seems so organized and people-oriented."

"She is, but she also got so fed up with people either not volunteering or not showing up at the things they volunteered for that she sent home a sealed parent letter listing the lovely field trips and playground equipment that the students could have had if the parents bothered fulfilling their commitments, but since they didn't, the PTA was going to provide copy paper for the school and that was it. I believe the parting line of the letter was, 'Enjoy continuing to sit on your collective butts doing nothing and blaming the school for not doing enough for your kids.' Well, Sara Lee didn't appreciate being accused of inadequate parenting and led a suddenly invigorated group of parents to impeach her. Of course, they didn't say it was because she accused them of being inadequate parents. They said sending a letter that included the word 'butts' where students could potentially see it was an inappropriate use of school stationery."

"You're kidding. Marianne was tossed out of office for using the word 'butts'?"

"Welcome to the Bible Belt. Marianne was lucky they didn't bar her from volunteering at the school library."

"The PTA is a hotbed of intrigue," she marveled.

He nodded. "Not as hot as the ladies' auxiliary, but yes."

Margot smiled and Kyle returned it. All that color rushed back into his cheeks and he looked down at his paperwork, shuffling it into a pile.

"I'll walk you out," he said, sliding the papers into his messenger bag. "I've got to go pick up the girls from piano lessons soon."

The school was eerily quiet with the hallways empty and the lights turned off. Kyle checked the office to make sure it was locked and led Margot out of the building. He locked the front door with a rather intimidating set of keys. That enormous ring of keys reminded her of how much authority Kyle held in Lake Sackett. She mulled that over as they crossed the darkening parking lot toward her truck. She didn't consider the escort necessary, unless she was attacked by the aforementioned Sasquatch, but it was a nice gesture. And it only left her more confused.

"I'm going to be honest, the first time I saw you, you looked so miserable and intense, I still wasn't convinced you were entirely real," she said, unlocking the truck. "And then, you're at school and it's all smiles and fist bumps to adorable little kids. And then there's the guy I met at the Dirty Deer. And I feel I know all of you and nothing of you at the same time. I'm just confused as to who the real Kyle is."

He scratched the back of his neck, staring off into the

purpling horizon as if there were some answers to frank and intrusive questions written there. "Well, nobody is ever just one person. When I'm at work, I'm the guy my students need me to be. I smile. I tell goofy jokes. I parent the kids who need it and make sure the kids who are parented get whatever they need. When I'm at home, I'm the guy my girls need me to be. I smile. I make banana pancakes with chocolate chips. I watch YouTube tutorials on how to do a fishbone braid. I focus on what they need and I take care of them. But when it's just me, I only worry about what I need. And sometimes that's just wandering around town, staring into space, drinking coffee in the Rise and Shine at six in the morning because Ike's told the whole staff not to talk to me if the girls aren't with me. All those things I won't let myself feel when my daughters are home or my kids need me, I let them in. I just feel. I don't have to worry about assuring anybody that I'm fine, that they don't have to worry or try to cheer me up. All that anger and despair and being pissed off that life is so damned unfair, that I'm raising these girls on my own when their mom should be here with us. I wallow in it for a while. And by the time the girls come back, I can turn it back off."

"Is it healthy, to compartmentalize like that?" she asked, leaning against the truck. The warmth from the metal seeped pleasantly through her jacket into her skin and she sighed.

"Says the woman who works with her estranged father but doesn't have actual conversations with him?"

"Did Frankie tell you that?" Margot asked. Kyle shook his head. "Marianne?" He shook his head. "Duffy? Too many people in this town have intimate knowledge of my personal life!"

"E.J.J. He comes into the Rise and Shine some mornings. He worries about you."

"I'm ignoring your attempts to redirect attention from you," Margot said. "You compartmentalize. It seems unhealthy to divide your life that way."

"It's not you!" he said quickly. "Or it is you, but it's not. That night at the bar . . . I wasn't drunk. I hadn't even had anything to drink. Honestly, I was there because it was a rare night off. I wasn't there with anybody. And I stuck with soda because I didn't have anyone to drive me home. That came out much sadder than I expected."

"It was pretty sad."

"I—I have had . . . oh, God, this is embarrassing. A couple of years after Maggie passed, people kept telling me it was time for me to date again, that I needed to 'get back out there,' and like a jackass, I ignored what my gut was telling me. I couldn't imagine trying to date a woman around here. I'd wait for the nights when the girls were with my in-laws and I would go to Alpharetta or Athens and meet somebody at a bar and go home with them. And I can't say that I wasn't enjoying myself in the moment, but it was uncomfortable. Because I was with that woman, but I wasn't *with* her. I didn't feel right, so I stopped. And then I met you and . . ."

"And?"

"I felt something. Not love at first sight or anything like that, but *something*. And I don't know if I'm ready to feel something. And I'm sorry."

"You don't have to be sorry. And it's okay. I'm not exactly in a relationship place right now . . . or ever, really," she said, straightening her shoulders. "I think I understand. Wait, no, I don't because I don't know anything about you. I know what people have told me about you. But nothing about you, from you."

"I could say the same for you," he said.

"So help me understand what's going on in your head, and I'll try to explain what's happening in mine."

He made a reluctant noise in the back of his throat.

"Come on, we've spent a lot of time together not talking or just sort of bouncing off each other in unnaturally uncomfortable social situations. I feel like a little revealing conversation isn't too much to ask. You said you're from New York. What part?"

"Manhattan. I grew up in one of those neighborhoods full of nice brownstones, where people always seem to get murdered in the first five minutes of *Law and Order*."

Margot glanced around at this tiny school in this tiny town and tried to imagine someone used to the hustle and bustle of New York City adjusting to the lack of bagels and sirens.

"You know how everybody always argues over where the *real* Original Ray's Pizza is? Well, I know. And because you've been, on occasion, sort of mean to me, I'm not going to tell you."

Margot scoffed. "Fair enough. Give me a deep-dish pizza over a folding piece of flaccid, half-cooked dough anytime."

Kyle gave her the stink eye. "I take it back. We can't be friends."

"I apologize for insulting your hometown's floppy edible shingles," she said. "For no other reason than I'd like to know how and why you left New York for Lake Sackett."

"My wife grew up here," he said. "I went to UVA because it was not New York and I wanted a change. That's where we met. We were every Facebook cliché about marrying your best friend. Maggie was one of the most fascinating women I ever met, just supersmart and funny. You'd think she would be intimidated, a girl from a small town on a big college campus, but she didn't take crap from anybody. I was studying to be a teacher. She was going into nursing. And when we got married, I got her to move to New York for a while. And she tolerated it, for my sake. She tried to make an adventure out of it. We'd been living in Brooklyn for a while when she got pregnant with Hazel. And then our walkup apartment was broken into for the fifth time and we decided maybe it would be a good idea to move out of the city and raise the baby in a place where we could be ninety percent sure there wasn't a human trafficking ring running out of the basement."

"I'm assuming that's in most parenting books," she conceded.

"Maggie's family is here. Parents, aunts, uncles, cousins, the whole bit. She wanted to be able to give the baby the kind of childhood she had. And since a lot of my childhood centered on warnings about not talking to strangers on the subway, I couldn't help but agree with her."

Margot nodded. "By the way, Hazel *and* Juniper?"

"There's a history of plant names in the family. My wife— whose name was Magnolia—was very susceptible to guilt-tripping by her mother and grandmother."

"Still." Margot snorted. "Don't you miss it, though? Not just the food and the museums and theaters that show more than one movie at a time, but the noise? I mean, I never thought I would miss the sound of traffic and police sirens, but I can't get a decent night's sleep without them."

"I miss some things. When we first moved here I was a lot like you, with the city shoes and the Starbucks withdrawals. But Lake Sackett grows on you—the people, the fresh air, the scenery, the fact that most of my neighbors wouldn't kneecap me over a parking spot. And the life here, it's just different. I got to the point where I wasn't homesick anymore and people stopped calling me 'that city fella.' My friends back home thought I was nuts, but I came to love it here. And when I lost Maggie, the people here are what got us through. I don't know what we would have done without them."

"So, city fella, how long do you think it will be before people call me by my first name instead of 'Stan's girl'?" she asked.

"Four, five years, tops."

"Great."

He cleared his throat. "So you now know my entire romantic history. Please, share some form of information with me so this isn't so one-sided."

Margot shrugged. "Um, there isn't much to tell."

"You mean you didn't leave some devastated upwardly mobile stockbroker in your wake?"

"No, I haven't really had a relationship in . . . four years. I mean, I dated. In college, I did the undergrad serial monogamy thing. But nothing came of it, much to my mother's horror. After I graduated, I started working and I was always busy. No one really seemed—and this is going to sound like an awful thing to say about my fellow human beings—but no one seemed worth the effort of being in a relationship? My mother always made it sound like it was so much work to take on another person, to make sure your life ran smoothly. And nobody really made me want to invest that kind of time. And just to increase the sad factor, I'm probably going to move again in a few weeks, so I'll have to start over with a whole new city full of men I will date but never commit to."

Kyle's brow furrowed. "I keep forgetting that, the part where you're leaving as soon as you can."

"So really, there's no reason for you to worry about a complicated relationship and hurt feelings, because I'm going to launch myself out of town at the earliest opportunity. I would use that punkin chunkin catapult if I thought it would get me out of here faster."

She paused, stood on her toes, and kissed him. Not a shy, polite peck on the lips, nothing that could be construed as a friendly gesture, but an honest-to-God kiss, with tongue and teeth and mingled breath. Her legs buckled slightly when he responded, sliding his hands down her butt and pulling her closer. She moaned into his mouth, threading her fingers through his messy hair. The beard was every bit as scratchy-soft as she remembered, bristling against her skin and leaving it just the right amount of raw. She bit down gently on his bottom lip just before pulling back from him. "Stop worrying so much."

And with that, she hopped into her truck, threw it into reverse, and backed out of the space, leaving Kyle standing there with his mouth agape.

It was nice to be on the other end of that expression for once.

10

$\mathcal{M}$ARGOT SUBMITTED HER planning strategy to Kyle and the committee within twenty-four hours. She'd chosen "Glory Days" as the festival theme, highlighting not only the establishment of the town but great moments in Lake Sackett's history. Margot believed the hopeful, nostalgic tone would attract more people than the previous year's theme of, well, nothing. She used design software on her laptop to mock up ads to place in regional papers and magazines, not to mention online travel sites. It was too late for a proper ad campaign, but she could still try to attract last-minute travelers looking for a pleasant outing before winter set in.

Overall, the committee seemed pleased with her progress. Sweet Johnnie, who turned out to be the town librarian, even spoke up in favor of the theme, exclaiming that she had all sorts of old photos that could be used in printables, posters, and displays. Dobb woke up long enough to say that he had some of the old tractors used by the construction crews who built the dam. His father had bought them cheap on a whim when the Corps of

Engineers teams left, and Dobb had spent years restoring them as a hobby.

"They're painted up and good as new," Dobb said. "We could put them out for show at the parking lot near the dam, put up one of those tents Miss Margot was talking about with pictures and posters on the construction for a—what'd you call it? A temp'rary exhibit."

"I think that's a wonderful idea, Dobb," Margot told him. "And if we spread the events and exhibits out over the town a little bit, it will definitely help with parking and traffic."

"So you want to draw attention to one of the most painful times in the town's history?" Sara Lee sniffed. "When people were forced to relocate from homes their families had held since the Civil War? Barely given fair market value for their land? Spoken like someone who didn't grow up here."

"It's a part of our history, just like anything else," Sweet Johnnie said, scratching the back of her neck. "'Sides, most everybody who was still bitter about it died off about ten years ago. Nowadays people are just grateful for the lake."

Sara turned on Dobb, demanding, "So why didn't you say somethin' about these amazin' tractors before, so we could use them?"

Dobb shrugged. "You never asked."

With support from the committee and Kyle, Margot overhauled the festival. And Sara Lee seemed to have figured out that openly bashing Margot's plans wasn't working, so she'd switched to more subtle methods of undermining. All subsequent meetings were attended by an entourage of Sara Lee's cronies, all just as delightfully rigid as she was, who crowded around the table and *tsk*ed over Margot's to-do list as if it was photographic evidence of a near-fatal car crash. It reminded her of her mother's friends descending on a Charity League meeting, but with far less Chanel involved.

Tootie and Leslie had received several phone calls from church friends "concerned" over what they'd heard of the changes to the festival. (No one called Donna, because Donna was scary.) Her family members were being told to get Margot in line while they still could. And Margot had to put password protection in place with the vendors she was using, because "someone" had called and tried to cancel the poster she was having printed, not to mention the ads she'd placed with the *Atlanta Journal-Constitution*. Other than that, and some nasty looks from the occasional mourner, she was sure she had the situation in hand.

She told herself that, right up until the "incident" with Animal Control.

Margot was driving home from work, humming along to one of Duffy's Blake Shelton CDs. Her jacket was thrown casually over a stack of large mailing envelopes in the passenger seat—envelopes she'd purchased herself, thank you. They were evidence of her latest round of job applications. She tried not to let the lack of responses to her inquiries bother her, but frankly, she was starting to think she might see a Lake Sackett winter. It was a singularly depressing thought and not just because of the lack of tourists or traffic.

She had to admit she'd had a pretty good day at the funeral home, despite her concerted effort *not* to upsell anyone. She'd managed to schedule services for Bennett Haskell and Garmin Rudd so the two families—who had been feuding for years over a hunting lease gone wrong and happened to have uncles who died at the same time—didn't run into each other once. And she'd actually managed to walk downstairs to deliver Frankie's lunch. Sure, she'd kept her eyes closed the whole time, dropped the grease-spotted bag into Frankie's hands, and run blindly toward the stairs—smacking into a wall. But she'd gotten down the stairs, which was more than she'd thought she was capable of weeks before.

Margot pulled the truck into the compound's driveway, rolling over the now-familiar ruts and bumps with practiced ease. As she rolled up to Aunt Tootie's place, she noticed the large white truck with SACKETT COUNTY ANIMAL CONTROL painted on the driver's-side door. The back of the truck was composed of kennels inset in the truck body. And a tall, rail-thin man seemed to be loading one of Tootie's dog pack into a kennel. Tootie was shouting and waving a rake at him in a threatening manner.

Margot threw the truck into park and tried to hop out before she even unbuckled her seat belt or turned off the engine. Taking a deep breath to steady herself, she freed herself and jogged across the gravel drive as quickly as she could manage in heels. The rest of the dog pack were going crazy, barking and yapping, but Margot noticed that none of them snapped at the animal control officer.

It struck Margot as odd that Tootie was alone in her confrontation with the dogcatcher. Normally one of the uncles would be on the compound grounds, but with a fishing bachelor party in town and the dueling funeral services, it was all hands on deck at McCready's. Margot had been released early because she'd arrived at the office in the predawn hours to accept delivery of Mr. Rudd's custom Harley-Davidson-themed casket. It seemed suspiciously coincidental that Animal Control's visit had been timed during such a busy afternoon.

As she got closer, she heard Tootie shouting, "Dougie Hazard, don't make me call your mama on you!"

Dougie Hazard's heavy Adam's apple made him look like a cartoon buzzard. He was backing toward the truck with Arlo in his arms, which was wise, considering the rake. Tootie might have been old, but she had a considerable amount of upper-body strength.

"Now, Miss Tootie, I know you take real good care of your animals. I have no objections to how you keep 'em. But once a complaint has been filed with my office, I can't just ignore it. That's the kind of thing that will get me fired."

"What's going on here? Put Arlo down now!" Margot demanded, prying the rake out of Tootie's grasp. "Really, Tootie, you're going to give yourself a stroke."

"He's taking Arlo!" Tootie shouted.

"Can you explain why?" Margot asked, turning on Dougie. "You can see that the dogs are all in good shape. They have clean conditions and ample food, and they're obviously getting plenty of exercise and socialization."

"Miss Tootie has thirteen dogs in her possession, which is one over the limit set by the county ordinance against hoarding," Dougie told Margot, hitching his loose belt over his narrow hips with one hand as he struggled with the wriggling dog. "That means I have to take one to the county shelter. And since Miss Tootie can't provide any papers proving this one's had his shots, I'm taking him in."

"Is it a kill shelter?" Margot muttered out of the side of her mouth.

Tootie nodded, glaring at Dougie. "After seventy-two hours."

Arlo squirmed in Dougie's arms, whining pitifully. Margot shot Dougie a venomous glare. "Really? You don't feel bad about this, at all?"

"I don't make the rules!" Dougie protested.

"Well, the rule doesn't apply anyway. Because that dog isn't Tootie's, it's mine," she said, taking Arlo from his grasp. Arlo's claws dug into her arms as he scrambled up her body. Also, she was pretty sure that warm wet spot spreading against her silk blouse wasn't sweat. Still, Margot didn't want to imagine how Tootie would react if she lost Arlo. Or really, how Margot would feel if she lost Arlo. She'd gotten accustomed to him finding a way into her home and onto her couch. He was like a warm, furry worry stone.

"He's yours?" Dougie asked in a tone that clearly communicated his desire to call "bullshit" on Margot's claim.

"Sure is," Margot said, willing herself not to shudder when Arlo's wet nose wedged under her chin. As much as she liked Arlo, that didn't make that sensation any more comfortable. "Goooooood boy."

Dougie's thin, graying eyebrows lifted. "Do you have any vet bills or paperwork to prove he's yours?"

Margot glanced at Tootie, who subtly shook her head.

"No. He's a stray. I just found him in the parking lot at the Food Carnival the other day. I haven't had a chance to file the paperwork yet," Margot lied smoothly. "I'll be sure to go do that as soon as possible. Surely you can't punish a good Samaritan for not having time in her busy schedule to run down to the courthouse, can you?"

Dougie frowned at her. "Put him down, walk about ten paces, and call him to you."

"What?"

"Prove that he's yours," Dougie said. "Call him."

"This isn't a scene from *Annie*," Margot protested. "I haven't had time to bond with him yet. And I'm just calling him Arlo because he didn't have any tags and it was the first name I could come up with. I don't know what he answers to."

"If you want me to go, call the dog," Dougie told her.

"Fine." Margot handed the dog to Tootie and walked ten steps away. Tootie whispered in Arlo's ear while Margot dropped into a crouch.

"Come here, Arlo. Come here!" Margot said in her best doggy voice. Tootie put Arlo on the ground. But for once, instead of instantly invading Margot's personal space, he sat on his butt, staring at her with his head cocked to the side.

"Uh-huh." Dougie snorted.

"Come on, Arlo! Come here, sweet doggy!" Margot cooed.

Arlo stayed seated on his furry butt.

"*Arlo*," she grumbled through gritted teeth. She rolled her eyes and smacked her hands against her legs in frustration. Suddenly Arlo perked up and came running. Dougie's jaw dropped, but not nearly as low as Margot's. She let the dog paw at her knees, but wary of further damage to her clothes, didn't pick him up. Arlo circled around to Margot's left hip and sniffed at her pocket with interest.

"You see there?" Tootie cackled. "That there's Margot's dog. I tried to tell you, but you wouldn't listen."

Margot blanched as a small plastic baggie slipped out of her pocket and Arlo clamped his teeth on it. It was a sample she'd picked up at the jerky store—mako shark with lemon and ginger flavoring—thinking that Duffy would get a kick out of it. She made a discreet grab for the jerky bag and stood, tucking it behind her back so Dougie couldn't see the meaty treat that had lured Arlo to her.

"Sit, Arlo," she told him firmly. Arlo whined a bit but planted his furry butt on the ground.

"Fine," Dougie muttered, scribbling angrily on his clipboard. "But you *will* get his papers in order by the next time I come out here. And Miss Tootie, you've been skatin' the line for too long, makin' me a laughingstock at county commission meetin's."

"Oh, I don't make you a laughingstock, Dougie, you do that well enough on your own," Tootie shot back. Margot nudged Tootie's ribs with her elbow.

Dougie grunted and waved her off as he stomped toward his truck. He peeled out of the driveway with the dog pack chasing the tires at a respectable distance.

"Oh, y'all stop that!" Tootie yelled, calling them back. "You don't chase stupid! It will find you eventually! Go on home now!"

The pack stopped the chase and took off running toward E.J.J. and Tootie's cabin; all except for Arlo, who seemed to assume that his fraudulent adoption was actually happening and planted himself at Margot's feet.

"Big lot of fuss over nothing," Tootie said with a sigh.

Margot asked, "Why didn't you just go get the dog's paperwork in the first place, Tootie?"

"You heard him, I'm over the county limit." She sniffed. "I'm old. I'm not stupid."

"So when do you think Dougie might come back to check on my completely fabricated story?"

"Oh, who knows? Dougie's harmless. Under normal circumstances, he'd probably just forget about it. But I think it's Sara Lee that's got him all stirred up. She's been jawin' to whoever will listen about how you're ruining the Founders' Festival."

"What does that have to do with anything?"

"Sara Lee was Dougie's high school girlfriend. He never quite got over her and she knows it. And she can't strike back directly at you, so she's trying to get to you through me."

Margot's brow furrowed. "High school romances run deep around here, don't they? So if I keep working with the planning committee, there's a chance you could lose your dogs? Should I tell Kyle that I need to back off from the festival?"

"Oh, honey, I have a long-standing feud with Animal Control. They're always threatening me with something. Don't let it rattle you."

"I am not used to being targeted by municipal agencies. I am comfortable with my being rattled."

Margot propped her hands on her hips, staring down at Arlo. "You're not sleeping at my house. My shoes *will* remain unchewed."

Arlo dropped his head to his paws, whining pitifully as he gave her literal puppy eyes. Margot rolled her eyes, and in doing so caught sight of the shabbier yellow house.

"Hey, Tootie, the house at the end of the row, the yellow one with the green roof? Who lives there?"

Tootie pursed her lips. "Well, um, you did, hon."

"I'm sorry?"

Aunt Tootie walked toward the unkempt cabin. "That was the cabin that your dad built for your mama. They moved in right after the wedding."

Margot absorbed this new piece of information. "But he

doesn't live there anymore? It looks like it hasn't been kept up in years."

"Right after your mama left, he moved into the sleeping cubby at the funeral home."

"He's been sleeping at the funeral home for thirty years?" she exclaimed.

"He couldn't sleep at the house anymore," she said. "Said it was too quiet. We tried to keep it up for him. Leslie and I do what we can so the inside doesn't get too musty. But he doesn't want us putting on a new roof or carpet. I think part of him was afraid you might not recognize it when you came home."

"I didn't recognize it," she said, shaking her head. "This doesn't look at all familiar."

She stared at the forlorn little cabin, its windows reflecting nothing, like blank doll's eyes. There was no life inside this house. There hadn't been life there for years. And she didn't feel the faintest tug at her memory while staring at it. Shouldn't she be able to remember the first place she called home?

"You wanna go inside?" Tootie asked. "I have a spare key."

Margot shook her head. "I think I'm going to go see Kyle, talk to him about this new development with Dougie. And then I need to look up how to file a dog license."

"Aw, honey, don't worry about it. I have the papers in my desk at home."

"Of course you do," Margot murmured. She patted Arlo's head and walked toward her truck. She paused midstep. "Tootie, when you decided where I was supposed to sleep, why did you put me in Marianne's old cabin instead of the one that belonged to my parents?"

"Well, first of all, I wanted someone close enough to hear me calling for help when I inevitably fall and break my hip when E.J.J. is out of the house. Stan's old cabin is too far away for that. And I did it because I didn't think you were ready to face that memory head-on, yet. You and Stan are still circling each other like cranky bears. You need some time."

"Thank you, Tootie."

"But mostly the hip thing. Those Life Alert commercials scare the hell out of me."

～

KYLE SAT AT his kitchen table, iced tea glass sweating between his hands as Margot gave him an account of Dougie's vigilant defense of animal licensing at Sara Lee's behest. Margot had obtained his address from Marianne, because in small towns, everybody knows everybody's address. The Archer home was an adorable recently built Cape Cod saltbox on the water, with blue shutters and enormous pots of mums growing on either side of the front door. Even from the driveway, Margot could see a dock stretching out behind the house. The wooden sailboat was tethered to the dock, bobbing lazily with the waves.

Hazel had opened the door, wearing a rainbow-striped shirt with a chimpanzee on the chest and electric-blue leggings paired with silver tap shoes. She hadn't greeted Margot in any way, simply yelled for her father and skulked off to her room.

The inside of the house was a little less well kept than the yard. It was clean but cluttered, with dolls—dressed like tiny drag queens?—and coloring books littering the polished wood floor of the large living room. The sofa was huge and squishy-looking, made of a sturdy, dark blue cotton. Paperback detective novels and academic journals were piled high on the coffee table. The degrees missing from Kyle's office were found here—a bachelor's in education from the University of Virginia, a master's from some private college in New York she'd never heard of. Big picture windows framed a beautiful view of the lake, but the long blue curtains that accented them could use a good washing. Overall, the effect was cozy, but it made Margot's hands itch to sort everything into some semblance of order.

Framed pictures were scattered over every spare surface, mostly family shots showing both girls at much younger stages, beaming from the arms of a beautiful dark-haired woman with laughing brown eyes. This must have been Maggie, she mused, noting with a twinge of shameful envy the easy, joyful grin on the younger version of Kyle's face as he stood with his arms wrapped around his wife. They looked like such a happy family. Even shy, solemn Hazel seemed to glow in the way only settled, happy children could. The only dark spot was a baby picture of June, dimpled and chubby, cradled in the arms of a thinner, paler Maggie. Kyle was smiling at the camera, but there were dark circles under his eyes and pinched lines around his mouth. This seemed to be the last picture they'd taken before they lost Maggie.

It was easier to grasp what Kyle had lost, and somehow harder, standing here in the home of a dead woman. Was she wrong to think about Kyle as a potential partner when she couldn't guarantee him anything? What about his girls? She'd never dated a father before. And it was simple to say it didn't matter when those girls weren't in the next room with all their expectations and adorable eyes.

The kitchen, where Kyle led her after he'd recovered from the shock of Margot showing up at his door, was equally homey. From the carefully coordinated spring-green tile and curtains and countertops, there was a sense that at one point someone— Margot guessed Kyle's late wife—had very patiently decorated this kitchen to be a magazine-perfect, "heart of the home"–type room, but since that time, the space had been filmed over with #1 DAD mugs and crayon drawings secured with alphabet magnets. It smelled of some buttery concoction that was bubbling in the oven. It was everything her mother detested in a home—in that there was evidence that people (and, horrors, children!) lived there.

Margot shook her head, somehow feeling guilty for thinking of her mother here, in the home of a woman who had loved her child so much she had literally died for her. So she focused on explaining Sara Lee and her weird struggle for power over what amounted to nothing.

"I can't believe Sara Lee would do this. Who tries to steal someone's dog because they're threatened over a community festival? It's like starting a knife fight over a telethon. It doesn't make any sense!"

"I can give her kids detention," Kyle told her, grimacing. "And head lice. I have that kind of power."

"While I appreciate your willingness to take my anger out on small children, my conscience demands that I say no," she said, sipping her iced tea. It was unsweetened, and therefore didn't make her throat close up when she drank it.

"I could just talk to Sara Lee about her *Game of Thrones*–style attempts to wrestle control of Founders' Day from you."

"I don't need you to fight my battles for me. I didn't come

here to tattle on her," she told him. "I just wanted to warn you that if you receive any mysterious e-mails from 'me' claiming that I want male strippers and a simulated-snow ski ramp in the town square, get a verbal confirmation."

"Well, the head-lice-and-detention offer stands. Sara Lee's oldest son cut four inches off of Hazel's ponytail on the first day of school. He has payback coming."

"How do you deal with this?" Margot asked. "All the petty squabbles and backbiting?"

Kyle rose and grabbed a bag of vegetables from his freezer. He put them in the microwave and set the timer. "You're telling me that you've never dealt with petty squabbles or backbiting in the Junior League set?"

"Yeah, but it was over . . ."

"Important things?"

"Well, more money. Yeah, there's no way for me to finish that sentence without sounding like a pompous ass," Margot conceded.

"Not really," he teased, smirking at her.

"I am never going to fit in here." She sighed. "And a few weeks ago, that really wouldn't have bothered me all that much."

"And now?"

"Well, it doesn't bother me a lot, but it bothers me more than I'm comfortable with," she muttered. He grinned at her and bent to remove a casserole dish from the oven. She couldn't make out the contents of the steaming dish, but she could see that it was crusted over with crispy-looking crushed cornflakes.

"I'm assuming that the programs and presentations are coming along on the kids' end, because I can handle a lot of crises, but mass stage fright from a bunch of third graders is sort of outside the realm of problems I can fix with a sewing kit and a sense of determination," she said.

"We're on track, I promise," he said. "I have a little more control over the staff, since I can fire them if they don't do what I tell them. I can't fire parent volunteers."

Margot lifted a brow. "Can't you?"

June burst into the kitchen in a flurry of yellow tulle.

"Daddy, I'm *starving*," she proclaimed dramatically, sagging against the fridge. The bright yellow tutu she was wearing was offset by a pair of purple-and-black-striped tights and a blue Monster Math Squad T-shirt.

"Oh, June, I don't know how you're still alive after only consuming three packs of Cheez-Its the moment you hit the door after school." June's jaw dropped, her big brown eyes wide with shock. "Yes, I know about the two extra packs. Because I am Dad, and I see all."

June turned her gaze to Margot, who grimaced. "I have no input into this situation at all."

June crawled into Margot's lap and put a hand on either side of her face. "Hi, grocery store lady."

Small children were not at all respectful of personal space bubbles.

Margot pursed her lips, if for no other reason than to keep June's thumbs out of her mouth. "You can call me Margot."

"Where do you live? How old are you? Are you married?"

"I live over on the McCready compound. It's not nice to ask a lady how old she is, and no, I'm not married."

June gasped. "You live with the *funeral people*? That's so creepy."

"June," Kyle said, his tone a little sharp.

"No, she's right," Margot said. "It is occasionally creepy."

"You talk funny," June told her. "Where are you from?"

"I'm from Chicago," she replied.

"Do we sound funny to you?" June asked, with her father's twinkle in her big dark eyes.

Margot nodded. "A little bit, but not like most of the people in town."

June asked, "Are you here to see me?"

"Absolutely, who else would I be here to see?"

"I like your hair. It's even lighter than mine. Is this your real hair or do you dye it like my teacher?" she said, taking the nearest of Margot's loose locks and stretching it across her own forehead, as if she was trying on the lighter shade of blond. Margot tried to ignore her immediate internal warnings about head lice and various germs that June could be carrying home from school, but she did gently tug her hair out of June's grip. And Kyle had brought up the head lice, specifically.

"It's real," Margot said. "But I do add some highlights every once in a while, just to keep things interesting."

"Ms. Marcum tells the other teachers that's what she's doing, when she's standing out in the halls, but she leaves on Friday with a bunch of gray and always comes back without any gray hair. So I think she's doing something else."

"You are very observant," Margot told her. "But you probably shouldn't say anything like that in front of other grown-ups."

June preened at the compliment and seemed to forget the rest. "I like you. Are you going to stay for dinner?"

"Oh, no, I just came over to talk to your daddy for a second. I should be going,"

"No, stay!" June insisted.

Margot glanced at Kyle, shaking her head. "Oh, I couldn't."

"Stay." June growled, flopping her arms over Margot's shoulders and sagging against her.

"What is happening?" Margot whispered, awkwardly patting June's back.

"How do you feel about macaroni and cheese?" Kyle asked, brows lifted as he watched his daughter. The microwave dinged. He pulled out the bag of vegetables and tossed it back and forth between his hands. "And broccoli?"

"I like macaroni and cheese," she said. "No comment on the broccoli because I don't want to be a bad influence on your children."

"Thank you," he said. "June, why don't you go tell your sister it's time for dinner?"

June detached herself from Margot's neck. She pointed her finger in Margot's face. "Don't move."

"I wouldn't dream of it."

"And wash your hands!" Kyle called after her as June ran out of the room. "With soap!"

As an afterthought, he added, "And water!"

"Is the tutu a fashion choice or is there a costume involved?" Margot asked.

"The tutus are an after-school-only accessory," he said. "We have a whole policy about it. We had to write one, after the great tutu war of 2015."

"I think I saw something about that on the news."

"Many lives were lost."

"I don't have to stay, if it's going to make you uncomfortable," she said. "I didn't mean to intrude. I didn't even think about it being dinnertime."

"No, you should stay," he said. "June gets something in her head, expecting that it's going to go a certain way, and then she gets rattled if it changes. As far as the girls know, you're a friend who's helping me plan something for the school. And if you wouldn't mind, I would like to keep it that way. I don't introduce them to women I spend time with . . . outside of the house."

"Understood. I am a mere distant acquaintance. What can I do to help?"

"Well, my cooking skills, such as they are, have been exhausted by this feast you see before you. But could you set the table? The dishes and silverware are out on the counter—I'll grab an extra plate."

June returned, waving her hands in the air and declaring them clean. She helped Margot put four place settings on the table while Kyle poured milk for the girls. Hazel slunk into the kitchen, watching Margot warily. It seemed the older Archer girl didn't like last-minute changes, either. She sat down and began quietly picking at her dinner.

Margot felt very awkward, sitting down with the little family. This was not her place, with Kyle's children, enjoying a home-cooked meal. She decided she would eat as quickly as possible and then make her excuses to run back home.

Kyle's baked macaroni was serviceable, but not much compared to the casseroles her family had left in her fridge over the last few weeks. Still, he'd made sure there was something green on the plate. And the girls were drinking milk without complaint. Clearly he was doing something right.

June kept up a steady stream of chatter about her school day, the mean boy in her class who stole a classmate's lunchtime cupcake, the picture of a dog she'd drawn in art.

"Daddy, can we hang my picture of the dog on the fridge?" June asked.

"Sure," he said, glancing at the crowded fridge. "We may have to cull out some of your earlier works. Your rainbow period is probably going to go."

"That's fine." She sighed. "Because having a picture of a dog is as close as we're going to get to one right now."

"Well played, June," Kyle said, frowning, turning to Margot. "The girls have been doing extra chores and keeping their grades up to prove that they're ready to have a dog."

"We've been waiting for*ever*," June groaned.

"Six weeks," Kyle told Margot. She wondered if she should bring up Aunt Tootie's abundance of dogs, but she was sure Kyle wouldn't appreciate her interjecting in this conversation.

So instead, she said, "My mom wouldn't let me have a dog when I was growing up. She was allergic."

"My mommy died," Hazel said, finally looking up at her as if Margot's response was some sort of personality test.

Kyle went tense, and for a second, Margot got a glimpse of that miserable stranger she'd seen wandering around town. His lips pinched together and he turned his eyes on Margot, pleading and apologizing all at once. He looked so miserable that Margot couldn't find it in her to be irritated by Hazel's indirect challenge. She was a little girl who was sad and angry over an absent parent, and that was something Margot knew something about.

She took a deep breath through her nose and focused on keeping her voice calm. "I know. I'm sorry about that. Do you want to talk about it?"

"Not really," Hazel said, stabbing at her macaroni with her fork.

"Okay, then." Margot scooped a bit of broccoli into her mouth, wincing at the bitter green. She didn't care if it made her a giant child, she would never like the stuff.

"Is your mommy alive?" Hazel asked.

Trying to demonstrate good table manners, Margot dabbed at her mouth with a napkin before answering. "No, she isn't. She passed away about three years ago."

Hazel stared at her long and hard, as if she thought Margot was lying. When Margot didn't blink, a tiny crack seemed to appear in Hazel's icy exterior and she nodded. "I'm sorry."

"Thank you."

"Do you miss her very much?"

Margot tried not to let too much of a conversational lapse go by, because that would be telling. "Sometimes I do."

"Do you cry?" Hazel asked, sounding childlike for the first time since Margot had met her. "Sometimes I cry. And Dad says that's okay."

"Every once in a while," Margot admitted. "And however you want to feel about it is okay."

"And how do you feel?" Hazel asked.

Margot's mouth dropped open, unable to find a child-appropriate answer to a very loaded question.

"Okay, you have mined all of the personal information I'm going to let you try to get out of our dinner guest," Kyle interjected, his bearded cheeks flushing. "What's next? Her Apple ID password? PIN numbers?"

"No one says PIN numbers, Dad!" Hazel cried. "Everything is done with PayPal now!"

"Kids grow up too fast," Margot said, grateful for the break in the conversational tension.

Kyle muttered, "Preaching to the choir."

~

AFTER DINNER, THERE was a nightly routine of baths and homework checks and complicated preventive tangle care to make hairstyles easier in the morning. Margot excused herself from this scene before she was asked to braid, a skill she'd never managed to pick up.

June was loath to let her go, attempting to cling to Margot's leg as she walked into the living room. Hazel wasn't quite as clingy, but her chilly reception had thawed just a little bit.

Kyle walked Margot to the door while his daughters scraped their plates into the garbage. "I'm sorry the girls brought up your mom. I'm sure that was awkward and painful. And I'm sorry about asking you to be . . . remote, but I don't think any of us is ready for someone new to . . ."

"Oh, no, it was fine. Thank you for dinner."

"If I've learned anything from all this, it's that you don't try to gloss over grief."

"I wasn't very close to my mom," she said. "The more I find out about her from people here, the more I understand why we weren't close."

"Well, if you ever want to talk about it—"

"I can guarantee that I won't," she told him, edging toward the open front door. She stepped out into the still-warm evening air, grateful for the bit of breeze coming off the lake.

Kyle's head cocked and his mouth opened, as if he was about to ask her an extremely personal question, but Hazel yelled from the kitchen. "Dad! June hid all of her broccoli in her napkin again!"

Margot burst out laughing, her nose bumping against Kyle's chin. He groaned, his hands coming up to slide around her shoulders and press her close in a quick hug. "I'm sorry."

"Duty calls," she said, smiling. "Good night."

"Duty calls," he agreed, pressing his forehead against hers. He sniffed, separating from her and shouting, "June! Sit back down and prepare for a double helping of broccoli for your dessert!"

"Aw, Dad!"

"No sweets! We're talking total ice cream lockdown!" Kyle called. "Don't make me get the kale!"

"NOOOOOO!"

IN THE SPIRIT of cooperation, Margot had arrived at the Founders' Festival Parents' Workday (also known as Saturday morning at the elementary school gym) with her best smile and her brand-new glue gun. Alas, her enthusiasm to help the locals put together booths and handicrafts was not returned.

First, Jimmy Greenway met her at the door and tried to tell her that the PTA officers were holding an official closed meeting, but Sweet Johnnie waved her in cheerfully.

"Hey, shug!" Sweet Johnnie cried, throwing an arm around her. "I'm so glad you're here, because we can't seem to get the easels to stay upright without supergluing them. The flyers are printed on the wrong color paper. And Sara Lee called all of the information booth volunteers and told them that they're not needed. And I'm havin' to make a lot of apology phone calls."

Margot sighed. The board had agreed to establish "Ask Me Anything" booths, staffed by volunteers, on every corner, to help tourists navigate the festival. Sara Lee hadn't seen the point in them, since "everybody around here knows everybody anyway."

"Okay, one thing at a time. How bad are the flyers? Could we use them even if they're on the wrong color paper?"

Sweet Johnnie pulled an example out of her back pocket. It was printed on dark blue paper, so the black print was barely readable, even up close. Margot shook her head. "So, no."

Sweet Jonnie muttered, "Sara Lee insisted that dark blue would show up best on bulletin boards. I bought some lighter blue paper at the Office Supply Warehouse."

"Does Mr. Archer mind if we use the school's copy room to make up some replacement flyers?"

Across the gym, Kyle was nailing together booths with some of the other dads. Between the beard, the white V-neck T-shirt, and the hammer in his hand, he looked like a commercial for extremely flattering jeans. As if he could hear her thinking dirty thoughts about his denim wear, Kyle turned and waved. She waggled her fingers.

"Yeah, Mr. Archer said we could use his copy code," Sweet Johnnie said. "He was very sweet about it."

"Great, I'll just go get started," Margot said.

"Oh, no need," Mr. Greenway said, holding up a thick stack of light blue flyers advertising the festival. "I just made the copies. My old copy code still works, you know."

"Thank you, Mr. Greenway," Margot said through gritted teeth. She turned to Sweet Johnnie. "Okay, what about the easels? What can I do to help there?"

Sara Lee sidled up to Margot with a sly smirk on her face. "Don't bother. My Robbie put them together. Some things just need a little force so they can find their place."

Margot sneered at Sara Lee. "Gee, thanks, Sara Lee."

She turned to Sweet Johnnie, who was watching the exchange with an alarmed expression. "If you give me the contact list for the Ask Me Anything volunteers, I'll call them and explain that they are needed, despite some misguided claims to the contrary. I'm used to making professional-grade apologies for other people's screw-ups."

"Oh, we don't need you for that," a skinny brunette with a startling amount of red highlights piped up from behind Sara Lee. "I already took care of it."

Margot's mouth dropped open. Were these people seriously conspiring to keep her from helping with a community festival? Did they not have better uses for their time? Margot glanced at Mr. Greenway, who seemed to be lording his ability to make copies at will over Kyle. No, apparently they did not.

"How did you even know to do that, Katie Beth?" Sweet Johnnie asked. "I didn't ask anybody to make those calls. How did you know what to say?"

"Sara Lee told me what was needed," Katie Beth protested. "She's in charge, isn't she?"

"No, she's not," Sweet Johnnie cried. "Mr. Archer brought Margot in because nothing was getting done. Because we keep arguing over silly things, like a bunch of dang children."

"Look, it really doesn't matter who's in charge," Margot said. "I'm only here to help. We're all here for the same reason, which is to make the festival as successful as possible and help bring visitors into the town."

"Well, we don't see the point in you being here," Sara Lee shot back. "We don't know you. You don't know anything about this town. And you don't even have kids at this school. You know, you really have to be a *mother* to help out around here. Otherwise you're just in the way."

"If you think childlessness is my soft underbelly, you are jabbing at the wrong spot," Margot said with a snort. Sara Lee rolled her eyes. "And sending the dogcatcher to Aunt Tootie's house? That's bush league. I'm not scared of you. I'm not going to be intimidated away from helping just because it makes you unhappy. Look, you're terrible at this. I'm not saying this to hurt you, you just are. Mr. Archer wouldn't have called me in, otherwise. I don't care who gets the credit. Take all the credit, as far as I'm concerned. But I refuse to let this thing fall flat because you're too shortsighted to realize when you're in over your head. There is one voice that matters here, one directive, and it's mine, and if you have a problem with it, there's the door."

"You can't throw me out of a volunteer work day," Sara Lee shot back.

Margot smiled brightly. "Watch me."

Sara Lee hissed, her asymmetrical hair clinging to her left cheek. "You're crazy, just like your daddy."

Margot's eyes narrowed.

"What's going on here?" Kyle asked.

Sara Lee's expression turned all peaches and cream. "Just a little debate about who does what."

"That's right, just a little difference of opinion," Margot said. Her hand had twitched around her glue gun like Clint Eastwood's in a spaghetti Western. Sara Lee flinched. But Margot merely smirked at her.

"I'll just go see if Robbie needs any help," Sara Lee simpered as she tottered off toward a man who looked like a jock gone to seed. Sara Lee's supporters peeled away, leaving Margot with Sweet Johnnie and Kyle.

"Why do I feel like I missed something important?" Kyle asked.

"I've never seen anyone talk to Sara Lee that way, not even when we were kids," Sweet Johnnie whispered.

"She's not nearly as scary as she thinks she is," Margot assured her. "I just can't believe she's putting this much energy into excluding me from the Founders' Festival. It's hardly the Field Museum Gala."

"Well, I don't know what that is, but you need to watch Sara Lee. She's mean as hell when you cross her." Sweet Johnnie cast an apologetic glance at Kyle. "Sorry, I know you have to work with her for the PTA. I don't want to put you in an awkward position."

"Oh, no, she's awful," Kyle agreed. "And Sweet Johnnie's right, she fights dirty. You saw what she did with Tootie's dogs. Last year, Ike's wife demanded to see the reports for the school's Christmas wrap fund-raiser and the Rise and Shine got ten health department complaints called in on them in the next week."

Margot frowned. "Did Sara Lee ever turn the fund-raiser reports over?"

Kyle shrugged. "I had to make my own breakfast for more than a week until Ike got the mess straightened out. That whole time is one big blur."

～

SEVERAL DAYS LATER—after Margot had removed most of the poster-board glitter out of her hair—she shuffled down the dock toward the Snack Shack in a distinct funk. Not even the sparkle of the early-autumn sun on the lake could cheer her. She slumped into the shack, sliding onto one of the stools at the counter, and balanced her chin on her hand. The Snack Shack was a cozy little space, decorated in red vinyl and early Coca-Cola memorabilia. The chalkboard behind the counter listed the deep-fried specials of the day. Margot had come to worship at this altar to cholesterol, hoping it would keep her from falling into some sort of vocational depression.

Leslie was standing at an enormous bubbling cauldron of oil, deftly turning some golden-brown lumps over with a pair of chopsticks. Donna was sitting at the counter, sipping a cup of coffee. "Hey, Aunt Leslie. Aunt Donna."

"Hey there," Donna said. "You look like a freshly smacked ass."

"What is wrong with you?" Margot asked, shaking her head.

"Why the long face, shug?" Leslie asked gently, plucking the lumps from their fry bath and popping them onto a plate.

"Well, I got a callback on one of the résumés I sent out," Margot said, watching as Leslie sprinkled powdered sugar on the plate and slid it in front of her.

"But that should be good news, right? It gets you out of town, and that's what you want," said Stan as he slid onto the stool at her right. Margot could hear the intentional gentling of his tone, as if he was struggling not to sound judgmental. "I need a refill for the coffee vats, Les. The Brooks visitation is starting up in twenty minutes."

Margot's lips pinched together. Damn it, why hadn't she heard Stan following her out on the deck? He wasn't exactly stealthy. And while she hadn't wandered to the Snack Shack looking for a sympathetic ear, she would rather lean on Leslie's shoulder without Stan around to hear about her latest round of humiliation. His knowing what had just happened would somehow make it that much worse.

"No problem," Donna said as Leslie set about making her specialty sludge in an industrial-size coffee brewer. "Margot was about to tell me why she looks like somebody just gave her socks for secret Santa."

"I did that *one time*, woman," Stan said. "Bob told me you were running low on socks."

Margot snorted.

"What's wrong, girl?" Stan asked, in a tone far gentler than he'd ever used in her presence. "Ya are looking pretty down in the mouth for someone who just got a job offer."

Margot pressed her fingertips between her scrunched brows. "I didn't get a job offer."

"Then why did they call back?" Donna asked.

Margot shoved her hands through her loose blond hair. She would not cry in front of her father. She might cry later, in her bathtub, drinking off-brand pinot noir from a Solo cup, but she would not cry now. Even if it meant staring at the ceiling and pretending that her contacts were dry.

"I got a callback from Soiree, a really great company in New York. I mean, one of my pie-in-the-sky dream jobs that I didn't think I had a shot at, but I applied for because I had nothing to lose. They sent me an e-mail yesterday and asked me to set up a Skype session this afternoon. I cleared it with E.J.J., and I set up the webcam at my desk so I could look all professional and impressive. And when I opened up the chat window, I thought it was sort of strange that there were six people sitting in the room, staring at the monitor. I mean, sometimes you have panel interviews when you're applying at some of the larger firms, but none of the people on the screen looked old enough to be managers or partners. Bethenny, the recruiter who e-mailed me, wasn't on camera, but she started asking me questions. They were normal interview questions at first, my educational background, my internships, early work history."

Margot pressed her forehead into her hands. "And then Bethenny started asking about the greenhouse gala, asking me what I thought led to the 'crisis' and what I would do differently now to prevent the same thing from happening. I thought it was normal for her to ask about it. I mean, I wasn't surprised they'd heard about the flamingo incident. And I didn't blame them for wanting to know whether I'd learned from it, if they were going to hire me. But then the off-camera woman started asking the people sitting in front of the camera where *they* thought I'd gone wrong, how they would have handled it differently, and what sort of office policies could be written to prevent a 'disaster' like this in the future. She was using me as a teaching tool for her underlings! I was giving a TED Talk without even realizing it."

"Aw, honey, that's awful," Leslie said.

"I interrupted their brutal postmortem of my every decision and asked whether this was standard interview procedure, and Bethenny *laughed*. She said she thought my application was a joke, that there was no way I really thought I would be hired on to their company after what I'd done. And she thought I understood that this was a 'learning opportunity' for her employees."

Donna frowned. "Tell you what. If anyone asks where me and Duffy are tomorrow, tell them we're on an all-day charter and don't offer any extra details."

"Why?" Margot asked.

"So we have an alibi when that snotty bitch's office burns down," Donna said with a shrug.

"As much as I appreciate the offer of carefully orchestrated arson, that won't be necessary."

"Oh, that's okay, we can downgrade to filling their office with bees. Rubbing every toilet seat with poison ivy. Hiding a dead bass under a couch cushion in what's-her-face's office so it will stink for weeks and she won't be able to figure out why."

Margot glanced at Stan and Leslie, neither of whom seemed fazed by Donna's speedy list of disturbing revenge tactics. "Again, thank you, but no. I went back and checked my e-mails with Bethenny and realized she hadn't called it an interview. She'd called it a 'session.' So I can't even get upset with them."

"Well, sure you can," Stan said, frowning. "They acted like assholes. You can get mad at assholes. Even Tootie 'Turn the Other Cheek' McCready accepts that."

Margot groaned. "I think I was more embarrassed than anything else. No, wait, I'm angry, too. You know what really makes me angry? I'm angry because those snot-nosed little *interns* were picking apart my work and my decisions, like they could have done any better under the circumstances. Like I could have psychically detected the chef's intention to serve the mayor's wife an allergen and then incinerated the shrimp tower with the power of my mind." Margot sighed. "No, that's not it. I'm angry because I let my guard down. I walked right into a humiliating trap and didn't even realize it. I used to be much more cynical. I had the detachment that would have protected my feelings in a case like this. I wouldn't have fallen for vague, misleading language. And even if I did, I wouldn't have let it bother me so much. I think living out in the country is making me soft."

"Not soft," Leslie insisted. "Softer, maybe. But you're still plenty cynical, sweetheart, trust me. People around here still talk about how intimidating you are."

"Thank you, Aunt Leslie." Margot sniffed. Stan, on the other hand, simply stared at her, frowning and saying nothing. Margot deflated just a little bit more. How disappointing for him, to find out the daughter who'd devoted all her time to her career was failing at keeping that career. She knew she shouldn't have said anything in front of him.

"You know what I've learned?" Stan asked.

Margot lifted her head and saw that, yes, it was her father who had just spoken and not some helpful bystander. "No, Stan, what have you learned?"

"Sometimes life just stinks like a bass in your couch," Stan said. "It's not fair. And sometimes it doesn't get better. And sometimes there's no reason for it. It just stinks. You can either lean into it and try to ride it out, or you can fold under the weight."

Margot didn't mean to frown at her father, she really didn't. But who was Stan to lecture her on pulling herself up by her bootstraps when he was living in a sleeping cubby at a funeral home? She almost opened her mouth to ask Stan to leave her with Aunt Leslie to discuss the matter, but he followed up with "I know I haven't spent much time around ya. But I don't think you're a 'fold under the weight' kind of gal. So you misunderstood an e-mail, big deal. You got embarrassed in front of a bunch of interns. Who cares? In a couple of months, some other catastrophe will catch their attention and they won't even think about your flamingo problem. You just keep plugging along. You'll be fine."

Margot mulled that over for a moment or two and nodded. "Thank you."

"Well, you don't have to be a smartass about it," Stan snapped.

"No, really, I appreciate it. That was helpful."

Stan seemed confused for a moment, like Margot was going to take it back. "Any time."

Stan didn't smile. There was no affectionate ruffling of her hair as he slid off the stool and carried the huge jug of Leslie's coffee down the dock toward the funeral home.

Leslie placed a tall Coke with lots of ice in front of Margot. "Here, hon, you're looking sort of pale."

Margot took a long draw from the foam cup.

"You sure you're all right?" Donna asked.

"I just had a conversation with a parent that didn't end in yelling or recriminations," Margot said. "It only took me thirty years."

"Oh, honey, most people don't get that until they're in their fifties." Leslie reached over the counter and patted Margot's hand. Margot grinned at her, shaking her head.

"What exactly am I supposed to be eating?" Margot asked, poking at the large fried dough ball on her plate.

"You know those chocolate cupcakes with the little white swirls on top?"

"You deep-fried a Hostess cupcake?" Margot marveled.

Leslie giggled. "Well, sure, if it works for Twinkies, why not?"

"Prepare yourself," Donna warned her.

Margot pushed her fork through the dough ball, eyes widening as a chocolatey ooze emerged from the center. The first bite was warm and crispy and sweet, like a doughnut and a hush puppy had a beautiful baby.

"This should not be as good as it is," Margot said with a sigh, digging in for a second bite.

Leslie smiled brightly. "See?"

MARGOT WAS WARY of opening her personal e-mail account for almost a week after the prank interview. She didn't want to be tricked into being an object lesson twice. She wondered if word of her "misunderstanding" had spread to her former colleagues. Was she even more of a laughingstock than she had been before?

Maybe she would end up staying in Lake Sackett long term after all. Her job search was still pretty much at a standstill, but was that such a terrible thing? She was getting used to her little cottage. She was getting used to driving twenty minutes when she forgot milk. The cost of living was low. She had pretty decent job security and a comfortable living situation. She was starting to appreciate her work at the funeral home, bringing order to the chaos that followed death, bringing comfort to people just by handling the little details that were beyond their grasp.

And she was making friends . . . okay, she was becoming closer with her cousins. She'd established a routine of going to Frankie's cabin on Saturdays for terrible mutant shark movies and fruity drinks. Marianne joined them when she could, but sometimes she called with excuses about the boys' soccer schedule—which Frankie interpreted as "sexytimes with the hot backwoods hubby." Inevitably, Arlo would find a way to skirt around Frankie's door and snuggle under Margot's arm on the couch. And if she happened to feed him a couple of kernels of popcorn she dropped, it wasn't a gesture of doggy friendship. She just didn't want to waste food.

Duffy had managed to talk her onto his boat on a few afternoons when he didn't have charters, but she absolutely refused to fish again. She was content to learn how to drive the pontoon and indulge in a long list of important Oprah-level books she'd always meant to read but never had time to in the city, while Duffy fished and chatted about nothing at all. She'd asked about Lana, the aggressively skanky ex-wife, but Duffy shut her down by offering her sweet tea and a deep-fried Twinkie and then ignoring the question. She would miss her cousins if she left. She would miss E.J.J. She would miss Uncle Bob and Aunt Leslie. Okay, she was still afraid of Aunt Donna, but she would miss that little ripple of fear down her spine when Donna made eye contact. And Tootie, how would she get along without Aunt Tootie being all inspirational and then snarky by turns?

Her father. Well, they'd had one nice conversation. That was more progress than either of them had expected.

And then there was Kyle. She had no idea what was happening there. Maybe it was a friendship. Maybe it was one of those badly timed flirtations that would never take off. But it didn't feel wrong.

Maybe it wouldn't be a fate worse than death, making Lake Sackett her permanent home.

When a Saturday night kept Frankie at work (a car wreck involving a local mechanic versus a deer) and Marianne at home (she claimed Nate had a soccer game, but Duffy saw her picking up strawberries and wine at the grocery), Margot decided to drop by Kyle's house. She didn't even use the excuse of planning for the festival, because everything was well in hand, thank you very much. She just wanted to see him and she wanted him to know that she wanted to see him. Pretense was going to choke the life out of whatever it was between them, and she wasn't going to have it.

She was surprised to find him sitting on the end of his dock, watching the September sun sinking into the horizon. The girls were nowhere to be seen, which made her a little uneasy. But she noted that Kyle was drinking a beer, something she guessed he wouldn't do around the kids. And he seemed to be scowling off into the distance. His hunched shoulders and angry expression reminded her of that troubled wraith she'd first met.

But now he wasn't just some fascinating possible phantom. He was a man with a history she understood, and she wasn't sure if that made it easier or more difficult to see him like this. He didn't move as she walked down the dock, though it was impossible that he missed her footsteps. The sound of crickets chirping was the only noise to compete with her boots against the wood.

Margot stood in front of him, offering him the large bottle of Gold City Growler, a local craft beer Duffy had recommended. Kyle reached up to accept it, his brow creased and his eyes lost. "Bad night?" she asked.

"Eh," he said, waggling his hand back and forth. She dropped to her butt, sliding against his side. He leaned his head against her temple. She waited for him to talk, not wanting to rush him, watching the sky turn the water purple and dull. Eventually he ended up draped bonelessly across her lap as she ran her fingers through his hair.

"Want to talk about it?" she asked, cracking open the fresh

bottle and taking a short pull. She wasn't much of a beer drinker, or any sort of beer drinker, really. But she could appreciate how the bitter bubbles complemented the setting better than fruity girly drinks.

"I'm confused by you," he muttered against her denim-clad leg.

She frowned but didn't stop stroking his hair. "Because?"

"I shouldn't want you. You're fancy and bossy and you're going to leave town at the first chance you get. I don't think I'm ready for whatever this is. But I want you. I want to see where this goes. I haven't wanted anything like it in a long time and that makes me feel sort of terrible."

"How drunk are you right now?" she asked.

"Eh," he said, sitting up and waggling his hand again.

"So this diatribe about you being scared of relationships is based on real feelings and not alcohol?"

"I'm not afraid of relationships. I'm skittish. Don't judge me."

"I don't have room to judge anyone about that. I haven't been in a committed relationship in . . . I don't think I've ever been in a committed relationship. I never had the time. Or really the desire. That's sad. Is that sad?"

"A little," he said, shrugging. "I thought that I would be safer if I didn't want anybody for more than something physical. I thought I could keep all the pieces of me separate. The dad. The man. The guy who wears a poncho to avoid a cafeteria food bath. The parts of me that laugh every time you open your mouth. The pieces of me that want to tear your clothes off. The even more complicated bits that sit in awe when you take down snotty soccer moms. But I can't. It's stupid to try."

He dropped his head to her shoulder. "I loved my wife. I'm always going to love her. And for a long time I thought that meant punishing myself for outliving her." He tipped his forehead against hers. "I don't want to do that anymore."

She palmed his jaw, tilting her head as she rubbed a thumb over his chin. "So don't."

The corner of his mouth lifted in a sad half smile. He leaned forward and pressed a hesitant kiss against her lips, and then another and another, each hungrier than the last. She rolled onto her knees, making him rise to meet her, returning those kisses with equal energy. She clutched at his hair, pulling him closer as the tension seemed to bleed out of his body.

The hands around her back relaxed and slid along her ribs. The kisses that had been so fervent just a minute before slowed into a lazy dance.

Kyle looped his arm under her legs and pulled them up from what could end up being a precarious position on the dock. He hitched her legs around his hips and walked her toward the house. And given the firm weight she felt wedged against her as they moved, she had a pretty good idea she wasn't being invited in for sweet tea.

"Girls?" she murmured against his lips, rubbing her cheek on the scruff of his beard.

"Sleepovers," he said, catching the line of her jaw between his teeth.

"You really don't have to carry me *all* the way to the bedroom," she said as he managed to open his back door with one hand.

"Oh, thank God," he said, dropping her to her feet. "I know it was romantic as hell, but I was reaching muscle failure somewhere on the back porch."

She snickered, tugging on his shirttail as she backed down his hallway. He kicked off his shoes and then bent over to yank at the button of her jeans. Giggling, she nudged off her own shoes and pressed him against the hallway wall to tackle his pants.

Stepping through the bedroom door, she yelped, jerking her foot up from the floor and nearly kneeing Kyle in the crotch. He dodged, throwing himself against the wall to avoid the crushing blow.

"What in the hell!" she cried, hopping on her good leg while she tried to dig a tiny sharp object out of the sole of her foot.

"Is this a tiny hooker shoe?" she said, holding up the offending bit of pink plastic.

"Barbie shoes," Kyle said, shaking his head and supporting her arms while she massaged her foot. "Everybody bitches about LEGOs. But those mini platforms are the real danger to parental feet."

"You get wordy when you're drunk."

"Not that drunk. Here, let me help." Margot cried out when Kyle lifted her off her feet, but instead of sweeping her up bridal style, he swung her onto his back and carried her piggyback toward the bed. It was unexpected, like most things about Kyle.

She noticed that while there were lots of dust catchers and photos in the common areas of the house, there was only one photo here—one of Hazel and June smiling from a pile of pumpkins. The room would have been considered spartan if not for the wide, inviting bed situated in front of a picture window. Moonlight streamed through the glass as he tugged at the catch on her bra.

"I haven't brought anyone back here," he told her. "Ever."

"I understand. It's been a while since I've done this," she admitted as he pushed her onto the bed. She scooted back on the mattress as he crawled along with her, caging her against the bed.

"It's like falling off a bicycle," he promised, then frowned. "Or something like that."

He trailed his lips over her jawline and she turned her head so he could get better access to her neck. Her panties disappeared over his shoulder. Warmth flooded her middle and she sighed at the lovely, slippery sensations between her thighs. She made "eye contact" with Hazel and Juniper's photo in the frame by the bed and winced.

Kyle lifted his head and saw where she was staring. He reached over and flipped the picture frame facedown on the nightstand. When she arched an eyebrow, he shrugged. The heat of his fingers burned her thighs as he parted them and slipped his hips against her. She leaned up and closed her lips over his. He sighed into her mouth, his beard tickling her cheeks as he wrapped her legs around his waist.

A deft hand skimmed over her belly button and between her thighs, the thumb ghosting around but never quite touching the little bundle of nerves there. She laughed, gasping, as she shifted her hips, chasing his fingers. He snickered, because apparently he was a tease.

"All right, then," she whispered, grasping him in her hand. He yelped softly and dropped his head to her shoulder.

"Okay, okay," he whimpered, pinching her lightly and making her cry out. Two long fingers smoothed the way inside of her and her breath came in short pants against his shoulder. He fluttered them inside her and she gripped him even tighter. He canted into her hand and the smile against his skin was full of wicked promise.

Margot heard the crinkle of a foil packet and was grateful that she didn't have to argue for one. Kyle paused just before the long, slow slide into her and said, "This may not last long. But what I lack in initial endurance, I will make up for in enthusiasm and repeat performances."

Margot's answering cackle was stopped short as he thrust home and pulled the blankets over their heads.

12

$\mathcal{M}$ARGOT STRETCHED OUT over the soft cotton sheets and groaned, throwing her arm across her eyes to protect them from the morning light. She hadn't slept so soundly since . . . ever, really. She hadn't dreamed. She hadn't woken up worrying about some random detail for work. She vaguely remembered hearing Kyle's phone ring sometime in the night and him climbing out of bed. But she'd just rolled over and gone back to sleep.

This, by itself, was unusual for her. In the city, she'd rarely slept over with any of her dates. She hated the phrase *hit it and quit it*, but she'd generally walked out the door before the sheets cooled. And she'd been careful to keep evenings from ending at her apartment, so she didn't have to worry about awkwardly nudging the guy toward the sidewalk in the morning. She couldn't decide whether her falling asleep so hard that she didn't scoot out the door was a sign of how Kyle had exhausted her.

She smiled, pulling the sheets over her face. She should probably have been embarrassed by the demands and . . . sounds she'd made. But she wasn't. While a lot of things about whatever she had with Kyle were complicated, in bed they were deliciously simple. And repetitive. She would face the rest another time.

Kyle slipped through the bedroom door and shut it behind him. She propped herself up on her elbows, holding one eye closed as she adjusted to the sunlight. "Morning."

He stopped and exhaled loudly. "Something came up late last night, and I don't want to be rude, but—"

A cheerful voice called down the hall, "Daddy?"

Margot gasped and contemplated throwing the blankets over her head again. Kyle tossed her a worn blue plaid flannel robe that smelled like him. Margot scrambled into it, belting it over her shirt and panties.

"Just don't panic and we can get through this," he said.

"Okay."

"Daddy?"

Margot's eyes went wide as the bedroom door swung open and Hazel bounced in. Margot tugged the belt just a tiny bit tighter. Hazel skidded to a halt, the tiniest bit of scowl mixed with the surprise on her face. Kyle grimaced.

"Hi, Miss Margot. Did you have a sleepover with Daddy last night?"

"Oh, uh—" Margot looked up at Kyle, silently begging him to give her some appropriate information to impart to his daughter. His face went blank, as if he was mentally transporting himself to a magical place where he *wasn't* getting caught with a girl in his bed like a naughty teenager. That was decidedly unhelpful.

"What happened to not panicking?" Margot asked.

Kyle cleared his throat. "Margot came by to visit because she knew I would be lonely without you girls here."

Hazel lifted a dark eyebrow and turned to Margot. "Really?"

Margot pursed her lips and nodded. "Mm-hmm."

"Hazel woke up sick to her tummy around four this morning," Kyle said, giving Margot a significant look. "I couldn't wake you up. You are a very heavy sleeper."

Margot blanched at the note of accusation in his voice. "I'm sorry. I'm usually a very light sleeper. I must have really dropped off."

Kyle's lips pressed together in a thin line. Margot's mouth assumed a similar pose. This was not good.

"You stayed all night?" Hazel asked.

Margot glanced at Kyle, who seemed to be frozen in horror. "Mm-hmm."

Hazel patted her hand solemnly. "That's better than I did. I had to call Daddy to come pick me up."

"Oh, well, that happens to everybody," Margot assured Hazel, who was tugging her away from the bed and down the hall. Margot walked carefully, trying to keep Kyle's robe from flapping open and revealing her pants-less state. "When I was a kid, I had to call my father to come get me from Brittany Lowell's slumber party because we watched a really scary horror movie and I didn't want to be there anymore. But I told everybody I had a headache and needed to go home to get some medicine."

"Did anybody make fun of you?" Hazel asked.

"No," Margot told her, glancing away. And in a way, it was true, no one made fun of her for leaving the party. But Mother wouldn't just let her go to bed. She'd questioned her like it was a job, demanding details. Was she really sick? Had someone said something mean to her? Had someone on the Lowells' household staff done something inappropriate? But even at age nine, she'd known it didn't come from a place of motherly concern. Linda was looking for something to hold over the Lowells.

Hazel plopped down at the kitchen table, interrupting her train of thought. "Was Mr. Stan mad at you when he had to come pick you up in his pajamas?"

Kyle pulled her chair away from the table and pressed a mug of coffee into Margot's hand. She took an experimental sip and was pleased that a beverage in Lake Sackett didn't threaten to melt her esophagus. Kyle began moving around the stove, grabbing pans and canisters and mixing bowls.

Hazel tugged at her sleeve, asking impatiently, "Miss Margot, did Mr. Stan get mad when he had to come get you from the sleepover?"

"Oh, it wasn't Mr. Stan," Margot said, shaking her head. "This was when I lived in Chicago. I didn't know Mr. Stan back then."

"But I thought Mr. Stan was your daddy."

Kyle glanced up from the stove, where he was pouring batter onto a griddle pan. Margot took a deep drink of her coffee to stall for time. "Well, my mom moved away with me when I was really little, and I didn't get to meet Mr. Stan until a couple of months ago. I had what you might call a 'bonus dad.'"

"Was your bonus daddy nice?"

Civil and distant could still be considered "nice," right?

Margot smiled. "Sure, he was."

"So does he live with you now?" Hazel asked.

"Actually, he lives in England right now."

"Where Queen Elizabeth lives?" Hazel exclaimed.

"Well, not in the same neighborhood or anything, but he lives in London, yes," Margot said.

Kyle slid a plate full of banana pancakes in front of Hazel. "Hazel went through a princess phase last year and got sort of obsessed with Queen Elizabeth. She did a class presentation on her. She did a book report on a Queen Elizabeth biography for kids. She dressed up as Queen Elizabeth for Halloween."

"You know, there are worse female role models. Any number of former Disney starlets come to mind," Margot said as Kyle buttered and cut Hazel's pancakes.

"Daddy, aren't you going to make Miss Margot something to eat?"

"Oh, no," Margot said, shaking her head. "I couldn't. I'm just going to go change."

Kyle nodded. "Sounds good."

Margot practically ran for the bedroom. Throwing on her clothes, she could practically hear her own angry lecture in her head. She'd never dated a single father precisely because she wanted to avoid awkward situations like this. It wasn't okay for a kid to see her father's date doing the walk of shame. Hazel didn't need to know that she'd slept over. Hazel didn't even need to know her dad was romantically involved with someone until that relationship was serious. Growing up, Margot had seen too many friends faced with a constantly revolving roster of "uncles" and stepmoms. She knew how confusing and upsetting that was for them. Margot didn't want to give Kyle's girls the wrong impression.

This had been a mistake. She'd been an idiot to think she could get involved with a widower without getting entangled in his family life. She wasn't prepared for this. Did she like his children? Yes. Was she ready for a package deal that included the most humiliating pancakes in history? No.

Margot caught sight of herself in the mirror and winced. Her hair was a total rat's nest and she had beard burn . . . in so many places.

Kyle met her in the hallway. "So, it's probably better if you went home."

As much as it stung, Margot nodded. "I was already on my way out."

"I'm sorry. I just— I don't want to confuse the girls, to make them think there's something more here. I just don't want them to get used to you being around."

"Right." Margot swallowed thickly.

"I mean, not because—you said it yourself, you're not staying. And I'm not ready. They're not ready. This was just too soon."

"Right, please stop explaining. I'll see you around. Tell Hazel . . . don't tell her anything. Never mind."

He leaned close, hesitating before his lips could touch hers. She pulled back and followed his line of sight over her shoulder to Hazel. She was watching the scene with a little furrow of worry between her brows. Margot's heart squeezed at the expression, remembering that little line as something she'd seen in her own reflection as a girl. Always worrying, never comfortable, never sure of her place. Margot stepped back from Kyle. "Goodbye, Hazel, have a good day."

"You, too!" she said, turning back to the kitchen.

"Uh, before you go, I got you something," Kyle said, reaching into the coat closet and pulling out a small silver gift bag. "I was going to give it to you last night, but we got . . . distracted."

"Oh, I couldn't."

"I found it online," he said as she opened the bag to find a box labeled URBAN SOUNDSCAPES SLEEP MACHINE. "Normally, people want nature sounds, the ocean, crickets, that sort of thing. But this one sounds like traffic or sirens or any sort of city noise you want."

"Thank you, that is very sweet," she told him. "It's one of the nicest presents anyone has ever given me."

And sadly, it was. She couldn't remember the last time a man had given her a gift that she needed, something he put thought into and purchased based on something she'd said. Her previous lovers usually stuck with the flashy items like flowers and jewelry. She felt a weird, warm rush of . . . something . . . in her chest, and pressed the heel of her hand to her sternum.

Was this what a heart attack felt like?

"I'll call you," he said absently, glancing over his shoulder.

"Mm-hmm," she said, scooting out the door as quickly as possible.

Margot speed-walked toward her truck, climbing into the driver's seat and wincing at the stiff ache in her thighs. And that just brought up mental images of all the things she and Kyle had done the night before. Things that she wouldn't be doing again anytime soon, because she was pretty sure she'd just received a very firm brush-off from a man who had no interest in presenting her to his daughters as a long-term fixture in his life. Which was fine with her, really, except that it hurt more than she expected.

She sighed and bounced her forehead against the steering wheel.

So. Very. Complicated.

~

SEVERAL EVENINGS LATER, Margot opened the front door to her cabin while talking on her cell phone and found Frankie and

Marianne standing in her kitchen, putting frozen orange juice concentrate, blue gummy bears, and vodka into her blender. Margot dangled her house key from her keychain and threw her arm up, as if to say *Why do I bother?*

Frankie and Marianne both shrugged in response and continued with their amateur mixology experiment.

"Manny, Manny, listen to me. I know that you don't do pro bono work. I wouldn't ask you to work for free, especially in this big of a rush. I'm asking you to work at a discount. A deep, *deep* discount."

Marianne winced.

"So I'm not going to remind you of how I introduced you to all of my clients in the charitable circles so you could climb out of the super-saver coupon basement and into the world of high-end printables—despite the fact that your office is located in the boonies."

"I'm forty minutes outside of Chicago, Margot."

"Same thing. And I'm not even going to remind you of the time your nephew-slash-unpaid-intern decided it would be hilarious to add extra Fs to the presentation folders for the Chicago Endowment for the Arts and I managed to catch them before they were distributed at CEA's annual luncheon."

Frankie's mouth dropped open into a delighted O and she silently clapped her hands. It was an odd contrast to her Grumpy Cat T-shirt.

Margot rolled her eyes at her cousin and grinned. "I will simply remind you that we're friends, and friends do favors for each other, especially when reciprocated favors are long overdue."

On the other end of the line, Manny sighed. "You just had to bring up the Endowment for the Farts, didn't you?"

"Yes, I did." Margot shrugged out of her suit jacket and put it into her tiny closet, along with her shoes. Marianne handed her a frosted glass full of orange slush topped with a layer of floating blue bits. Margot took a sip of the tart, delicious blend, trying her hardest to steer her lips around the cold chewy orbs of gummy candy. She loved her cousins, but there were limits.

Behind Marianne, Frankie held up a DVD copy of *Sharktopus vs. Whalewolf.* Margot shook her head vehemently. Frankie pouted. Marianne held up a copy of *The Vow.* Margot shook her head just as hard. Marianne pouted.

While this pantomime played out, Manny was still speaking. "You're asking a lot, honey. Four-color glossy for seven different brochures? You know that's a chore."

"But they're short runs, Manny. And I'm uploading the files to your FTP site as we speak. I did all the design work myself and they've already been proofed. I just need you to hit print. I'll drive to Moncrief myself to pick them up. And you know I hate Moncrief."

Manny exhaled through his nostrils. Loudly.

"It's going to help a lot of people, Manny," she added.

"Gah, okay. But I'm using this as a tax write-off, Margot."

"I will swear an affidavit that you are Moncrief's foremost humanitarian."

"I miss you, doll. None of the girls at Elite Elegance give me nearly as much shit as you do."

"I prefer to think of it as challenging you, emotionally and morally," she said.

"That, too. Talk to you soon, okay?"

"Absolutely. Love to Maria and the kids." Ending the call, Margot drank a good portion of her grown-up slushy, blue bits and all, and raised it in victory. "I don't want to be obnoxious right now, but I am amazing."

Frankie said, "So that's what you're like in your natural habitat."

"What do you mean?"

"Well, usually you're uncertain and edgy in that 'lion with a thorn in its paw' sort of way. But you couldn't have been more self-assured just now. Like Jesus himself had come down and said, 'Order as many brochures as you want, Margot,'" Marianne said. "I just get the feeling that's more 'you' than you've been since you got here."

"Does Jesus really involve himself in printing orders?" Margot asked. "Also, why do I even bother locking the door if you two are just going to break in and abuse my small appliances?"

"We don't know, really," Frankie said. "Everybody knows where the spare keys are."

"Also, why gummy bears?" Margot asked, holding up her drink.

"We were going for an alcoholic bubble tea sort of thing. But tapioca is disgusting," Frankie told her.

Margot shrugged. "On this, we agree."

"So you're really kicking ass and taking names. I don't want to say I was totally right, emotionally blackmailing ya into helpin' with the festival. I'll let other people say that for me," Marianne said, nodding toward the large corkboard Margot had tacked to her living room wall. The corkboard meticulously outlined Margot's overhaul of the festival plans, focusing on bringing tourists into Lake Sackett. She'd arranged for boat tours where participants would be subtly routed to see all the shoreside inns, marinas, and restaurants while enjoying Lake Sackett's scenic beauty. Hayrides would show the visitors the more land-bound locations where they could deposit their money. She'd added a Taste of Lake Sackett event over the weekend so local restaurants could make a little extra cash and get some free marketing. The usual carnival company set up their rides and games on the school grounds. But Margot had offered them a higher percentage of the gate to give local products as prizes instead of the traditional cheap stuffed animals and trinkets. If the participants somehow managed to win at ring toss, they would get a small plant from Nan's Nursery, cookies from the bakery, or a sample from the Jerky Jamboree.

The children had their own dedicated stage. The signs were ordered and matched, as opposed to homemade glittery crazy quilt signage. The vendors were ruthlessly bound by their contracts.

"This is just like planning a party," Margot assured them. "A really big party."

"If I move this note card, will you freak out and start cursing?" Frankie asked, reaching out for the card listing the order of the children's presentations with a teasing smirk.

"I wouldn't test her," Marianne muttered out of the side of her mouth. Frankie shrugged and unwrapped a tray of deviled eggs and little baked sausage balls, setting them out on Margot's counter.

"A love offerin' from Tootie," Frankie said, tossing the cling wrap away with a flourish. "She wants to make sure we have something in our stomachs to soak up the booze."

"I am a little protective of the board," Margot admitted, taking her hair out of its careful chignon. "I know it sounds paranoid, but I was afraid that Sara Lee would break into my office and try to change things. Bless her heart."

"Oh, no, that's reasonable," Marianne assured her. "Especially after you wouldn't let her take over at the parent work day. Sara Lee's warpath has gotten that much steeper."

Margot groaned and scrubbed her hand over her face. "It did not go well," she admitted.

It would go less well, Margot knew, if she discussed some of the discrepancies she'd found in the previous years' records. She'd come across spending patterns and receipts that just didn't make any sense, but she was keeping her theories to herself until she had sorted through all of Sara Lee's files.

"Well, Sara Lee has moved on to trying to convince the local businesses that you're gonna screw the pooch something awful and they'll lose money on the festival. She tried to get on the agenda at the Chamber of Commerce meeting, but Uncle Bob told her personal attacks didn't count as new business," Marianne said.

"She's too late, I made all the vendors sign contracts. But I'll touch base with them, reassure them in my sweetest Sunday tones that I truly appreciate every little bit of their help." The last sentence was Margot's best imitation of the molasses-thick accents of her neighbors.

"That wasn't bad," Marianne told her. "Just try to ease back on the twang a little bit, that's more of a Tennessee/Kentucky thing. Also, speaking of contracts, here are those papers you asked about, for Aunt Tootie."

Margot accepted a manila folder full of forms marked with the Sackett County seal. "Thanks, this is going to be a huge help."

"And in another awkward segue, speaking of vendors, you might want to talk to Bud down at the bakery," Frankie said. "He's closing up shop."

"Oh, no, he was supposed to provide the cupcakes for the festival's opening ceremonies!" Margot cried. "And prize cookies!"

"Well, he's still closing. He's getting older. His sales have been on a downswing for years and his son is an idiot. It would be pointless to put Bud Jr. in charge of a business that would burn down within a month. He just can't make it work anymore."

"That's so sad," Marianne said. "But yes, Bud Jr. is an idiot."

"I'll talk to him, make sure he'll honor the sales contract," Margot replied, writing herself a note on a Post-it and pinning it to the "to do" section of the board.

"More and more businesses are gonna close down if tourism doesn't pick up." Frankie sighed. "We're gonna end up like one of those creepy ghost towns in horror movies, where the only buildings not boarded up are the police station and the shop of a questionable mechanic who has no intention of fixing your car so you can get out to a safe distance."

"As the wife of the town's mechanic, shut your face," Marianne told her.

"The mechanic is always questionable!" Frankie insisted while Marianne made a rude gesture.

The trio sat at the tiny kitchenette table and enjoyed their drinks and snacks, debating their DVD choices.

"Frankie, I love you. But I don't think I can sit through another movie where a shark gets sucked into a weather system or crossbred with another animal, creatin' an 'eff you, science' hybrid," Marianne told her cousin.

Frankie gasped, affronted, and turned to Margot, who shook her head. "Why do the tornados only affect sharks? Why not a Squidnado? Or a Dolphinado?"

"Because people would be *happy* if a bunch of adorable dolphins were dropped into their backyards! I'm pretty sure that's the plot to *Free Willy*," Frankie protested.

"It's really not," Margot told her.

Frankie rolled her eyes to the fullest extent her thick mascara would allow. "Okay, fine, I will watch one non–Nicholas Sparks movie with Ryan Gosling in it—"

"Yay!" Margot and Marianne chorused.

"*If* . . . Margot spills all the gory details of her tawdry affair with the school principal," Frankie finished.

"It's not tawdry! I don't even know what that means!" Margot spluttered.

"Everybody in town knows you two have taken up together," Marianne said, prodding her ribs. "Tootie and Aunt Leslie are already planning your wedding cake."

"Everybody?" Margot groaned. "But we've been so careful and discreet!"

"Well, not as careful as you think. Sweet Johnnie practically swoons when she talks about the looks you two send each other during the planning committee meetings," Frankie said slyly. "And Hutch Gershaw was running crappie jigs last weekend and saw the funeral home truck parked out in front of Kyle's house at six in the morning."

Margot slumped against the table and buried her face in her hands. "That was *one time*."

"Also, Nate came home the other day and asked when his aunt Margot could come have a sleepover at our house. Because Hazel told all the kids at school that you'd had a sleepover at her house and Nate didn't think that was fair."

Margot's forehead thunked against the table while Frankie

cackled. Marianne patted her shoulder. "Welcome to small-town dating. There are no secrets."

"So *everybody* knows? Even those judgmental church ladies in Tootie's card group? Sara Lee? My father?"

"Most likely," Marianne said. "Aw, hon, it's not a big deal. Most people are pleased for you both. And those that aren't? Well, screw 'em."

Margot thunked her head on the table again.

"Um, this seems like more than embarrassed head-thunkin'," Frankie said. "Is there something you want to talk about?"

Margot mumbled a string of indistinguishable sounds into the wood.

Marianne smirked. "What was that?"

"I don't know *what* I'm doing," Margot said. "I don't think we're dating in the traditional sense, but I'm not quite a booty call. It was going so well the other day and then Hazel came home early from her slumber party and I was wearing her dad's robe and it was just so awkward. And then Kyle basically tossed me out of the house, which hurt, but I can't really blame him because his girls have lost enough as it is and they shouldn't see him dating. Plus I don't know how to talk to children anyway and that just makes it worse. I just don't know how to navigate this. I am unprepared."

"Do you want to date Kyle in the traditional sense?"

"I don't know. He's funny and smart and kind of drives me crazy but in that intellectually challenging way I like so much. I've never met a man who can manage as much chaos as I do, and I find that attractive in a slightly disturbing way. And he feels things and lets me know what those feelings are. He doesn't hide them behind a glib mask that lets him keep his dignity. He doesn't sugarcoat it, even when it would be better for both of us. And that is so . . ."

"Endearin'?" Frankie suggested.

"Sensitive?" Marianne added.

"Bizarre!" Margot barked. "Even though I know it's coming, it catches me off guard *every* time. There are times when I think a little sugarcoating would be nice."

"So why wouldn't you want to date him?"

"For one thing, I don't have a lot of experience with real relationships, not the kind that are meant to go anywhere. And for another, there are his kids."

"What about them?"

"I don't know anything about kids. I've never dated anyone with kids. I don't know how to act around them. I definitely don't know how to take care of them. I've killed off so many houseplants, my assistant at my last job gave me plastic cacti to keep in my office."

Marianne patted Margot's hand. "But Hazel and Juniper seem to like you, from what the boys tell me," Marianne assured her. "And if I can keep Nate alive for seven years, you can supervise two well-behaved kids who want to impress you."

Frankie grimaced. "Besides, his girls are part of who he is. That's his life. Trying to divide up that life into parts you can manage and ignore the rest, that doesn't work."

Margot muttered, "That sounds oddly similar to something he said."

"So if you're thinking of dating Kyle, does that mean that you're not gonna be bolting out of town like your ass is on fire?" Marianne asked.

"It's possible," Margot admitted. "But that has nothing to do with Kyle. It turns out I'm unmarketable to employers who are not related to me."

"Yay!" Frankie cried. "I mean, sad for you. But yay for us!"

"You could be less thrilled about my inability to find work," Margot told her.

"I don't think so," Frankie said, shaking her head so her pigtails jiggled.

"Keep it up and I will vote for *The Notebook*," Margot told her.

Frankie slapped her hands over her eyes. "Noooo!"

AND OF COURSE, the moment Margot began to accept that she might be staying in Lake Sackett, she got a nibble on one of the dozens of résumés she'd sent into the professional ether. She was sitting at her desk in the funeral home, gloating over the completed forms for the very first funeral service she had planned from start to finish, including selling the casket and arranging for the grave excavation. She had mastered all the paperwork, managed to give the bereaved Jenkins family comfort and help during their planning process, *and* sold a bright pink sparkle-finish Duchess casket at a deep discount for eighty-two-year-old MayJean Jenkins, who had adored all things pink and rhinestone covered since her childhood. The glittery, satin-lined casket made her family smile, and that had made Margot happy, knowing that she was doing this weird family job well.

That self-satisfied grin was still plastered across her face when she answered her desk phone. "McCready Family Funeral Home and Bait Shop, how may I help you?"

"Funeral Home and Bait Shop? That's really a thing? I thought that was a typo," a female voice drawled on the other end of the line.

"I'm sorry?"

"I was tryin' to reach Margot Cary," the caller said. "She listed this number on her résumé."

"Yes, ma'am, this is she," Margot said, a little flutter of anticipation taking wing in her belly. "How can I help you?"

"Well, aren't you charmin'?" the voice declared. "I wouldn't expect that sort of Southern syrup in a Chicago gal."

"Oh, my family's from Georgia. I've been spending a lot of time with them lately, so I guess the niceties are rubbing off on me. I'm sorry to ask, but who's calling, please?"

"Where are *my* manners?" the woman cackled. "This is Rae Temple, the *R* in RAB Events in Dallas? I'm head of corporate shindigs."

Margot lifted her brow. She vaguely remembered filling out an online application to RAB through JobLink during one of her late-night submission binges in Chicago.

"Yes?" Margot squeaked.

"Well, we just had a position open up in my division and your name was at the very top of our callback list. How would you feel about doing a Skype interview in the next few days, and if that goes well, we can fly you down here for a face-to-face chat?"

"Of course, that would be great," Margot said, working hard to keep her voice from trembling as an unwelcome thought occurred to her. She cleared her throat. "Are you sure you have the right Margot Cary? There isn't some other Margot K-E-R-R-Y that's supposed to get this phone call, is there?"

Rae snickered. "No, hon, we tend to do a pretty thorough background check on our applicants before we call them."

Margot sighed. "Oh, so you know about . . ."

"The birds? Oh, sweetheart, that was the funniest thang I've ever seen. We have you-themed GIFs on file to attach to interoffice e-mails when we're afraid we're gettin' too serious."

"Ms. Temple, is this a joke interview?" Margot asked carefully. "Because I don't think I could handle another one of those."

"No, no! We'd love to have you," Rae exclaimed. "We'd be lucky to get someone who can wrangle shrimp-crazed birds with one hand and call 911 with the other. That sort of disaster happens all the time in our business. You've got people drinkin' too much when they don't have enough food in them, while wearin' uncomfortable shoes and tryin' to impress each other. That's a recipe for disaster. Besides, it's not considered a party down here until someone falls into a pool wearing a five-thousand-dollar cocktail dress. The difference is we see the humor in it, and we appreciate someone who can handle those situations quickly, without losin' her damn mind and making it worse. You've got style and you've got grit, and we need both. What kind of people have you been dealin' with up there, darlin'?"

Margot actually felt her eyes tear up a bit. All this time, she'd assured herself that one disaster didn't negate her entire career, that she still had talent. But she'd needed to hear it from someone in her industry. She didn't know what that said about her as a person. She was sure it had something to do with chasing the approval of her difficult-to-please mother and absent father or some Freudian bear trap that would cost her thousands at the therapist's office. But for right now, she was just grateful not to feel that crushing disappointment in herself.

"Thank you. That is the first time I've heard that," she said. "I haven't had a callback on an application in months."

"Well, isn't that lucky for us, then? Look, I'll send the details for the Skype interview to your e-mail address. And really, we're interested in workin' with you, Margot, as long as you think you might like the culture 'round here. Give movin' to Texas some serious thought."

"I will," she promised. "Thank you."

Margot hung up the phone and covered her mouth to contain the ecstatic squeal that would have raised the nearby dead. After months of nothing, she had an interview, with someone who sounded like a reasonable employer. The life she'd been trying to steer back onto the tracks ever since the Night of the Flamingos was finally coming back together. She could live in a city again. She would have access to more than one grocery store and dependable cell coverage and not have to worry about possums breaking into her garbage. Or worry about Sasquatch as a real possibility instead of possums. She would be herself again.

As her eyes landed on the McCready Family Funeral Home and Bait Shop stationery stacked on her desk, that euphoric thrill ebbed from her chest. She could be leaving this place. What would she tell her family? They would be so hurt that she was leaving, after everything they'd done to make her part of their lives. She couldn't have that easy, comfortable relationship with Marianne and Frankie over Skype. She'd prove everyone who'd said she was just like her mother right.

Her father . . . wasn't as much of a consideration. The progress she'd hoped for with him just wasn't happening.

Oh, hell, what would she tell Kyle? The fragile green shoots of whatever sort of relationship she shared with her favorite principal would collapse under the pressure of a nebulous long-distance relationship. He wouldn't want to be with someone who was a fly-by-night presence in his girls' lives, confusing them even further.

She would have to start all over, again, just after she'd become comfortable in the life she'd started in Lake Sackett.

Margot slumped down in her chair and, for the first time ever, said, "Dang it."

13

MARGOT STOOD AT Kyle's front door on a bright, cloud-less Saturday morning, debating whether to knock. In her hands she held the finalized schedule for the student presentations at the History Pavilion. It was an excuse, really, to talk to Kyle, to casually drop into conversation that she could be leaving town and gauge his reaction to that.

Rae had set up the Skype interview for the following week. Margot hoped that if she ended up being offered the job, she would be able to negotiate a start date after the festival.

Though it seemed impossible, the festival had taken on even more importance after Uncle Bob reported the Chamber of Commerce's totals for summer tourism. The town's visitor numbers were down 8 percent from the previous year and more than 15 percent from five years before. Rental income was down for the third year running. And Harley Ramsett, owner of one of the biggest boat rental companies in town, was thinking about closing, taking ten jobs and an incredible amount of tourist appeal with him.

Sara Lee had used the *Lake Sackett Ledger's* coverage of

these grim numbers to try to wrest control of the festival out of Margot's hands a whopping two weeks before opening ceremonies. She'd called an emergency meeting of the PTA to ask members to sign a petition to fire Margot. Fortunately for Margot, volunteers couldn't be fired and only ten people signed the petition—all of them Sara Lee's cronies. So for now, she still held the reins to what could be the biggest show in town. She did notice, however, that her card got declined more often than not at local businesses owned by Sara Lee's friends. And all four of her tires seemed to go flat every time she parked her truck in town. Carl, bless him, had put an air pump behind the bench seat so she could blow them back up without his help.

She'd almost retracted her hand and decided to silently scuttle back to the truck when Juniper opened the front door, wearing sparkly purple tights, neon-green Crocs, and an orange life vest. Margot lifted a brow.

"Is there a flood warning or is the life vest a fashion statement?" Margot asked.

"We're going sailing today, Miss Margot!" Juniper cried, grabbing Margot's hand and dragging her into the house. "It's the last sail of the season before we have to put the boat up for winter. We do it every year. Daddy always packs a special lunch and we have a picnic on the fairy island."

"Wow, that sounds great, Juniper—"

"JUNE."

"That sounds great, June. But maybe I should just come back at another time." Margot tried to back away toward the front door, but June's grip on her wrist became Teamster tight.

"Noooo!" she howled. "You should come with us, puh-lease? It's always more fun when another grown-up comes with us because Daddy doesn't worry about us falling out of the boat when he's working the lines."

"Does that happen a lot?" Margot asked as June locked the front door, then dragged Margot through the house to the back door, looking over the water.

June threw the glass sliding door open with the force of someone who had never made home insurance payments and screeched, "DADDY! MISS MARGOT IS HERE!"

"Your ability to speak in all caps is astonishing," Margot told June, who just grinned at her.

Down at the family's dock, Kyle's head popped up behind the hull of the little sailboat. He appeared to be stowing ropes in a small hold at the front of the boat, while Hazel was untying the knots that kept the sail tightly rolled. He smiled and waved at Margot as June yanked her down the length of the dock by her wrist. How could someone that small be *that* strong?

Kyle hopped gracefully over the hull and landed on the dock with both feet. He was wearing jeans and the green utility jacket he'd had on the first time she saw him. The sight of the jacket kick-started a warm flicker in her chest that she tamped down by remembering that Kyle's children were standing *right there* and it would not do to ogle their father right in front of them. Even if they wouldn't realize it was happening. Probably. Maybe a little ogling wouldn't hurt.

No.

Margot broke eye contact and stared at the sailboat. It was even prettier up close. She knew very little about these things, but it seemed well cared for with its glossy wood and polished brass fittings. It was the sort of thing constructed in what Tootie would have wistfully described as the "good old days," when everything was built to last. A careful hand had painstakingly painted MAGGIE'S LITTLE TREES on the bow in gold and white.

"June, honey, we've talked about trying to dislocate people's shoulders," he told her, though his tone wasn't at all stern. "It's not nice."

Margot's lips twitched as June reluctantly loosened her death grip. "Sorry," June mumbled. She brightened considerably in less than a second. "Guess what, Daddy? Miss Margot is going to come with us!"

Kyle glanced up at Margot and she shook her head back and forth. "Oh, I don't think so. I mean, look at me. I'm not dressed for sailing."

The family looked at her jeans and light green sweater, combined with the only pair of sneakers she'd brought with her to Lake Sackett. Kyle asked dryly, "You're afraid you'd end up turning an ankle in those fancy shoes?"

"My sweater is very absorbent," Margot said, clearly searching for an excuse. "It would weigh me down if I went in the water. Also, you weren't planning to feed me and I don't want to make lunch too sparse."

"No, no, Dad always packs a few extra sandwiches and drinks because we drop them in the water. Puh-*lease*?" June begged.

Margot grimaced. "I don't think so."

"You're welcome to come with us," Kyle said, though his tone clearly meant the opposite.

"Oh, I couldn't."

"Please!" June cried, making big anime eyes at her.

"Okay," Margot said, through an uncomfortable smile. "But I just want to point out that this is how *Gilligan's Island* started."

"Get in the boat," June said, pushing at Margot's hip until

she stepped onto the bow. Kyle was quick to take her hand and help her get on board without falling into the lake. The boat pitched a bit under her feet and she stumbled into Kyle. He gave her a light squeeze before picking June up under her arms and setting her down on one of the bench seats by the tiller.

Kyle looped a thin, narrow life vest around Margot's neck and clipped it closed. "It inflates when it hits the water," he told her. "It's a little easier to move around in than the neck pillows for the kids."

"This is some sort of practical joke, isn't it? I'm being filmed?"

"Just wear it," he said. "And sit there, where you won't get smacked with the boom."

She nodded. "Will do. Not getting hit in the face with a sail is a big priority in my life."

Margot sat next to Hazel, who was also wearing a colorful but mismatched outfit topped off with a bright orange life vest. She gave a halfhearted flick of her hand. "Hi, Miss Margot."

"Hi, Hazel."

Kyle asked, "Everybody ready?"

"Aye, aye, cap'n!" June cried as Kyle cast off lines and bustled around the boat doing things Margot didn't quite understand.

"Everybody got their life vests buckled?"

"Aye!" the girls yelled.

Kyle helped June pull the cord for a small motor that pushed them away from the dock. Margot gripped the edge of the hull and the sailboat shot forward. This boat seemed so much less stable than the pontoon. While this was clearly something the Archer family enjoyed, Margot thought she preferred the room and stability of a pontoon.

Once the boat had cleared the Archers' little inlet, Kyle cut the engine and pulled a cord that tightened the sail. The boat pitched forward again, diving into a wake. June squealed as the sailboat skimmed across the surface. Even Hazel was grinning like mad. The colors of the other boats, the happy shouts, the sunlight sparkling over the water—what would it have been like to grow up doing this as a family? Would she and Stan have taken boat trips like this on the weekends? Would she have learned how to bait her hook properly from Stan? Or would Linda have hauled her to Atlanta every weekend for museums and ballet?

No, it wasn't likely, given her parents' marriage. And she didn't want to think about that right now. She wanted to focus on feeling good for once. Margot turned her face into the wind and closed her eyes. She was right. This did feel like flying.

"So what brings you to my door on a Saturday so my daughter can kidnap you into a family outing?"

Margot's jaw fell open, something she remedied immediately when a bug nearly flew into her mouth. She wanted to tell him everything. She had a job interview. She could be leaving town. She wasn't sure that she'd still be around for the festival and was doing her best to have everything ready so Sara Lee couldn't derail it all if and when Margot left town.

But she couldn't. They were on the water and the girls were so happy and Kyle looked so relaxed and content. She couldn't ruin that. Their family didn't have enough of these happy moments.

Besides, if he got angry, she didn't have anywhere to go except over the edge of the boat.

"Oh, I just brought some papers by for you. The finalized list of the kids' events," she said as he sat next to her. He kept the guide for the tiller in his hand, holding their path straight across the width of the lake. "So what's the fairy island?"

"It was Maggie's favorite island when she was a kid. She used to take a little rowboat out there on sunny afternoons and read under the trees. She said that she felt like the queen of her own fairy kingdom on that island. And the girls get a kick out of looking for fairies while we're out there."

"That's sweet."

"We do this every year. Um, Maggie's birthday is this week," he explained quietly. "It's hard to explain to the girls sometimes. I mean, they understand in the abstract, I think, but tying it in with the final sail seems to help."

"And I've intruded. I'm so sorry."

"No, it's nice, having another adult here who understands what I'm trying to do. Maggie's parents came for a couple of years, but I think it hurt too much. It's nice having *you* here. Part of that 'decompartmentalizing' thing."

"Thanks," she said.

Margot relaxed against the seat, listening to June's excited chatter. Even with the cooling weather, there were some boats on the water. Margot spotted Duffy on the pontoon, with a group of older gentlemen fully outfitted in the flashiest fishing gear. He waved and grinned so wide she could see it from yards away. Margot and the girls waved back.

Hazel warmed up slowly, enjoying the fact that she had to explain the parts of the sailboat to Margot.

"Jam cleat. Sail ticklers," Hazel said, pointing to the various parts of the boat. "Gooseneck."

"You're making this up," Margot said, scrunching up her face, making Hazel giggle.

"Kyle, what are those ribbons up on the sail called?"

"Sail ticklers," Kyle said, grinning at her.

"Told you!" Hazel cried.

"Who comes up with these names?"

"Weirdos," June told her solemnly.

They traveled the length of the lake before finally entering one of those little pronged inlets. Near the shore were several small islands, barely big enough to support grass and a few trees. The largest was closer to the lake proper and roughly the shape of a kidney. Several scrubby trees shaded the mossy terrain.

Kyle anchored the boat and tethered it to one of the thicker trees. The hull settled easily against the muddy knoll of the island, allowing the passengers to hop off onto land. It was quiet here, away from the engines of the fishing boats and the wind. Scraps of ribbon, some only slightly faded, others bleached bone white by time and sun, hung from the branches overhead.

"Mommy started hanging these up when she was little," Hazel told her while Kyle unpacked their lunch. "For the fairies. We hang more every year on the last sail."

"Fairies do like their colorful decorations," Margot said as Hazel nodded.

"Will you rebraid my hair?" June asked, handing Margot a brush from her backpack. The wind had done a number on June's braid, leaving her with a halo of flyaways. Margot grimaced. She'd never really braided anyone's hair but her own, and she wasn't great at that. Her own hair was so fine, it slipped when she tried to maneuver it. She wasn't sure her hands would "remember" how to do it from a different angle.

But she dragged the brush through Juniper's thick sandy

hair, careful not to catch her ears. The tangles were insane, but June didn't whine once as Margot worked through them. She separated the fall of blond into three sections and began twisting them into a simple braid.

"When you don't live here, do you live in a big city like Daddy came from?"

"Yes," Margot said, frowning at her uneven braiding and undoing her work to start over. "It wasn't as big as the city your dad came from, but it's superior in many ways. Many, many ways."

Kyle cleared his throat in an exaggerated fashion as he spread an oilcloth on the ground. "Don't lie to my children."

Margot smirked at him, but before she could answer, June was firing more questions at her. "Did you ride a subway? Did you go to museums with dinosaur bones? Did you live in a big tall building?"

"Yes. But we called the subway the 'el train.'"

"Do you miss it?"

"I miss some parts of it. I miss things that you can't get here, like sushi and reliable Internet. But there are things I like about this place."

"Like what?"

Margot considered her answer as she tied off the passable braid with a hair elastic. "Fireflies. We get fireflies in Chicago, but you can't always see them because there are too many lights. And Aunt Leslie's deep-fried things. And my cabin. I like my cabin."

"And my daddy?"

Margot looked up to find Kyle smirking in return. "Your daddy is something I like, yes."

"Well, be still my beating heart," he drawled, pressing a hand over his chest.

"So you're not going to go back?" Hazel asked, watching Margot's face carefully. Margot's lips parted to give an answer, but the breath remained trapped in her throat.

Kyle frowned and tugged gently on Hazel's ponytail. "Lunch is ready!"

The girls scrambled over to the picnic blanket to chow down on peanut butter and jellies, lemonade, and pink-frosted cupcakes. But Hazel's unanswered question hung heavily in the air between the adults, turning the too-sweet canned frosting to ashes in Margot's mouth.

⁓

UNNERVED AND EXHAUSTED by the sailing trip with the Archers, Margot pulled the truck to a stop in front of her cabin. The afternoon had been as delicate as a soap bubble, treading the line between respecting Maggie's memory and making the day a happy occasion for the girls.

When they'd anchored the boat to Kyle's dock, an older couple had emerged from the back door, waving. Margot saw the exact moment when the couple spotted her, because their arms froze midair and sort of drooped to their sides.

"Oh," Kyle said, his eyes cutting toward Margot.

"Meemee and Pawpaw!" June cried, waving her arms.

Margot winced, both at the idea of meeting Kyle's in-laws *and* some of the strangest grandparent nicknames she had ever heard. Kyle looked so uncomfortable, he actually turned pale.

Kyle murmured as Margot helped him tie off the line to the dock, "They're very nice people. It's going to be fine."

Margot thought about how she would feel if her daughter had died an unfair and tragic death and she found that daughter's husband taking up with a stranger just a few years later.

"That seems so unlikely," Margot told him.

The Kellers did their best to keep pleasant, welcoming expressions on their faces as Margot and Kyle herded the girls up the dock. Vaguely, Margot remembered her Aunt Tootie mentioning Maggie's father by name—Hank? Henry? Hal! And Rosie. She distinctly remembered Tootie saying that Maggie's mother was named Rosie.

June leaped at Hal, knocking him back on his heels and nearly sending them both careening into the lake. Margot gasped, expecting Kyle or Hal to reprimand her sharply for acting like that near the water. But Hal just laughed while Rosie leaned in to blow raspberry kisses on Hazel's cheeks.

Both girls chattered happily about their day on the water, the new ribbons they'd tied on the "fairy trees," the cupcakes their daddy had made, burned, and remade. Margot approached the older couple with all the apprehension of an apprentice snake charmer.

But Hal reached out and gave her hand a very firm shake. "Hi there, I'm Hal Keller. This here's my wife, Rosie."

"Margot Cary," she said, returning the handshake with the sort of pressure she'd used for meetings with CEOs back in Chicago.

Rosie nodded and Margot gave her a lighter, less squeezy handshake. "Tootie said you'd met the girls."

"She came sailing with us," Hazel said. "We took her to the fairy island."

Rosie's face took on a speculative expression. "Did ya now? And how'd you like it?"

"It was really lovely," Margot said carefully but firmly, staring into Rosie's frank brown eyes. "I feel very fortunate to have been invited to see it."

Rosie pursed her lips for a long moment and then nodded. "Good."

With a considerably lighter tone, Rosie grabbed both girls' hands and said, "I brought a big pot of Brunswick stew and put it on the stove. I figured y'all would be hungry, being out on the water most of the day." The girls cheered and ran up the steps to the house.

"Rosie's Brunswick stew is the stuff of local legend," Hal told Margot.

"Your aunt Tootie's been trying to get the recipe out of me for years," Rosie said. "And I'm gonna take it to my grave, just 'cause I love to see the look on her face when she tries to figure out my secret ingredient."

"That seems fair," Margot agreed.

"You're joinin' us for dinner, aren't ya?" Rosie asked as the grown-ups walked toward the house.

Margot glanced at Kyle, who said, "Oh, no, she was just on her way home."

"I was," Margot assured them. "I shouldn't have taken the afternoon off. I have work to do."

"Margot is organizing the Founders' Festival," Kyle said quickly. "That's why she came over this morning. She had festival paperwork."

"Mm-hmm," Rosie said, examining Margot closely.

"Well, I better go," Margot said, practically bolting for her truck, even when June called after her. She couldn't keep doing this. Kyle had made the boundaries around his family clear, and she needed to respect them. No more dropping by with papers or news. If she had festival business to discuss, she would e-mail him. It was time for her to start her exit strategy from Lake Sackett.

—

LATER, MARGOT WAS standing in the purpling shadows in front of her cabin, watching the wind play with the tree at the end of the cabin row. The wind had picked up considerably since they'd docked earlier, tossing the branches back and forth and smacking the roof of the dingy yellow-and-green cabin. She began walking toward it.

Arlo, who seemed to think of her as his person ever since they'd conspired to trick an animal control officer, trotted along with her, sniffing her shoes.

She wished she could say that the cabin tugged at her memory, but not one cell in her body recalled it. It was the first place she'd been taken from the hospital. She'd spent her first three years under the damaged green roof, but she didn't recognize it. Shouldn't she remember it? She stepped up on the creaky, sun-faded porch.

Arlo seemed to realize that the old cabin was not a place for goofball dogs and slunk away with a pitiful whine.

"Coward!" Margot called after his retreating furry butt. She reached under the empty flowerpot nearest the door, knowing that, as with all the other cabins on the compound, she would find the spare key there. Taking a moment to steady herself, she turned the doorknob and flipped the light switch.

The house hadn't been abandoned. The tables weren't dusty. The floors were swept. The kitchen counters were bare. It did look like some sort of museum exhibit to early eighties decor. A cheap imitation–Laura Ashley couch and matching chair took up most of the living room, flanking an oak coffee table. Brass geese waddled across the mantel between framed photos. A reproduction Tiffany lamp glowed in the corner nearest the kitchenette. It was as if Stan had just walked out and never bothered moving the furniture.

She recognized the people in the portraits as much younger versions of her mother and Stan. But it seemed so alien to see the two of them standing with their arms around each other. She stepped forward, spotting a framed photo of Stan with a baby on his lap. His whole body was oriented around that infant, as if he was trying to shield her from the whole world. A happy grin lit his mustachioed face. She wondered for a second who that baby was, until she spotted the bib around her neck. It spelled out MARGOT in bright primary colors.

Too late, she heard heavy boots on the porch. She turned to see Stan in the doorway, frowning at her.

"I saw the light on." He glanced down at the photo. "What are you doing in here?"

To her surprise, he didn't sound upset. He sounded . . . nervous, embarrassed, like this house was some secret he was keeping from her.

"Tootie said that I used to live in this house with you and my mother, but I can't remember anything about it. I thought maybe if I looked around . . ."

Stan carefully placed the photo back on the mantel, running his thumb along the silver-tone frame. "You were so little when your mama left, it's not a big surprise that you don't remember."

"So why don't you stay here? It's a perfectly nice house. It has to be more comfortable than sleeping at the funeral home."

Stan stuffed his hands in his pockets, unable to meet her eyes. "I tried for a while. It was too hard, too quiet. For the first couple of years, I thought maybe if I waited, if I kept it how it was, your mama might come back and see that I waited on her. And then I thought maybe if I kept it the same, you would be more comfortable when you came back. Anyway, I just couldn't stay like that anymore, and I couldn't face changing it.

"Your aunt Donna comes by and cleans every once in a while, just to keep the critters at bay. Your room's down the hall, if you want to take a look."

Margot glanced down the hall and found that, no, she had seen quite enough of the house for one evening. "No, I'm fine. Why wouldn't you just move the furniture? Change things up so it didn't remind you of us?"

Stan jerked his shoulders. "It was easier just to leave it."

"Why?"

"Because it was."

"But why?" Margot pressed.

He turned, his expression tense. "Because if I changed it, it was like admitting that you weren't ever coming back, even when it was better that you didn't. I accepted that your mama didn't want me anymore. We weren't suited, as much as I hated to admit it. She wanted more from life than I could give her. I don't know why she ever took up with me. I was young and stupid and drank too much, had nothing to offer her, other than maybe she thought I was gonna get more of a share in the business than I'm entitled to. And she'd always had a hankering for city living—fancy restaurants, the theater, that sort of thing. I thought we could make it work, but deep down, I knew that she might leave. But knowing I would never see you again? That was too much. And I fell even deeper into the bottle. Because that's what I did then."

"What? What do you mean it was better if we didn't come back? Why would you say that?"

"I didn't deserve you. I didn't deserve your mama, miserable as we made each other. I wasn't the type of man who got to go back to a nice house and daughter who loved him at the end of the day. I was a drunk, a sloppy one. Lazy, distant, kind of a jackass sometimes. You wanna know what made her leave? You got sick, just a stupid stomach flu that almost any parents could handle, but I couldn't, so your mama was left to deal with it. And she got sick herself and she just charged on, because that's what she did. But then your fever spiked and she needed someone to drive you to the clinic because she was in no shape herself. And I was too damn drunk to get behind the wheel, so she had to ask Bob. She couldn't even depend on me to *drive* you somewhere where she would end up doin' all the parentin' anyway. She had to ask my brother. And so I came home a few days later and found you gone. And I understood. That love you had for me when you were little? I would have let you down. You would have ended up hating me, and I don't think I could have lived with that." He put his hands on her shoulders and cupped her chin, forcing her to look up at him. "At least this way, there was a chance that someday you might come back and I might be cleaned up. Your mama did the right thing, Margot."

She nodded. She'd spent a lot of years frustrated with her mother, resentful of her mother, but now, she felt *sorry* for her mother, having to make that choice, to take a daughter away from the father who loved her, knowing that even if it was painful, it was for the best. Linda Cary hadn't been a nurturing, cuddly mother, but she'd made one loving gesture that counted, even if it left them all feeling destroyed.

When she came out of her haze of thoughts, she realized there were tears dripping down her cheeks. Stan dabbed at the water tracks with his thumbs. "Aw, Sweet Tea. It's all right."

"I'm so sorry," she whispered as he wrapped his long arms around her and pressed her into a shirt that smelled of Old Spice.

"I did it to myself," he mumbled into her hair. "It wasn't ever anythin' you did. I was a grade-A dipshit, and it took your mama leavin' for me to see it. Hell, it still took a year or two for me to dry out. And even then, I couldn't get over the guilt."

Margot relaxed into him. She didn't think she could ever remember getting a hug like this from a relative. She wasn't being held at a careful distance to protect emotions and expensive clothes. She was being enveloped, anchored, and comforted. And she could have had this for years if her mother hadn't left. Then again, who knew how long it would have lasted if Stan had continued to drink. There was no perfect outcome. There was no win-win. She probably would have ended up a mess no matter how her mother had handled it.

"I'm sorry. I have to go." Margot ripped herself out of her father's arms and dashed out of the cabin.

14

$\mathcal{M}$ARGOT FELT LIKE she was standing on a cliff with her toes hanging over the edge.

The morning had started off normally enough, if normal was being caught between several different paths in life and feeling unable to choose any of them. Her father had been gently distant with her for days, bringing coffee to her office in the mornings and chatting but not pushing her for anything more. Kyle had been texting her off and on all morning, checking in, making her smile.

The last-minute details of the festival were coming together nicely. The early reservation numbers for local hotels looked good. The liability insurance on the carnival rides had come through. The online advertising was showing an encouraging number of click-throughs. Margot was going to host one last informational meeting with the volunteers running the booths and games and then she would consider the success of the festival out of her hands.

And then Rae called for the interview they'd scheduled. Margot was on Skype, talking to a panel of people from RAB Events as they asked interesting but pointed questions about her organizational methods, her thoughts on alcohol consumption, and her predictions on the coming trends in food and drink. It felt like Margot was stretching muscles she hadn't used in months, discussing her planning timelines and how she might develop good contacts in a city she'd never even visited. She relaxed into the conversation, but in the back of her head, she wondered whether this was what she really wanted, moving to Texas and abandoning the life she'd built. She'd agreed to the interview without a second thought. Did that say something? Wasn't your gut reaction supposed to be the right decision?

While one of Rae's subordinates was asking a question about her stance on budget versus vision, a text notification chirped from her phone. Marianne had sent her another text. It was a picture that June had drawn in a school art class Marianne volunteered for, a rough shape sort of similar to a sailboat with four circular smiley faces sticking up over the hull. June's teacher had very helpfully printed names over the little faces: *Daddy, Miss Margot, Hazel,* and *Me.* And at the bottom of the paper, June's teacher had printed *My Family Went on a Boat Trip.*

And instead of the heart-melting sensation she was sure most people would feel upon seeing this message, a cold flush of dread ran through her belly. June had drawn her as part of her family.

And then she realized that she hadn't answered the interviewer's question about party budgets yet.

THE REST OF the interview had gone well, so well that Rae had offered her the job before they hung up. She'd sent Margot a compensation package that included a handsome salary, excellent insurance, moving coverage, and housing at a nice local hotel until Margot found an apartment. And Rae was kind enough to give her some time to think the offer over.

So here she sat at her desk, staring at the wall, wondering what the hell she was going to do. On one hand, she'd just been offered an awesome job in an actual city. She would be using her real talents. She'd be making three times the money the family paid her to work for the funeral home. On the other, there was her family, and her father. It was lovely that she felt like she had some closure about her issues with her mother, but how could she walk away from her dad when she'd just reestablished some understanding with him? And then there was Kyle . . . and his girls.

She hated to admit it, but the idea of staying here and seeing where things might progress with Kyle scared her. She wasn't qualified for this sort of emotional responsibility. She wasn't prepared to be part of a nuclear family. She didn't have any experience remotely resembling a happy one. She had very limited mothering instincts. Hazel and June were adorable, but she was not ready for this. She might never be ready for this. They deserved better. She'd been deluding herself, having sailing outings with the girls, going to Kyle when she was upset, thinking she was keeping things casual between them. They'd been building toward something, and she was about to back out of it, in a big way. They would be better off if she left now, before more expectations were built up, she told herself. She'd never intended to stay in Lake Sackett long term. She was only following the plans she'd always had.

"Did the wall make you angry?"

Margot turned to find Marianne standing in the doorway, with Frankie and Duffy peering over her shoulders.

"What?"

"You're staring at that wall like it owes you money," Frankie said.

"Lots of money," Duffy added. "Bass boat money."

"I've just got a lot on my mind, that's all."

"Well, I have a rare child-free evening—thank God for in-laws—and we came to see if you wanted to go down to the drive-in and watch cheesy 1950s B-movies while eating inadvisable amounts of popcorn," Marianne said. "Carl's gonna bring the flatbed, so it will be like sitting on our own parade float."

"Oh, that sounds like fun," Margot said absently.

"So what's on your mind?" Frankie skipped into the office and threw herself into the nearest chair.

Margot sighed. "I'm thinking about moving to Texas."

"What? Why?" Marianne cried.

"We just got you back!" Frankie yelled.

Duffy frowned and pointed to the ladies. "What they said."

"I got a great offer from a really nice company. It's the kind of work I'm used to, the work I'm good at," she said. "And it would mean moving back to a city, somewhere I'm more comfortable. I love you all. I really do. I never thought I'd get to have a big extended family. And you gave me that. But I don't belong here, and I need to go back to where I belong."

"Well, I can't say we aren't disappointed." Marianne sighed.

"And as a gesture of our enduring cousinly love, we're giving you the least scary of the paint-by-number Jesuses," Frankie said brightly.

Margot shook her head so vehemently she almost lost a hairclip. "No, thank you."

"Have you told your daddy yet?" Marianne asked.

"No," Margot said, leaning back in her chair. "I don't know what to tell him. He just now opened up to me. But that can't be enough of a reason for me to keep living here."

"Well, that's a bunch of horseshit," Duffy grumbled.

Margot snorted. "Thanks for your support, Duffy."

"It is!" Duffy exclaimed. "You belong here. You're loved here. You don't need to run off to some city to find out that you're not as happy there as you were here."

Margot raised an eyebrow. "Well, don't sugarcoat it for me."

"You *are* happy," he insisted. "I'm the one who picked you up from the airport, remember? I saw how wound-up and miserable you were, checking your phone and the time every two minutes. And you're different now. You smile. You look people in the eye during conversations instead of staring at some screen. You should stay here."

"Where is she going?"

Everybody in the room winced as Kyle appeared in the office doorway.

"Kyle, hi!" Margot said, her voice cracking as she stood from her desk. "What are you doing here?"

"I may have called him to invite him to the drive-in with us," Marianne said with her eyes closed. "I told him to meet us here."

"Oh, thank you, Marianne."

"Why is everybody acting so weird?" Kyle asked, his eyes narrowing.

"We're gonna, uh—we're just gonna go somewhere else," Duffy said, hustling away and dragging his cousins with him.

Kyle's head kept turning back and forth between Margot and her retreating relatives. "Margot, are you all right?"

"I got a job offer," she said carefully. "At a really great company in Dallas. They're doing huge corporate events and these crazy extravagant private parties—right in my skill sweet spot. And they don't care about the flamingo disaster. They like my ability to handle myself in a crisis."

Kyle's face went from warm and concerned to the neutral, professional mask in seconds. "Oh, well, that's great for you. I'm really excited for you."

Margot felt her shoulders sag with relief when he didn't start yelling. She gave an awkward little smile and said, "I am, too. And I'm sort of used to Southern quirkiness now, so really, my time here was like a training camp."

"Well, I'm glad that we could be of some use to you," he said coldly.

"You know I didn't mean it like that."

"How did you mean it?" he asked.

Margot chewed her lip. There was really no good explanation for how she'd intended that statement.

"So I'm assuming you've already accepted the offer?" Kyle's face was starting to take on that cold, miserable expression it had held when she first saw him. She was hurting him all over again, just as she'd feared. She was as bad as her mother. It was best to do this quickly, to get it over with so Kyle could move on and find some other woman who could make him and his girls happy.

She dug her fingernails into her palms and tried to keep her voice as calm as possible, even while her stomach twisted itself inside out. "Not yet, but Kyle, I always made it clear that I planned to move on from Lake Sackett, that this wasn't permanent for me. I told you from the start that I was looking for a job somewhere else."

"But that was before you really knew me or the girls—and

what about your family? You're always talking about how much you love spending time with Marianne, Frankie, and Duff. And Aunt Tootie. Why are you throwing that away so easily?"

"I'm not throwing it away. I can still keep up with them over e-mail and Skype and—"

"Oh, sure, that's exactly the same."

"It's more than I had a year ago, Kyle. And it's not up to you to judge whether it's enough for me or not. Besides, you can't say you're upset about this. You've been pulling away from the moment Hazel found me in your room. I'm just finishing the job for you."

He dropped into the chair across from her desk. "You're right, I'm not being fair . . . You know what? No. This is bullshit. I don't want you to go somewhere else. You're the first woman who has come into my life since Maggie that I've even wanted to try a real relationship with. I know I've been an ass since that morning, but you've got to give me some time to figure all this out. This is new for me, Margot. I can't say I'm madly in love with you just yet, but I was hoping that we were heading toward that, that we were heading toward some sort of life together, that you would *want* to stay here and make that life together with me and the girls. I mean, you talked about bonus parents with Hazel; you don't think that they inferred some stuff from that?"

"I never meant to mislead you or the girls. I tried to be up-front with you about everything. Getting to know your daughters was great, but I never tried to give them the impression that I was going to join their family. You talk about your wife and it's this epic, tragic romance, the kind they write songs about . . . I don't know how to be that to someone. I don't know how to love like that. I don't even know how to be someone's dependable live-in girlfriend. That's not how I'm built. I wouldn't begin to know how to be someone's wife or mother. I literally had no good role models for that, growing up. And I'm not about to use you and the girls as guinea pigs. I would only end up messing it up or leaving. It's better this way, before everything gets all confused and enmeshed."

"Oh, yeah, this is super easy. I don't feel hurt at all." Kyle scoffed, shoving up from the chair and moving toward the door.

"I'm sorry, Kyle."

"I'm sorry, too, Margot. I'm sorry I screwed up and hurt you. And I'm sorry that you're a coward. I'm sorry that you're a quitter. I'm sorry that I let you into my head. I'm sorry that I let you spend time with my girls when I've never let a woman do that before. I'm sorry that you're afraid. I'm sorry you don't trust me enough to even try to love me. I'm really, really sorry."

And with that, Kyle walked out of the office.

Margot let out a breath she didn't realize she'd been holding and put her shaking hands on her desk. She was fine, she told herself sternly. She inhaled deeply through her nose, gritting her teeth and blowing the breath carefully out of her nostrils. This thing with Kyle was bound to end sometime. She was fine. Really. Fine.

Except that her heart seemed to be lodged in her throat and she couldn't breathe. And Kyle's face had been twisted in such a horrible mix of disappointment and disgust and she didn't want that to bother her but she was pretty sure she wanted to throw up. And she couldn't make it up to him, because there *was* no making up for making someone feel like they weren't worth the effort of staying around.

Desperately, she wanted to go back to a few minutes ago,

before she'd broken them—broken something she hadn't even realized was important to her until she was faced with the terrifying reality of not having it anymore. She couldn't go chasing after him. What would she even say? There was no coming back from this. No more teasing smiles out of Kyle. No more funny texts in the middle of the day. No more being held like she was something precious. No more feeling like—just once—she could be enough.

Margot's shoulders sagged under the weight that seemed to be dragging through her chest.

A faint knock sounded at her office door. Margot lifted her head to see Stan standing in the doorway, his brows furrowed. "You okay?"

Margot nodded and tried to smile, but her facial muscles didn't seem to move the way she wanted them to. "Sure. Why do you ask?"

"Well, uh, the Willet visitation is upstairs . . . in the chapel . . . right over your office . . . and your vents are open . . ."

Margot looked up to see that the air vents over her desk were indeed open. And those vents led to air ducts shared with the chapel, meaning that everyone attending the Willet visitation had overheard her argument with Kyle.

"I'm fine," she said, even as her vision burned and tilted on its axis. Stan's mouth pulled back into a grimace. "I'm fine."

"Sweet Tea, you don't have to pretend you're fine if you're not." Stan crossed the room and closed the vents.

"I'm fine," she insisted, her voice wobbling.

"Margot."

"I'm fine," she said again. She collapsed in on herself, curling around her stomach, laying her head against her desk. Stan patted her back awkwardly as she cried, huge racking sobs that shook her whole body. She threw her arms around her head, trying to hide, from her father or the world, she had no idea. She cried like she hadn't cried since she was a little girl. And when Stan put his arm around her shoulders, she didn't even have the strength to shrug him off.

15

THE NEXT FEW days were just as uncomfortable as Margot had suspected they would be. As word spread that she would be leaving town for a "fancy city job," each of her family members—even Aunt Donna—stopped by her cabin to tell her how much they would miss her, but that they were glad she'd found a job that would make her happy. Except, of course, for Aunt Tootie, who informed Margot that she was a "damned fool," but Tootie loved her anyway. Stan supported her quietly, giving her hugs when she needed them and assuring her that they'd find a way to keep talking, even if she did move away. She spent a lot of nights on her couch, with Arlo cuddling against her chest, trying to remember why she'd returned RAB's call in the first place.

Every time she dared appear in public, people stopped talking, and not just in the "stranger among us" way they had when she'd first arrived in town, but in a specific way that Margot had earned on her own. Kyle barely looked at her. Any additional materials for the festival she left in his office with Clarice with instructions on how to get them back to her.

It hurt. She missed him more than she thought possible. She missed the way he teased her and the way her head fit under his chin. She missed the girls. She missed the way Hazel saw through the pretentions of adults and got to the heart of the matter. She missed June's weird humor and overwhelming enthusiasm for everything. And Kyle, oh, how she missed every bit of Kyle.

Even now, as he sat in the back of the crowded school auditorium, staring through her like she was a piece of glass, her chest ached with regret. But she was a professional. The blood of Tootie McCready flowed in her veins. Sort of. She could handle this.

Margot cleared her throat and stepped up to the small microphone. "Good afternoon, everybody. Thank you for taking the time to come out for this volunteer meeting. We've only got a week before the festival starts, and I think it's important for us to get everyone's roles assigned and clear so we don't get bogged down in last-minute details on opening day. Now, can we start with booth setup?"

"I don't see why ya think we need this," Sara Lee complained loudly from the front row of seats. Jimmy Greenway sat to her right, his arms crossed over his LSES Staff polo shirt. "There is such a thing as overpreparing, ya know."

Jimmy smirked. "We've never had to have one of these special meetin's before. Unless you don't think us small-town folks are smart enough to follow your instructions."

Margot's fingernails bit into her palms, the pain keeping her focused. Her expression was so much like Frankie's maniacal "before nine a.m." face, Marianne whispered, "Oh, shit" from the second row.

"Is there something you would like to say, Sara Lee?"

"Only that there's really no reason for you to be here." Sara Lee stood up and shrugged innocently. "You've laid everything out so clearly, in small sentences, so even we can understand it. Why don't you just let us handle our own from here? How about you go back to the funeral home and wait for your daddy to fall off the wagon? Or maybe I'm supposed to say, fall off the hearse?"

If ever there was a moment in Margot's life when she heard a record scratch and all time seemed to stop, this was it. Her cheeks flushed hot as every person in a twenty-foot radius seemed to gasp and clutch their metaphorical pearls.

Under normal circumstances, Margot would simply give Sara Lee a smile as warm as lake-effect snow and make some stinging observation that would leave the woman wondering for hours.

But not today.

Sara Lee had just insulted Margot's father, insulted him in a way that tarnished the sobriety he'd worked so hard for, and Margot found that she took that very, very personally.

A smile so acidic that it burned her lips spread across Margot's face. Several parents stood up and backed away from that smile, clearly unsure of what was to come. Even Sara Lee looked a little unsteady, but she didn't move out of Margot's sights. Marianne only grinned and rubbed her hands together. Because Marianne still remembered what happened when she was ousted from the PTA leadership, and she sensed McCready vengeance on the wind.

"You think we should go back to your way of planning things?" Margot asked.

Sara Lee nodded, looking to Jimmy for support. Jimmy merely stared at Margot, leaning back in his chair. "We didn't seem to have so many meetings and steps. I just got things done."

"Oh, I'm sure your small dictatorship over the PTA made it much easier to run. I mean, your experience in the ladies' auxiliary certainly trained you for your time as president, didn't it?"

Sara Lee cooed, "It sure did."

"Is that where you learned to change the plans so often that no one knew how much you were spending, how much had been refunded from canceled vendors? Was that something you learned at the feet of Margene Moffat? Because I couldn't help but notice that you served as treasurer of the ladies' auxiliary while she was in charge. You know, all of those years when she was embezzling enough money to go to prison?"

Sara Lee turned a shade of chalky white found only in kabuki theater, and then flushed bright purple. "I don't know what you're talking about. You're just crazy big-city trash. You see crime everywhere. You think everybody's out to get you. I hear drunks get real paranoid like that when they're on a bender."

"Oh, so I'm the drunk now and not my father? Sure, I'm just being silly." She sighed. "I mean, all those canceled checks from the festival account that I found from the last couple of years, written out to 'cash'? That could have gone toward anything. There's really no way of proving where that money went. Surely Mr. Greenway would have said *something* if he saw checks being written for prizes that were never bought and vendors that didn't exist."

Next to Sara Lee, Jimmy's eyes bugged out. "Hey now, don't drag me into this."

"She's crazy!" Sara Lee screeched. "Everybody sees that she's crazy, right?"

"You're right, my crazy allegations would be impossible to prove. Except that when I reconciled the books, there's about twelve thousand dollars missing that can't be accounted for through the receipts. And according to Sweet Johnnie, you did just put in an in-ground pool, despite the fact that your husband's been out of work for a year."

For a second, Margot thought Sara Lee was going to punch her. The blonde stood there, clenching and unclenching her fist while giving Margot a face-melting glare. And taking a page from Tootie's book, Margot said, "Sara Lee, honey, bless your heart."

Sara Lee seethed, stomping within striking distance, her arms tensed. Behind her, Marianne stood up and stepped around the chairs, prepared to tag in if necessary. But Margot shoved her hand against Sara Lee's advancing shoulder and leaned in close enough that she could whisper.

"Don't ever talk about my daddy again, Sara Lee," she said, surprising herself with her own Southern pronunciation, much less the use of *daddy*. "And don't go screwing around with my aunt or any other member of my family. I know where the bodies are buried. And for once, I am not talking about grave sites."

Sweet Johnnie stood to her full five feet, four inches and looked Sara Lee in the eye. "I think it's time for you to go, Sara Lee. I think we can get along just fine without your kind of help. But I'm gonna be calling an emergency meeting of the PTA on Monday. You should probably be there, ready to answer some questions."

Sara Lee sniffed, trying her hardest to look dismissive, but she seemed rattled and pale.

"I don't know what she's talking about. And I won't stand here and be accused of something I didn't do."

With her nose in the air, she swanned out of the auditorium. The screech of tires from the parking lot followed. Jimmy stood up and quickly, silently made for the fire exit. Kyle's face was alight with barely contained schadenfreude, so barely contained that he held his meeting agenda in front of his face to keep people from seeing it. A cacophony of chatter filled the auditorium as Marianne and Sweet Johnnie rushed to Margot's side.

"Did Sara Lee really steal from the PTA?" Sweet Johnnie asked.

Margot nodded. "It took me a while to unjumble the books and figure it out. I'm not an accountant. I'm just compulsive about receipts."

"Why didn't you say anything?"

"I already turned it all over to the sheriff's department," Margot said. "They've hired a forensic accountant to go through and track the money and determine whether Principal Greenway was involved. I wanted to wait until after the festival before I accused her and caused even more complications."

"But instead you chose now?"

"Well, the accountant texted me this morning to say that he'd confirmed everything I found, so the investigation is progressing now, no matter what," Margot said. "Besides, she took a jab at my dad. She had it coming."

"We expected the McCready to come out of you at some point," Marianne said. "We just expected it to involve booze and farm equipment."

"Farm equipment?" Margot asked, glancing over her shoulder to Kyle's seat. The sight of the empty chair brought a frown to her face.

Marianne nodded solemnly. "It would be the last thing we'd see comin'."

~

FOR THE FIRST time since Margot arrived in Lake Sackett, a cool breeze drifted through town. October had finally fought back the humidity and heat to create some semblance of reasonable weather. That wind carried the smell of smoked meat and frying dough, making Margot's mouth water.

Opening day for the Founders' Festival dawned bright and cool (with cupcakes gently wrangled out of Bud Sr. before his retirement). Main Street looked downright Rockwellian with each building coated in new paint and the signs refreshed. Every stationary object was festooned with patriotic bunting and informational posters. The Ask Me Anything volunteers had already started to man their posts.

The food vendors had arrived hours before dawn to start their prep work. The smell of the Holy Smokes pork shoulder was enough to make a vegan beg for mercy. Aunt Leslie had opened a tiny-house version of the Snack Shack, with Bob and Marianne running the counter. She was offering some of her newer recipes, trying to determine which would be best to take to the state fair. Margot had no idea how you deep-fried s'mores, but she was eager to see how it turned out. She'd promised herself a big plate of them if she survived this first day with dignity—or at least without punching Sara Lee in the cleavage.

Margot had her clipboard. She had her walkie-talkie. She also had butterflies moving like unmanned drones through her belly. She rubbed at her stomach. She realized that for the first time ever, she was worried about how an event would turn out, not because her job or some bonus was at stake but because she would be personally disappointed if it didn't go well. She wanted to see her neighbors having a good time. She wanted to see the town make some money and get some interest from potential tourists. And if that didn't happen, she would be very put out.

"It's gonna be just fine."

Margot turned to see her father standing behind her with his hands in his pockets. His bright green MCCREADY FAMILY FUNERAL HOME AND BAIT SHOP T-shirt was a cheerful contrast to the somewhat sheepish discomfort on his face.

"Hi!" she exclaimed. "You look great!"

"I feel like an idjit," Stan grumbled, pulling at his collar.

"Well, I for one am happy to see you out of your usual black-and-white ensemble. Next thing you know, I'll get you into pastels."

"Don't push it," he told her while she grinned.

Across the street, the carousel played a tinny version of "Let Me Call You Sweetheart." Margot hoped that the operator switched it up a bit throughout the day, because that song was going to drive her nuts. She made a mental note to check the operator's maintenance records one more time before the official kickoff, because Tootie's talk of untrustworthy carnie folk was making her nervous.

"This all looks real nice, honey," Stan said, his tone careful. "I think this whole thing is gonna turn out just right. Everybody's real proud of how you pitched in . . . *I'm* proud of how you pitched in. You worked hard. And it shows. I like to think you got the bullheaded work ethic from me, but Lord knows your mama had plenty of that, too."

"She did," Margot conceded. "But I believe I got some of my better traits from you."

"Aw, thank you."

"Mostly the bullheadedness," she added.

"Smartass," Stan grumbled.

"I got that from you, too," she told him.

"That you did." He sighed, slapping his McCready's ball cap on his head. He slowly leaned over and pecked her cheek. "I'm gonna go help E.J.J. on the corner of Beecham Street."

"Make sure he drinks plenty of water and gets some time off of his feet," she said, returning his cheek buss. "I know he's tough as nails, but Tootie will worry. And that goes for you, too. Hydrate."

"The bossiness is not a McCready trait!" he called over his shoulder.

"Yes, it is!"

Over the course of the morning, Main Street grew crowded with people. The mayor's official cutting of the burlap ribbon to open the festivities was met with thunderous applause. The band shell's constant rotation of bluegrass and country acts kept the atmosphere lively. The candy shop's Win Your Weight in Fudge contest had cleaned out their supply in less than an hour. The boats and hayrides kept up a steady traffic, and Margot had to refill the brochure stand twice. Aunt Donna and Fred Dodge had stopped arguing long enough to try to beat each other at spraying water into a bear's mouth for prizes. All around her, children clamored for sweets and toys. Adults were laughing and stuffing their faces. If there was any better sign of a successful venture, she didn't know it.

She would miss this, she realized. Lake Sackett wasn't exactly home, but it felt far less alien than it had when she rolled into town all those weeks ago. She would miss the slower pace, and the view from her porch, and being able to go to a restaurant and be fussed over by Ike for not eating enough. She would miss Arlo.

"So, everything turned out just as you said it would."

Margot turned to find Kyle standing behind her. His hands were shoved in his pockets and he looked almost as awkward and miserable as Margot felt. That only made her day a little bit better.

"How are things going over at the school?" she asked.

"Fine, we've done two skits and a choir concert without incident. The kids and their parents have been very well behaved. And Jimmy Greenway is losing his mind, he's so upset that he had nothing to do with it. Thank you."

"You're welcome," she said, her lips quirking up into a hesitant smile. "I hope that this display of power helps with your perceived authority."

"I know it sounds sad, but it just might," he said.

Silence hung heavy between them, a little island of unhappiness in a swirling ocean of squeals and excitement. She couldn't tell him she would stay for him. She couldn't bear to hear him tell her that her apologies weren't enough or that he was still disappointed in her. She couldn't send him away, because she didn't know when she might have the chance to talk to him again. And he wasn't making this any easier by filling in the blank space with words.

"So, uh, how are the hotel numbers?" he asked. "Are they good?"

Margot was wrong. Maybe she should end this conversation. It was getting painful.

"Margot!"

Margot startled as Juniper bounded up to her, her little round face painted with an elaborate butterfly design, the glittering wings stretched from cheekbone to cheekbone. "I got my face painted!"

"You did!" Margot said, catching June before she managed to bowl her over. Her voice rang with false cheer but her smile was sincere as she took in June's elaborate face decor. "And it's absolutely gorgeous. You look like a rainbow and a unicorn made a baby on your face."

Kyle blanched and shook his head as Hazel scoped out the prizes at a nearby ring toss booth.

"I'm still working on my child-friendly patter, okay?" Margot whispered.

"It was a little weird," June told her.

Hazel inched closer, catching Margot's eye. "And what about you, Hazel? Are you a . . . wolf? A cat?"

"I'm a fox," Hazel whispered.

"Ah, sneaky and mysterious, without being so gauche as to wear a mask like the raccoons. I like it."

Hazel grinned at her. "So no rainbows and unicorns?"

"Can we go back to when you were shy and didn't tease me?" Hazel giggled.

"Good call on the face-painting lady," Margot told Kyle. "She's not cheap, but her line is wrapped around the funnel cake stand."

"If I've learned anything from our trips to the zoo, it's that you should never underestimate children's overwhelming desire to have glitter paint slapped on their faces," he said.

"And, by the way, all of the local hotels are booked solid for the next three days. We're running at near maximum capacity on just about everything. We're estimating a crowd in the ten thousand range. So I'm going to consider this a success."

"That's a huge increase over last year!" Kyle raised his hands in triumph and yelled. "Suck it, Jimmy Greenway!"

Several people turned around to stare at Kyle's display. He shooed them away. "As you were, people. Move along."

"Congratulations," Margot said, smiling as she handed June over to Kyle's waiting arms.

"I better get going," she continued. "I'm sure there's an emergency involving the petting zoo or porta-potties that I should be dealing with."

Kyle frowned. "That sounds . . ."

"Smelly," Hazel supplied.

"I'm sure it will be," Margot said. "I'll see you around."

Margot turned away from him and took a deep breath. "See? You got through it just fine, Margot. Just fine."

She had to find a new word to define herself or she was going to go insane.

~

THAT EVENING, STAN found a sunburned, tired Margot on the porch of his old cabin, sweeping the dead leaves aside with Tootie's push broom.

"Tootie said you wanted to talk to me? Is it about the festival?"

Margot grinned at him and swept the last of the leaves off the porch.

"We're never going to get those years back, and trying to

pretend otherwise is hurtful for both of us. But we can build something new." With a flourish, Margot opened the door to show him what she'd been working on in secret ever since their conversation at the mantel. With Duffy's help, she'd gotten rid of the faded floral couch and the tacky oak table. She'd replaced them with comfortable, more current pieces from a liquidation sale at a furniture store outside Atlanta. She'd also replaced the dishes and glasses, the coffeemaker, the bed linens and dish towels. She'd stocked the fridge and pantry with heart-healthy foods. And she'd framed photos from her teen years, her college graduation, and a few candid shots with her cousins and left them around the living room.

"I'd like you to stay here," she said. "Close to your family. You shouldn't be living your life at a funeral home. That's a place for the dead, not for living."

"This is really nice," he said, nodding. "This is beautiful. Thank you."

"I like to think I took away some of the bad memories that kept you from staying here before and replaced them with new ones." She nodded toward the mantel, where her childhood photos were spread. "Also, the carpet, because that was outdated and infested with mold."

"Thank you, Sweet Tea," he said, putting his arm around her shoulders. "I was gettin' kinda tired of sleepin' at the funeral home."

"I can't imagine why," Margot said, eyes wide.

Stan dropped to sit on the new nubby brown couch and put his Coke on one of the Trout of the World coasters Margot had purchased.

"I'm not actually decided one way or the other, whether I'm going. I thought it would be easy to make that decision once I finally got an offer, but I can't seem to make myself pick up the phone and call Rae."

"The big decisions are never easy," he told her. "And I think you know it's about more than a job or money or big-city livin'."

"What would you think of me moving to Texas?"

"Well, I can't say I like the idea. I'd miss ya. But we could call and write, and I could get Tootie to show me how to use that webcam thing. It wouldn't be like having you live here, but it's more than we had before."

"That's what I told Kyle. And he got so angry with me."

"And you can't figure out why?"

Margot crossed her arms. "No, I know why. He wants more from me than I think I can give him. And he's mad at me for being too scared to try."

"Why would you be scared? Kyle seems like a nice boy. Good job, smart, likes kids."

"I thought you were supposed to be discouraging me from being interested in boys."

"I'm still figurin' out this whole dad thing," he said, elbowing her lightly in the ribs. "Come on. Why are you scared?"

"I'm scared because I like him too much to hurt him. Because I don't even know how to begin to give someone the kind of love he would require of me, and rightly so, because he deserves it. I'm afraid of confusing his girls, or hurting them. I am fundamentally unable to have a committed relationship involving grown-up feelings."

"Well, I wouldn't go that far."

"The last guy I dated, I dumped him before dessert on the third date because I was afraid he was going to take up too much of my weekend time during the holiday party season."

"Okay then." He pursed his lips, trying to contain his laughter. "Look, I'm clearly not the expert on romance."

"Clearly."

"But it strikes me that you're not a coward. You didn't back down from coming here to a strange place full of people you didn't know. You didn't back down from your aunt Donna, and she scares everybody. You didn't back down from Sara Lee Bolton and her harpies when they tried to assassinate your character over a stupid party."

"Watch it."

"My point is that you don't back down when you're faced with something scary. So why would you back down when you're faced with something that could make you happy?"

Margot's nose scrunched up and she buried her face in her hands. "I wish that didn't sound so profound."

"Stay or don't stay. I want you to do what's gonna make you happy. But I don't want you to make a decision based on what you think *should* make you happy. There's nothin' wrong with being happy living in a small town. There's nothin' wrong with being happy workin' for your family. Your mama thought livin' in a big city would make her happy because she thought it would be embarrassin' to be content with a small town. But from what you tell me, she wasn't all that happy no matter where she was."

"Again, please stop making excellent points that force me to reconsider my world view," she said, sagging back against the couch.

"Sweet Tea, what do you want to do with your life?"

"I want to stay!" she exclaimed. Her eyes went wide. "I want to stay. I really do. I didn't expect that, but I do. Not because of Kyle, though that would be nice. But I don't want to leave because I have friends here and family. And a job that doesn't send me into a panic if I get something wrong. And people I actually look forward to seeing every day, as opposed to people who would love to see me fall on my face so they could post it on Facebook. I like living here. I don't want to leave. Oh my God, I don't want to leave. Dad, I don't."

"So you're going to stay?"

"Yes."

Stan grinned. "Well, don't tell your aunt Leslie."

"Why?"

"She'll activate the gossip phone tree. Your fella will know your decision quicker than a jackrabbit on a date."

"Ew."

"So you want to order a pizza? Mama Ruby's is doin' a triple bacon special this week."

"How about that veggie lasagna Aunt Leslie sent over?" Margot asked, pointing to the kitchen, where the lasagna was warming in the oven. "I would really like to know that you had some vegetables with your dinner. Or at all today."

"Is this how it's gonna be from now on? You bossing me around and fussing over me?"

"Probably," she said, nodding.

"I guess that will be all right."

She gave him a lazy smile. "Thank you."

"You called me Dad, back there. Did you notice?"

"I did. I can't say it's a habit I'll get into, but I'll try."

"Well, that would be all right, too," he said, carefully keeping his face still, though the corners of his mouth were quivering into a smile.

"Your enthusiasm is overwhelming. Stop, I'm blushing."

"Come here," he said. He put his arm around her shoulders. She leaned against him and found that she was comfortable. And for the first time in her memory, she propped her head against his shoulder and closed her eyes.

~

IT TOOK MARGOT more than a week to work up the nerve to call Rae and admit she wasn't taking the job. It wasn't a terribly professional or emotionally mature response, but Margot figured her recent personal growth granted her a little wiggle room.

"I'm really very sorry to turn down the position, Rae," Margot said, sitting on her front porch, watching the last boaters of the season brave the cooling winds of October. "I think I would have enjoyed working for you."

"Well, we're sorry, too, shug. Are you sure there's nothing I could do to tempt you to Texas?"

"No, thank you. Your salary package was more than generous. But I just got an offer I couldn't refuse." Margot grinned down at Arlo, who had his head on Margot's knee, graciously accepting her scratching behind his ears.

E.J.J. telling Margot that she was off her probationary period and was now entitled to a dollar more an hour and two weeks' paid vacation counted as an offer, right?

"Keep us in mind if you decide to send applications around again," Rae said.

"I will, I promise."

Margot bid Rae good-bye and hit END. She sat back in her rocker and propped her feet on the porch railing. In her heart, she knew she'd made the right call. She wouldn't regret passing up Dallas. But she would have regretted leaving her family. She would have regretted losing the life she had here on the lake. And Kyle . . .

Well, she would figure that part out. She hadn't had the nerve to call him about her decision. She didn't want him to come back to her just because she'd made what he considered the right choice. She was sure that made her fickle.

But still, she was happy with her choice, no matter what.

She glanced down the row at what used to be the shabby yellow house. Stan was officially moving back into the formerly unhappy home, which Duffy and Bob were painting a soothing blue-gray. A crew from town had scraped the shingles off the aging roof and replaced them with a dark slate. Between that and the complete change of furnishings every McCready with an available truck was moving inside the house, it was barely recognizable as the same place.

Frankie's head poked around the corner of the porch, her pigtails swinging merrily. "So, did I just hear you turn down the fancy city job so you could stay here with us?"

"Not you, specifically," Margot insisted. "I would miss Sara Lee's hearings. And I couldn't have that."

Marianne's head appeared just above Frankie's. "Admit it. You love us."

"I don't recall ever saying that."

Duffy's head appeared above Marianne's. "Come on, if you admit that you love us, we can have cake."

"How many more of you are back there?" Margot asked.

"Just me," Carl said, walking around to the porch. "I wasn't comfortable standin' that close to Duffy."

"Good call, man." Duffy nodded.

Carl shot finger guns at his brother-in-law and then turned to Margot. "So are ya stayin' or what?"

"Yes, I am staying," Margot said, grinning.

Her cousins exploded into cheers, and yes, they did have a cake with them on the other side of her cabin. They carried it to her while Carl lit gold sparkler candles. Frankie, wearing capri fatigue pants and a shirt layered from many synthetic fabrics, was careful to keep her highly combustible casual wear away from the open flames.

The cake read TEXAS SUCKS ANYWAY.

"Very nice," Margot cackled before blowing out the candles.

Marianne slid her arm around Margot's waist. "If you decided to go, you weren't going to get any candles. And we would have scraped off the icing so the cake said, 'Texas Sucks.'"

"Classy."

"Mom and Tootie are cooking up a storm. We're havin' an official, old-fashioned 'welcome home, Margot' pig smoke for you this afternoon."

"This afternoon? Not months ago, when I got here?"

"Well, we figured all of the McCreadys *and* a whole roast pig would have been a bit much for you to handle," Duffy said.

"You're probably right," she admitted.

"Just prepare yourself for the inevitable 'sugar in the cornbread' fight between Mama and Tootie," Frankie told her.

"I've already seen it," Margot said. "It doesn't scare me. But before we start partying in earnest, I need your help with something. Actually, I need Carl's help with something."

16

THOSE WHO WITNESSED what became known as the City Girl Apology would claim that Margot came speeding across the water right up to the dock behind Kyle's house in a seaplane trailing a banner that said I'M SORRY I'M A BIG-CITY IDIOT. Others would claim it was a jet boat with a banner that said YOU'RE AN IDIOT, BUT I'M SORRY ANYWAY.

The truth was that Kyle was standing on his dock, prepping *Maggie's Little Trees* for winter storage, when he saw a large shape moving slowly across the water. It was backlit by the afternoon sun, and at first Kyle couldn't tell that it was a McCready's pontoon boat, much less a pontoon boat driven by Margot.

Margot cut the engine long before she got near the dock, allowing her to float safely close enough for Kyle to read I'M SORRY written on the sheet she'd stretched over the left side of the boat. The words seemed to be written in dark, metallic . . .

"Is that *duct tape*?" Kyle called.

"Yes, it is," Margot said. "Carl helped. He says duct tape is the solution to all problems."

Kyle walked slowly to the end of the dock, giving Margot a chance to tie up safely before jumping down to the platform. He looked apprehensive as she moved closer to him.

"You defaced your family's boat," he said.

"Only temporarily," she told him. "But they helped me do it. Hell, Duffy taught me how to drive it, which was the most terrifying experience of my life. Look, I did a terrible job of talking to you about the Texas offer. I'm staying, not because of you, but because it makes me happy to be here. When I said I don't know how to love you, well, I wasn't wrong. I'm going to screw this up somehow, I'm certain of it. But I'll do my best not to hurt you on purpose. And I would never hurt the girls. If that's not enough of a promise and you're done with me, I understand."

Kyle's lips pressed together into an apprehensive line. Margot's stomach rolled, anxiety turning her insides to water. What if he said no? What if after putting herself out there in rather dramatic fashion, he said no? She'd thought she'd considered this, but realized now that she'd been dangerously optimistic. Romantic comedies had led her terribly astray and she'd made an enormous fool of herself in a small town where she planned to live for quite some time. She was going to be a cautionary tale at the Rise and Shine.

She was right, tragically so: She didn't know how to be in a relationship. She couldn't even make a romantic gesture without looking like a lunatic. She should just slink back to the boat and end what seemed like an eternal awkward pause while she had some tiny bit of dignity left, go home and wait for Tootie's phone to start ringing with gossip about "poor Margot pining after a man who don't want her."

"Okay."

Margot shook her head, chasing away the image of Ike Grandy serving her a side of pity with her Rabbit Food Special. "I'm sorry, what?"

"Okay. I want you to stay," he said, pulling her close. "I shouldn't have said all of those things about you being scared. I'm scared, too. And I'm not sorry that I introduced you to the girls. I'm not sorry I let you into my space. I lashed out because I was losing someone all over again and it turns out that I am sort of an asshole when I'm going through that."

"Well, I wasn't exactly the picture of emotional maturity and open communication, either. I'm still scared, Kyle. I'm still so afraid, but I think I'm more scared of what will happen if I don't try."

He chuckled into her neck and squeezed her.

"I mean, I could end up with some local who doesn't appreciate my sarcasm nearly as much as you do."

"I wouldn't say I *appreciate* it," he said, wincing when she dug a knuckle into his ribs. "Please stay with me. Don't leave. I'm not saying we have to get married right this second or even this decade. Just stay and help me figure it out."

"But someday, if you ever propose, leave duct tape out of it."

"I make no promises." He kissed her soundly. "Duct tape seems to be very effective."

~

THOUGH SHE HAD been warned about the whole hog—smoked slow over hickory all day—it was still overwhelming to see poor Porky laid out in all his full, delicious glory, surrounded by every conceivable starchy side dish. With the sun setting over the water, the family—including Kyle and the girls—dug into this pork-based treasure trove and lounged on a hodgepodge of lawn furniture gathered on Tootie's porch.

Kyle was stretched out over Margot's lap, rubbing at a belly distended from eating three pieces of pie. He didn't want to upset either Leslie or Tootie by showing favoritism.

"You're going to have to either learn to accept pie-based glares from little old ladies or say good-bye to those washboard abs," Margot told him.

"Duffy took just as much as I did. How does he not weigh four hundred pounds?" Kyle moaned.

From his cane rocker, Duffy pointed to the dogs, lolling in the nearby grass with coconut pie filling smeared across their contented muzzles.

Kyle gasped. "You cheated."

"Learn the system, newbie," Carl drawled. "Wait until Thanksgiving, when there's three different kinds of gravy."

"I don't know whether to be alarmed or a little aroused," Kyle said, making Margot shudder.

In the distance, Margot saw the white Animal Control truck bouncing along the gravel driveway. The dogs sent up a howl, running alongside the truck and barking all the way. "Um, Tootie," Margot called across the porch. "You didn't acquire a new dog, did you?"

"No." Tootie scoffed. "But I did ignore the summons that pinhead Dougie posted on my door. I'm not about to be forced into court by a boy who used to eat crayons in my Sunday school class."

Marianne tried and failed to contain the frustration twisting her facial muscles. "What did the summons say, Aunt Tootie?"

"Something about me coming to the county commission

meetin' to discuss my noncompliance with the spirit of the animal codes."

"Was this last week, before . . ." Margot shook her head. "Never mind, Tootie, we'll take care of it."

As he got out of his truck, Dougie spotted the crowd of Mc-Creadys crossing the lawn and drew himself up to his full height. "Now, y'all, I don't want any trouble. I'm just here because Miss Tootie hasn't been compliant with the county codes. I told her I was gonna have to step in and fix it one of these days, and today is that day."

"So, what, you're gonna haul her off to puppy jail?" Carl asked, fixing his most intimidating glare on Dougie. The poor man's enormous Adam's apple bobbed as he swallowed heavily.

"No, but I am gonna have to take two of the dogs into custody," he said.

"I thought we resolved that when I took custody of Arlo," Margot protested.

"Ma'am, I've checked the county records. You haven't filed for dog tags or taken Arlo over to Dr. Warner's office for shots or a checkup. How about we cut the crap and just admit that you lied about him being your dog?"

"Watch your tone when you talk to my daughter, Dougie," Stan snapped.

"No, Dad, he's right. I did lie. Arlo's not really my dog," Margot admitted, making his jaw drop. "I love him and I'm willing to take him in, but I got so busy with the festival and other stuff that I forgot to file the papers."

"Oh," Stan grumbled. "Well, still. You're talking to a lady, Dougie. Act like it."

"It's fine, Dad. Dougie, what if I signed papers that made

me Arlo's owner officially?" Margot asked. "Under a legal animal rescue?"

"That would do it," Dougie conceded.

Marianne came dashing out of Margot's cabin with a manila file folder in hand. "I have articles of incorporation for a nonprofit animal rescue called the Lake Sackett Animal Haven. It's been filed with the county commission and was approved in a special session on Tuesday. Eloise 'Tootie' McCready is named director and given full powers to approve animal adoptions as she sees fit."

Margot smiled, all peaches and cream and innocence. Dougie didn't need to know how good Marianne was at impersonating Aunt Tootie's signature.

Dougie scanned the folder, chewing on his lip.

Tootie snatched the papers out of Dougie's hands. "What in the Sam Hill?"

"Surprise . . . ?" Margot said weakly.

"Explain yourself, girlie," Tootie told her.

"We were thinking you could open a real animal rescue," Margot said. "I know you like having your pack running around the compound, but this would get Dougie off your back. And you could help place your dogs with loving families."

"You know I have a hard time giving my puppies up. I barely let Arlo go to you, and I like you. I don't know if I would be able to send them all away with strangers."

"You can do all the background checks and home visits you want. And opening a shelter would allow you to help even more dogs," Margot said. "And cats and ferrets and turtles and whatever else shows up on your doorstep. Marianne's handled all of the paperwork with the county. She found a really nice building near the county line and she's working on getting you a lease. It was a vet's office, so there's already plenty of equipment and fencing and kennels. People around here know your reputation and how committed you are to helping animals, and they know they can trust you to do a good job. People will respond if they know you're in charge."

Tootie's face softened for a moment before she gave Margot a weak glare. "I'll think about it."

"I did mention the paperwork is already filed, yes?" Margot asked.

Tootie snorted. "You're a piece of work, you know that?"

"Well, you brought me down here and helped convince me to stay, so really, you have no one to blame but yourself."

Dougie cleared his throat, to draw their attention back to him. "Look, Arlo's adoption will help, but the limit for maximum dogs owned has been lowered to eleven for any single home. So until you've moved into the shelter building ya mentioned, ya still have one too many dogs."

"When did the limit get lowered?" Tootie demanded.

"At the meeting you got summoned to," Dougie shot back.

Marianne slapped her hand over her face. And that was when Margot remembered that Sara Lee had mentioned a cousin on the county commission. Was this revenge for Margot uncovering Sara Lee's fraud? And she thought *Chicago's* political system was corrupt!

"But if Tootie was to place another dog with a loving, responsible family . . ." Margot said, jerking her head toward Kyle.

"That would put you under the limit, yes," Dougie said.

Tootie frowned at Margot while she jerked her head toward Kyle again. "Sweetie, is there something wrong with your neck?"

Hazel and Juniper came running up to their father, the pack barking at their heels, which didn't exactly help argue against Tootie's dog hoarding tendencies.

"Dad! Dad!" Hazel yelled, petting Lulu the pit bull. "I got Lulu to do a pirouette in her little tutu."

"I think this one likes me, Dad," June said, as Brutus the Chihuahua licked at her face.

Margot gave the girls another pointed look. Tootie's face softened. "Kyle?"

Kyle's sandy brows winged up as he observed the canine chaos around his ankles.

"Doggy kisses!" June sighed as Brutus nuzzled her cheeks.

"You have been talking about getting a dog," Margot noted.

"Fine, they've done the chores, earned the grades. They haven't knocked over any liquor stores this month. I guess it will be okay."

Tootie grinned and bent so she was eye level with the girls.

"Ladies, what's your favorite food?" Tootie asked.

"Bacon," June answered quickly. "Daddy says it's nature's glorious meat candy."

Margot turned on Kyle, who shrugged and looked up at the trees.

"And what's your favorite time of day?"

"Right after bath time," Hazel said. "When I smell all clean and I put on new pajamas and we read."

"And what is your favorite song?"

"'Brown Eyed Girl,'" June said. "Daddy sings it for us when he makes pancakes."

"Aw, that's adorable," Margot said.

"His dancing is terrible," Hazel noted.

Margot shrugged. "Less adorable."

Tootie looked Hazel over carefully and then pulled June close. She pursed her lips, studying both of them, and then whistled. "Charlie!"

Charlie, the little chocolate-and-tan dachshund, came trotting forward through the pack ranks, sniffing at the girls' hands. Tootie stooped and then groaned as she stood up with him. "This is Charlie. He's the runt of his litter. One of his front paws is smaller than the other, so he always heads slightly left of whatever he's running to. But he's a sweetheart. He's not a show dog. He needs a family that he can take care of. Do you girls think you could let him take care of you?"

The girls nodded solemnly, sneaking glances at their father.

"Can we take him home, Daddy? Please?" Hazel begged.

"Um, well, we really hadn't settled on a breed or an age for the dog yet, girls. Last week you wanted a Saint Bernard," Kyle said.

"Liquor stores, Kyle," Margot said, nudging at his ribs.

"All right." Kyle sighed. "Yes, we can take him home."

Tootie scratched behind Charlie's floppy black ears. "Charlie, how would you like to go home with these nice girls? They like bacon, just like you, and they like being clean. And they appreciate musical classics. What do you say?"

Charlie sniffed Hazel's ear and licked June's face. He gave one short yap before wiggling his butt enthusiastically and launching himself at the crouching girls, smothering them with kisses.

Charlie then turned his attentions to Kyle, sitting on his butt and giving Kyle the full tragic puppy eyes.

"Cute doesn't work with me, sir," Kyle told him. "I work with kids all day."

Charlie tilted his head and the size of his eyes seemed to double.

Kyle growled. "Oh, you're good. You evil adorable jerkface."

"Well, Mr. Hazard, since Aunt Tootie's pack is now down to eleven dogs, she is no longer in violation of the county ordinance," Margot said.

"Well, how do I know you're not just fibbing again, and when I come back, I won't see Arlo and Charlie running around with Tootie's other dogs?"

"I've got it!" Marianne said, bursting through Tootie's front door. She handed a sheet of paper to Margot and one to Kyle. "This is the Animal Haven's standard adoption contract, a very simple written agreement to make sure the dogs are cared for medically and neutered. All Kyle and Margot need to do is sign copies for Arlo and Charlie, have them witnessed by Dougie, and the county commission should accept it as proof of the adoption until they file for tags."

"Which I *will* do," Margot promised. "This time."

Dougie sighed. "Just sign them."

Kyle and Margot each signed their copies, which were then signed and dated by Dougie.

"Congratulations, you're now dog owners." Marianne handed Dougie the documents with a smile. "Dougie, the next time you come out here, it better be for a social call and not to harass my family members."

Dougie took the signed contracts from Margot and Kyle. "Yes, ma'am."

"Dougie, would you like some pie to take home with you?" Tootie asked.

Dougie hesitated for a moment, but finally said, "Yes, ma'am."

~

LATER, AFTER A second round of leftover pie, the girls were lying in a heap on the floor in Kyle's living room, with a dog clutched to each of their chests. Kyle and Margot sat on his couch, beer in hand, marveling at the cost of dog gear.

"How is it that something so small has such expensive taste?" Kyle asked, examining the pricey dog food Tootie had insisted Charlie had to have, else his stomach would be thrown into chaos. "Just since we've been home, that dog has tried to drink from a toilet twice."

"Well, you shouldn't fall for your daughters' cute begging faces if you're going to question the cost later."

"They are awful cute," he said, peering down at them.

"They are." She sighed, curling into his side.

Margot tucked her face into the crook of Kyle's neck. Her life was near unrecognizable from the one she'd left in Chicago. She still wore her designer suits, though she had to be a lot more careful about where she sat. Her shoes were still impractical. But she spent a lot less time getting herself ready and way more time braiding other people's hair and talking small people out of poor tutu choices.

She was happy in a way she had not expected. Her relationship with her dad would never be what it could have been, but it was more than she'd anticipated. She didn't feel the need to compete with her friends for who had the best life, the best job, the best shoes. She was . . . content. Open to what life was going to throw at her. She drew the line at moonshine, though. She thought that was pretty reasonable.

Kyle kissed her forehead. "So, I was thinking that I might take you and the girls on a trip to the greatest city in the world over Christmas."

"You're going to take me back to Chicago?" she said, gasping in exaggerated joy.

"Funny. I said 'greatest city,' not 'deep-dish wasteland.'"

Margot made a nasty face at him. "That's it, relationship over."

He grabbed her around the waist as she pushed from the couch to walk away. "I was thinking New York. We could take the girls and hit the landmarks for Christmas? The Rockefeller tree. The Fifth Avenue shop windows. Serendipity 3. And then maybe we could go visit my folks? I know it's hard for you to plan that far in advance, but—"

"I'll be here," she told him quickly. "But meeting your parents? That's a big step, isn't it?"

"Nah, you've met Maggie's parents and they love you. Actually, I think they're happy knowing that there might be a woman around the house to help match the girls' clothes. And they were always going to be way tougher on you than my parents. The only fault my parents are going to find with you is that you're not going to convince me to move back to New York."

"Not terribly reassuring. But I'll think about it."

Kyle pulled her close. "In the meantime, Charlie might get lonely over here by himself. He's used to having the whole pack around him. You might have to bring Arlo over for playdates."

"I can do that."

"And maybe overnights and weekends."

"That's moving awfully fast."

"It is," he admitted. "But if I've learned anything, it's that life is short. And when you find someone you could love, you hold on to them."

"I will think about it. I'll have to ask Arlo."

"Arlo's good opinion can be bought with bacon."

"So you better stock up."

He kissed her thoroughly and she didn't even notice the scratch of his whiskers. "I'll do that."